# *Biting the Apple*

# *Biting the Apple*

Lucy Jane Bledsoe

Carroll & Graf Publishers
New York

Biting the Apple

Carroll & Graf Publishers
An Imprint of Avalon Publishing Group, Inc.
245 West 17th Street, 11th Floor
New York, NY 10011

First Carroll & Graf edition 2007



ISBN-13: 978-0-78671-927-3
ISBN-10: 0-7867-1927-3

9 8 7 6 5 4 3 2 1

Interior design by Maria Fernandez

Printed in the United States of America
Distributed by Publishers Group West

*For my coaches and teammates*

# *Molly Malone*

*In Dublin's fair city where the girls are so pretty,*
*I first set my eyes on sweet Molly Malone.*
*She drove a wheelbarrow*
*through the streets broad and narrow,*
*Cryin' "Cockles and Mussels alive, alive-o!"*

Chorus:
*Alive, alive-o, alive, alive-o,*
*Crying "Cockles and Mussels alive, alive-o!"*

*She was a fishmonger, but sure 'twas no wonder,*
*For so were her father and mother before,*
*And they each pushed their wheelbarrow*
*through streets broad and narrow*
*Crying "Cockles and mussels alive, alive, oh!"*

*She died of a fever, and nothing could save her,*
*And that was the end of sweet Molly Malone;*
*But her ghost wheels her barrow*
*through streets broad and narrow,*
*Crying "Cockles and mussels, alive, alive, oh!"*

# *Contents*

## Acknowledgments

A huge thank-you to Alison Bechdel and Kanani Kauka for invaluable feedback on drafts of *Biting the Apple*. I'm also grateful for the friendship, support, and counsel of Jane Adams, Suzanne Case, Elana Dykewomon, Robin Ellett, Margaret Evenson, Bob Finney, Martha Garcia, Margot Gibney, Mary Goglio, Sheri Krams, Olivia Martinez, Jane McDermott, Barbara Sjoholm, Shannon Smith, Nancy Suib, Karen Sundheim, and Herb Wiseman. I'd still be writing with a stick in the sand if it weren't for the technical support of Bob Dang and Vinh Chu. Another huge thank-you to Charles Flowers, editor of *Bloom*, for publishing an excerpt from *Biting the Apple*. The Multnomah County law enforcement officers who gave me a tour of the Portland jail and booking process generously answered all my questions and more. I can't thank Don Weise enough for his warmth, vision, and dedication to books. Most of all, love and thanks to Pat Mullan for living in the heart of her music, for listening to all my literary angst and joy, and for putting up with the casts of characters I live with always.

## *The Beginning:*
## *Spring, 1973*

Nick stood on the side of the track while his girls, an unlikely herd of horsey, shy, raucous, and flirtatious teenagers, ran their first 1,500 meters of the season. The head coach, George Winston, who had kept the boys' team for himself, lectured his athletes in the middle of the muddy field. Miraculously, the first day of sunshine in weeks coincided with the first day of track-and-field practice in Nick's first year of teaching at Kennedy High School in Portland, Oregon. The sky was a wet blue, deep and oxygen-rich, and the cold air sparkled. Nick just couldn't believe his good fortune: only twenty-one years old and already coaching. How many years would it take to make head coach at U of O? He laughed out loud, knowing it was possible, even inevitable, and swept his gaze around the track, taking in the whole beautiful world and looking for his runners.

Most of the girls were on the far side of the field, running in a pack, their sneakers splashing in the big puddles on the graveled track. But there were two girls coming around the bend, well in the lead. In fact, they were nearly three-quarters of a lap ahead of the pack. The girl in front, though by just a couple of paces, was beautiful, with her long legs and thick, honey-blond hair dusting her shoulder blades. Her running style was even more beautiful than she was, damn near prophetic, as if she had been trained by some oracle from the ancient Greeks themselves. Her arms made right angles close to her sides, swinging loosely back and forth, hanging from her perfectly relaxed neck and shoulders. Her slim hips moved forward in a straight line, no energy lost to wobble or sway. And her legs! Long golden winged legs. A shaft of sunlight, as if coming from a window high in the room of the world, lit her, singled her out, as if she were the only sight his eyes would ever need. Nick's appraisal of his life, which a moment before had seemed perfect, leaped to an even higher level, hope made manifest. He had an athlete he could polish, a star runner, a winner. Just this moment itself would be enough, the golden joy of it.

As Nick marveled, the other girl, the one with fierce elbows and a mop of sandy curls, who was running as if her life depended upon it, as if crossing that finish line first were the only thing that mattered, sprinted past the golden girl. As she did so, she reached out a hand and tapped the small of her competitor's back, a gesture both tender and challenging, and then crossed the finish line first.

Nick checked his sign-up sheet and matched the numbers on the girls' backs with their names. The golden girl: Marianne Wade. Mop-head: Joan Ehrhart.

Years later, he'd remember the hitch in his stomach, the briefest moment of unease, as he overlooked Joan and allowed his attention to be wholly absorbed by the graceful Marianne. He would tell himself that crossing the finish line first wasn't nearly as important, not at this early stage in the game, as style, coachability, *potential*. Joan's face was planted on the grass as she convulsed with exhaustion, but Marianne was hardly winded as she turned to him and smiled. At twenty-one, Nick Capelli believed in destiny, and the golden girl was his.

---

Joan noticed Marianne the new girl right away. Everyone did. At first kids said she was stuck-up, but that was only because she was so beautiful. Then people said that she'd changed high schools midyear because she'd gotten pregnant and had an abortion. Some had seen her dad on her first day and said that he was a gypsy, which made her long blond hair difficult to explain, but allowed for lots of speculation. Someone even told Joan that Marianne was some sort of descendent of Scandinavian royalty, sent to Portland, Oregon, to retain anonymity while she finished her education. Something about Marianne Wade required myths. But there wasn't any hard evidence for any of these stories, since she rarely talked to anyone, and so eventually, the student body at Kennedy High School returned to its first assessment, that she was just stuck-up. Even so, the boys kept looking. And the girls wished with all their hearts that they could be her. In the desert of high school, her cool was a sea breeze.

Marianne was seated next to Joan in Mrs. Fisher's Advanced Placement English class. It was Joan's habit to slouch at her desk and make frequent wisecracks to anyone who listened. She got away with it because of her high academic test scores. Mrs. Fisher had told her that she "wrote like a dream." Joan was amazed when beautiful Marianne started laughing at her classroom commentary. One day, Marianne sat next to her in the social studies lab during study hall, and for two weeks after that, the girls met every day.

The friendship was a near crisis for Joan, who wore faded Levi's and big black T-shirts every day. Suddenly she was looking at herself in the mirror before leaving for school in the morning, but felt incapable of figuring out what changes she should make to accommodate this new effervescence in her life. That's how she thought of it, a great bubbling, brought on by someone who laughed at the same things she did. The girls talked about absolutely nothing every day, but they laughed so hard they cried.

When they got kicked out of the social studies lab one afternoon, Joan took Marianne to her favorite place under the track bleachers and was amazed that the perfect girl accepted a cigarette. Joan began to get the feeling that Marianne would do *anything.* It was as if she had some source of knowledge that Joan hadn't yet discovered. At night Joan wrote a lot of poems trying to understand Marianne. Finally, she just had to taste her.

Joan would spend decades trying to remember Marianne's

reaction to the kiss. Not only had she accepted it without reserve, she'd followed Joan home to her bedroom that afternoon where, for what felt like an eternity, Joan basked in the glow of Marianne. For Joan, the afternoon had been not just a revelation, but a first understanding of miracle. She wouldn't remember touching her friend so much as the sensation of flying, literally flying.

The next day in Mrs. Fisher's Advanced Placement English class, Marianne was her usual cool spring self, laughing at Joan's jokes, lounging in those hideous desk-chair contraptions like a jaguar in a crate, with that look in her eye that placed her on another continent.

But she didn't show up in the social studies lab. Nor did she show up the following two days. Joan tried to pretend she didn't care, but on the fourth day, she couldn't help herself. She stopped Marianne in the hall after English class. Marianne scowled slightly as if she didn't understand why Joan would be detaining her. She shook her head at Joan's question, as if Joan had spoken in a language Marianne didn't understand, and walked away. Joan's poems that weekend described medicine balls swinging into her gut, a world devoid of color, the death of God. On Monday morning she wrote in her notebook, "A kiss impregnated a girl with a monster / the monster grows in her womb."

When Marianne had told her the previous week that she was going to try out for track, Joan had chided her for even thinking of hanging out with jocks. She hadn't believed Marianne would actually do it. But on the first day of track practice, when Joan checked the sign-up sheet outside the new teacher's room, Marianne's name was there. Joan wrote her own name at the bottom of the list. For the rest of that afternoon, she tried to talk herself out of it. She knew she would only humiliate herself by trailing Marianne, but that monster grew bigger in her womb, shot monster legs down the insides of her own legs, and at 3:30 she walked to the track. Mr. Capelli pinned a number to the back of her T-shirt and told her to run a couple of warm-up laps.

Joan balked. She couldn't quite believe she was trying out for a *team*. What if someone on the literary magazine saw her down there with the jocks? She was about to leave when the monster thrashed. Marianne of the fairy-tale hair and jaguar grace was coming around the bend toward her. Joan wanted to roar and abduct her. Monster girl carrying off princess to her lair. She was afraid she was about to do something utterly wrong, and so was relieved when Mr. Capelli blew his whistle.

"Everyone warmed up?"

Joan wasn't, but she didn't care.

"Line up on the start line. Fifteen hundred meters at full speed. On your marks."

Joan stepped up to the line, on the far side of it from Marianne, and let her arms dangle at her side. Maybe running wouldn't be so horrendous after all.

Mr. Capelli blew the whistle.

In the course of those 1,500 meters, Joan got the idea that if she could catch Marianne, or even better, run faster, she would win back her attention. Her legs were on fire after the first 500 meters. After 1,000 meters, her heart and lungs felt as if they would heave up her throat and out her mouth. Still, she didn't let up. The monster pumped fuel into her and she gained ground on Marianne, who turned out to be the fastest girl on the track. Sheer desire drove Joan. The moment of passing Marianne just before the finish line, *beating* her, was unbearably sweet. It proved everything.

She turned off the track and fell to her knees on the field. Her head dropped to the grass, and she was impatient for the heaving in her stomach to stop so she could find Marianne. Joan struggled to her feet, still gasping for breath.

It had worked. Marianne was walking toward her. Smiling.

"Now look what I've done," Joan cracked. "He's gonna make me be on the team."

If Marianne had been about to answer, she didn't get a chance, because Mr. Capelli jogged up with an enormous grin on his face. Joan was glad that Marianne was present to witness the congratulations he was about to give her. She put her hands on her hips, tried to look like a jock, prayed again that no one from the literary magazine was anywhere nearby.

Mr. Capelli got down on one knee in front of Marianne. "I want you to stretch, like this. Your hamstrings." He tapped the back of his own thigh and then demonstrated the stretch. "I can tell already they're tight."

Mr. Capelli didn't even look at Joan.

He gestured for Marianne to come with him, and shouted for the other girls to run a couple of cooldown laps. Joan watched him unfurl a mat on the wet grass so that Marianne could stretch in comfort. Mr. Capelli stood over her, arms folded on his chest, talking nonstop, like he owned her.

Joan's monster put an arm around her shoulders and led her off the track. Out of the arena. Up the hill to the school.

Her monster talked soothingly to her. As hard as she tried, she couldn't shake it off.

---

Marianne knew from an early age that she had a gift. It was quite apparent to her, an actual transcendent light that she felt glowing inside her. As if, when making her, God had gotten distracted and left His hand on her a few moments longer than He left it on other people. But Marianne's gift was never nurtured, and it grew wild and free. People noticed it, oh yes, and they used it. Everyone wanted a piece of Marianne. By the time she arrived on that track in Portland, Oregon, in the spring of 1973, she had way too much experience for a girl of sixteen. People projected their dreams onto her and tried to extract what they perceived to be her secrets.

At sixteen, Marianne didn't have a clue what her own secrets were. Sure, Joan frightened her. Who wouldn't be frightened? The girl was intense. But more to the point, Marianne didn't have the luxury to indulge her own feelings. She'd learned to accept the best offer. To look only for opportunity. The coach looked like a good bet. The kindness on his face. His need to develop—rather than to use—her. That felt, at the time, like salvation.

Later, she would say that this moment in the spring of 1973 was the beginning of her life. She would say that her first sixteen years, constantly moving around with her itinerant preacher father and string of stepmoms, didn't matter. She would credit Nick and Joan and Alissa for delivering her back to herself, a process that started with Joan tapping her back before crossing the finish line ahead of her. A process that took twenty-five years.

---

A couple of thousand miles away, in St. Louis, Missouri, an eleven-year-old girl played Vivaldi on her violin while her teacher watched with dismay. Talent like that almost frightened the public school teacher, as if she had opened a trunk in her attic and found a lost Rembrandt. The teacher racked her brain trying to figure out how to best preserve and nurture Alissa Smith's extraordinary endowment. She needn't have worried so much. The girl would soon give up the violin. She would grow up to be a very successful marketing and publicity director.

And she would be the barreling train that eventually cleared the track for Marianne Wade.

## *A Glimpse:*

## *Joan*

Joan had been working on a long piece for the *Willamette Week* when her editor at the *Times* called. "Joan, how's it going? Look, I have a story I think would be perfect for you. Have you ever heard of that motivational writer, Eve Glass?"

Joan had an office with a view of the Willamette River. It was a brisk, not quite yet spring morning, sailboats on the water, Rollerbladers gliding along the waterfront. If she opened the window and leaned way out, she could see the mountain, too. A dead calm came over her. The peace she felt right then almost frightened her.

"I think I've heard of her," Joan said.

"She has a new book. *If Grace Is the Goal.*" The editor brayed a full minute at the absurdity of the title. "Have fun with this one. I want a feature, not on the book, but on the woman. Maybe some dirt, anything you can dig up. This Eve Glass has an interesting past. She was in the Olympics, I think it was Montreal, and a big media star for five minutes. I don't know. I just have this feeling there's a good story here and I thought your wicked humor would fit it perfectly. Surprise me with something sensational."

Of course Joan wouldn't do the story. She didn't believe in revenge. Anyway, that had been a lifetime ago. Still. Her rule was to never commit, one way or another, on the phone. "I'll think about it."

"Don't think about it. Do it, Joan. This one's perfect for you."

Joan rocked back in her chair and put her feet on the desk so she could see only the sky out her window. She remembered perfectly walking down those cold halls to the principal's office, thinking that she had probably won some new academic award. Mr. Ubik stood up, dark gray suit and hair pomaded straight back, and gestured toward the other side of his desk. "Have a seat, Joan. How are you?"

"Fine."

"Joan, you get straight As. You're a very bright girl."

She looked at her hands and mumbled, "Thanks."

"Why would you engage in this kind of behavior?"

Joan looked up quickly. Was he talking about smoking? Sassing a teacher?

"You have a lot of opportunity ahead of you. You don't want to throw it all away." Mr. Ubik leaned to the corner of his desk and picked up the telephone. "Sally, get me Mr. Frisch, please."

Joan stood up.

"Sit down, young lady. I'm here to help you."

"No." Joan slung her book bag over her shoulder and headed for the door.

"You have two choices. Meet with the counselor or—"

"I'll take the or."

Joan swung her feet to the floor of her Portland office overlooking the Willamette River. "Ah, I'm sorry. I can't do the story. I'm completely booked with work."

"There's no hurry on this one. Any time in the next six months. Really, Joan, your voice is perfect for this. Also, Glass is right there in Portland." She allowed herself another long bray.

The laughter kindled something fierce in Joan, something so profound it felt biological. It occurred to her that the ax that had been held over her head twenty-five years ago was now hers to hold over their heads. She had nothing to lose. They had everything.

As soon as she hung up, Joan punched Meredith's number. "You'll never believe what just happened." She could hear Meredith continuing to type and pictured the headset on her partner's head. "Are you listening?"

"Mm. Yeah. But I'm on deadline. What's up?"

"Something really strange." Joan listened for a second to the clacking of keys. "I got an assignment from the *New York Times.*"

"Honey, that's *great.*"

"To do a story on Eve Glass."

"Who's she?"

"She's the *one.* From high school."

"That one you went ape-shit over?"

"You could say that. She changed her name. She used to be Marianne Wade."

"Why the hell would the *Times* want a story on her?"

"I've told you. She's a motivational speaker and author now. I'd say minor-league, but maybe on her way up."

"Obviously, you can't do it."

"I think I could be unbiased."

"*Joan.*"

"I'm feeling very compelled. Besides, I don't want to say no to the *Times* editor. She might not call again."

"That's bullshit. Just tell her the truth."

"The truth sounds very silly."

Meredith laughed, and Joan laughed with her. Only when you're sixteen do you leave whole trees' worth of unanswered notes at a lover's locker. Beg with tears streaming down your face. Throw rocks at her window in the middle of the night. You do that when you're sixteen because you haven't given up on the truth yet. You believe the truth is stronger, much stronger, than all the lies everyone else lives by. That kind of passion makes funny stories a few decades later.

"I gotta go," Meredith said. "I'll see you later. Much later. I don't know when I'll get in tonight. That deadline is suddenly in my face. Call your editor. Tell her no. Just say you had a relationship with her."

"Right. She'd turn around in a nanosecond, hire someone else to do the story, and *I'd* be the subject. That woman loves dirt."

"Gotta go." And Meredith hung up.

Joan thought she ought to feel disquieted, unnerved. But she didn't. She felt a measure of tranquility, as if resolution were at hand.

*Part One*

# Nick's Golden Moment

Nick sat at Judith's kitchen table with a cup of coffee and listed the mistakes he had made in his life. He used a small blue notepad and a black felt-tip pen. His letters were blocky and masculine. The list was short, but every item on it hurt. He hated fucking up. What he really wanted was to understand the relationship among the mistakes. If only he could make a flow chart that would show him where he could have cut each one off at the pass. Or organize them into a significant matrix that, once formed, would cause the mistakes to retroactively vanish.

Judith sat in the living room, her feet tucked beneath her, a novel propped on her knee, a cup of coffee cradled in her lap. Her short pixie hair was wet from the shower, and she wore her weekend leggings with a long yellow jersey. Even from the distance of the kitchen, Nick felt the aching sweetness that was Judith. At the top of Nick's list of mistakes was his behavior on the night he met her, six months ago. He came this close to completely botching what at the time was only the possibility of Judith.

After a good run and weight workout, Nick had showered and then met Bart Jowalski at O'Brien's. Bart also coached high school track and field. Their schools were primary rivals, and over the years they had developed a public show of enmity which their students and the press loved. In fact, Nick and Bart were good friends. Bart was recently divorced, which was why he was available on a Saturday night, and Nick had promised to show him the ropes to meeting women. O'Brien's, an Irish cafeteria-style bar with kitchen tables, hard chairs, and athletic events blaring on the ceiling-mounted televisions, was not a likely place for finding a date. But that was one of Nick's tricks, meeting women where they didn't expect to be picked up, because women, at least the interesting ones, usually didn't like the idea of being picked up. If you met a woman where she didn't feel she was being picked up per se, there was a much better chance that she would be friendly. The problem with O'Brien's, compounded by Bart's postdivorce melancholy—and Bart wasn't the cheerful type to start with—was that it was an easy place to get very drunk. Not just drunk but manic drunk, on account of the killer Irish coffees. At O'Brien's, one tended to talk about grand life decisions, longings made enormous by the whiskey-caffeine combination, and long-spent passions. Nick and Bart were on their third Irish coffee when Nick told Bart the entire story of his golden moment that day on the track at Kennedy High School, where he still taught and coached.

Of course Bart had heard the story before, a few times, but Nick tried to add new details in each telling so that his friend at least got something in return for his kindness in listening. That night in O'Brien's, because he was so drunk, Nick immersed himself in the story, once again becoming that twenty-one-year-old boy who had had a moment of grace with a girl. One of the things Nick liked best about himself was his loyalty to the pledge he had made on that day, that no matter how many years passed, he would remember the feeling of that moment, he would use it as a reference point of possibility. And he had. He had never forgotten.

"Ya gotta understand," Nick almost begged Bart. "She was just so pure to me then. It was a huge, explosively beautiful moment."

"You're drunk, pal."

"So? That doesn't change anything about what she has meant to my life. At least symbolically."

"Correct me if I'm wrong, but the woman has been one big pain in the butt, from what I can see."

Nick sighed. He threw back the last of his Irish coffee. "I *said* symbolically, didn't I?"

Not wanting to be dismissed, Bart rallied. "So you didn't, I mean, as the coach and all . . . ? I'm talkin' back then."

"No, I didn't," Nick said. "You know that."

"You were twenty-one. People do crazy shit when they're twenty-one. Maybe you did but you've been too ashamed to tell me."

"Marianne and I didn't sleep together until after Montreal, three years later." Nick swept a finger in his glass to get the cream on the bottom. He could have told Bart that she was nineteen by the time they slept together. He could have told him that they were already engaged. That he felt no shame about anything that had happened back then. That was the deal, his pact with the golden moment.

"You called her 'Marianne,'" Bart accused.

"Yeah, well, I do sometimes when I'm drunk. I'll admit, I never liked that she changed her name."

"It's just part of her whole shtick."

Nick ignored that. Bart's problem was jealousy. He'd been married for too long. If he wanted to meet women, good-looking women, he had to lose the pot. He had to trim the bushy eyebrows and update his haircut. He had to lose the suspicious expression he often wore, as if every encounter were a potential con. Nick doubted Bart was a good lay, and that, *that,* was the secret to women. If you knew how to make love to them, if you really knew, that knowledge informed your every movement. It radiated off your skin, was delivered in your voice. Women could tell. Or at least they could get a whiff of it. Hint number two was listening. Nick had learned a lot of this from her, from the way she was with her fans. Women loved listening. Which didn't mean that Nick listened to them only as a manipulative way to get them into bed. He found women interesting. He found women more interesting than men. Men talked too much because they were trying so hard to impress. Listening was a lot easier. If you insisted on doing all the talking, you had to find the topic, out of an infinite number of possible topics, that would interest your date. If you listened, the topic was her, and everyone, men and women, were interested in themselves. It was a sure thing, you had her interest from the start, if you just listened.

During his fourth Irish coffee, Nick leaned across the table and told Bart all of these tips and any others he could think of. Bart watched his friend under his big eyebrows and occasionally said, "Huh!" which Nick interpreted as a cross between an interested, "Is that so?" and "What bullshit." His distrust spurred Nick on. He wanted Bart to believe him. Nick sandwiched tantalizing stories of recent sexual encounters he had had between pieces of advice to keep him listening.

"Okay," Bart finally interrupted Nick's drunken monologue. "There's a woman sitting behind you that I wouldn't mind, you know . . . doing. I want practical advice. Step one, step two, step three."

Nick reached up and placed a hand on his friend's jowly cheek, and gently swung his head back so that he was looking at him. "Number one, don't stare. Number two, say 'meeting' or 'getting to know,' not 'doing.'"

"Shit, Nick. This is man to man right now. I didn't say 'doing' to her, for Christ's sake."

"It's all attitude, pal. You're *thinking* 'doing,' and that's going to come across."

"Of course I'm *thinking* 'doing.' What, when you pick up a woman, you convince yourself it's for the conversation?"

"Okay, okay," Nick said. "I'm going to have a look at her."

"Not now. Wait."

"You're the one who was staring."

"Exactly. That's why it would be obvious if you craned your neck."

"Okay," Nick said again. He put his elbow on the back of the chair and pretended to be casually taking in O'Brien's. The place was full of all kinds—elderly folks dining on the inexpensive turkey, gravy, and mashed potatoes, workers who met their cronies there nightly, young people who found the old-world atmosphere charming, and people who just knew there wasn't a better Irish coffee in Portland. Slowly he pivoted until he could see the woman. "Shit."

"What?"

"I know her."

"You *know* her?"

"Yeah. She's a runner. She runs every morning at the Y." Damn. Bart's first statement of interest since his divorce, and it was Nick's best fantasy. Not best sexual fantasy, but best real-life fantasy. He could see taking long early Sunday morning runs with her, then having extended, messy afternoons with coffee and the newspaper. He liked her tousled short brown hair and cute but infrequent smile. Something about her seemed a bit sad, reluctant about all things in life, and yet her running style, as well as the fact that she did run, early each morning, was like a decision, a choice to be in the center of her own life. He said to Bart, "Come on. Let's talk to her."

"What? Are you crazy?"

"It's a perfect opportunity for me to demonstrate the concepts I've been trying to describe to you." Always the teacher and coach.

Even as he pushed himself out of the hard, wooden cafeteria chair, even as he approached the table she shared with a woman who was leaning forward engrossed in telling a story, he knew it was a mistake. Which it was, a huge mistake. Judith would never forget that part of him, the man who picks up women in bars.

It got worse than that, though. He was drunker than he thought. He said, "I wondered if I could ask you ladies for some advice. It's about Marianne."

Bart hovered behind Nick, a look of horror on his face.

Judith looked at her friend, an ample woman in lots of gold jewelry and postmodern glasses, who reached for her purse. But Judith laid a hand on her friend's forearm and said, "We don't have to go. He does." Then to Nick, "We don't want your company. Please leave."

He couldn't make it any worse than it was, so he persisted. "We know each other." And then, even though he was standing still, he stumbled a little. "The track. I see you running at the Y. Uh, in the mornings."

Bart would never listen to another word of advice from him again.

"Oh, yeah," Judith said. "I recognize you. Jeez, you're bombed for someone who runs so much."

"My friend here just got divorced, so we're sort of, you know . . ."

"Thanks," Bart grumbled, his barely audible voice full of fury, "thanks a lot."

The other woman laughed, pulled out a chair. Nick could tell that he and Bart had just become a good story for the two women. He was trying to focus his thoughts enough to decide if he would do better in the long run by staying or leaving, when Judith's friend asked, "Who the hell is Marianne?" She looked at Judith and laughed, apparently thinking Nick was too drunk to care if someone laughed at him, or maybe he'd been so rude she figured he deserved it.

Judith didn't think Nick was so entertaining. She gnawed a fingernail and looked off across the bar.

"I'm really sorry," Nick said. "I'm not usually like this. I'm actually not an idiot."

"You didn't answer my question," the ample woman in gold jewelry said, reaching across the table to squeeze Judith's hand as a signal to relax, to play along with her game with the drunken fool. Nick felt like a squirrel to whom they were holding out bread crumbs. Maybe they'd snap a picture of him, show it around the office in the morning.

Still, he sat down and ordered black coffee, no whiskey, from the waitress. "My wife. Well, actually, my ex-wife."

The woman who introduced herself as Roberta said, "What's the problem?"

Nick scooted forward in his chair. "My buddy there, Bart, thinks I should forget her, and maybe I should, but have you ever experienced a moment with someone where you swear life is *exactly* how it should be? A golden moment?"

Judith shook her head no. Roberta waited for details. Bart had disappeared.

"She's sort of a public figure," Nick said, trying to bolster his position. "You've probably seen her book. *Going the Distance: Endurance for Achievers.*"

Judith said, "You're kidding. I've read that book." Then she paused, snorted. "But it's by Eve Glass. Not Marianne Somebody."

"She changed her name. When I met her she was Marianne

Wade." Nick was not supposed to be talking about this publicly. Why didn't he shut up, and why had Bart abandoned him?

Both women scrutinized him. Then Judith burst out laughing. "Eve Glass your ex-wife? No way."

Nick felt quite suddenly sober. He stood up. "I've bothered you two long enough. I really do apologize. I better find my friend and get home."

Judith and Roberta exchanged a look, communicating silently but quickly about whether or not they should detain him. How interesting was the drunk fool? Judith shook her head. Not interesting enough. Nick didn't even say good night. It took all his concentration to walk to the lit green exit sign without stumbling. At the door he turned, and sure enough, both women were watching him, so he waved and let himself out.

The following weekend, loneliness forced Bart to forgive Nick and they went to a regular downtown pickup bar. "So how'd you do with the runner?" Bart asked sullenly. Nick shrugged. She did smile at him at the track on Monday morning, and her smiles were rare enough to be worth something. He didn't try to talk to her, though, not once all week. As always, he arrived at the track a little later than she did, ran his laps, and barely made eye contact after the initial Monday-morning smile.

Despite Nick's performance the week before, Bart let Nick lecture him again. He emphasized that bars were not good places to meet women. The sex following bar pickups was usually fairly perfunctory, even cold, always awkward, and most often left both parties feeling empty. The look in the woman's eyes, when you left, could haunt you. But once in a while, like the occasional cigar, a bar pickup was fun. That night Nick made sure he didn't drink much and also that he didn't flirt ahead of Bart. Luckily, Bart met someone within an hour, an attractive, nervous woman from Tennessee who was visiting her Portland sister. "Where's the sister?" Bart asked like a tenth grader, like they needed a pair of girls between them. Nick winced. "Oh, she's gay," the woman said. "She's spending the night at her girlfriend's." "As long as you're not gay, ha ha ha," Bart said, and Nick winced again. But the pleased look on his friend's face as he left with the woman made it all worthwhile, even the anticipated bus ride and long walk home alone. As it turned out, though, Nick found himself in bed with a twenty-five-year-old woman who claimed to be the personal secretary for a high-level Microsoft executive. She said she was in Portland on business. She also said that she loved Nick's body, which she described as "deliciously hard for a man your age," and was a very enthusiastic lover. Happily, nothing about her would haunt Nick. He left her hotel room early in the morning (another rule: always stay the night), after they shared a quick cup of coffee.

That, it turned out, was Nick's last sexual escapade. He began dating Judith two weeks later and the relationship was serious, from Nick's point of view, from their very first run together. It took several dates to convince her that his claim to have been married to Eve Glass wasn't a gag, and it disturbed him a lot that Judith just couldn't believe that he could have been married to such a luminary. Back then, when Nick and Judith first started dating, Judith thought very highly of Eve Glass and her book, believed her to be "the only one of those types who actually says something, who isn't just a bunch of psychobabble." When he did finally convince her that he'd been married to Eve, there was a nice payoff: Judith learned that, as foolishly as he had behaved at O'Brien's, he hadn't told her a single lie.

But he had told her one too many truths that evening six months ago, and this morning he wrote that one at the top of his list of mistakes. *Drunkenly mentioned to J. my pact with the golden moment.*

Monday morning, Nick skipped his run and got to school early. He would work out with his track team in the afternoon. He hadn't even looked at the World War II papers he'd promised his students back today. Not that he would be able to read them all between 7:00 and 9:00, but it'd be a start. The custodian hadn't arrived yet, and Nick had to unlock the big front doors himself, clamping his briefcase under his armpit, shaking his ring of keys until he found the right one. The air in the dark hall was coldly rank, as if the rows of metal lockers were refrigerators with vents, releasing the chilled rot of sweaty clothes, old food, and older books, and, worst of all, the stench of adolescent desire. Without the clang of those locker doors opening and shutting, the beefy kid energy stomping the linoleum, the sound of his name—*Hey, Mr. Capelli! Did you grade the tests? I can't make practice today. My mom said*—without the commotion to hold him up, he was overwhelmed by a familiar sense of failure. Teacher. Working with youth. Some of his colleagues made themselves feel better by inhabiting a personality of heroism, but Nick hadn't chosen to work with kids and he wasn't going to lie to himself about it. He'd meant teaching to be the first step of his coaching career. Back then he'd assumed he could ascend the rungs by sheer passion, by his belief in an ideal, the Greek ideal of the perfect athlete. He was the only straight man he knew who worshiped Michelangelo's *David,* but he did, for the sheer beauty of form. Nick loved the human body, and he loved it best in the most classic of sports. All the track-and-field events fired him with a kind of aesthetic lust, a feeling of transcendence he got nowhere else. As a child, sitting through Mass, what he understood best was the priest's exhortations about man being made in God's image. That made sense to Nick. The human body *was* divine.

But not the teeming larvae that filled these halls day after day, with their bad skin, poorly fitting clothes, unharnessed energy. Sometimes there would be a kid Nick would watch through the years, freshman through senior, if he or she even graduated, whom he knew could be a great runner. If it weren't for the poor nutrition, the smoking and drinking, the utter lack of discipline, the abhorrence of himself or herself. Unless they came out for his track-and-field team, there was nothing, not one thing, Nick could do for those kids. Sometimes he did get borderline kids out for the team, and occasionally he had shown one or two of them the beauty of their bodies, and it had made a difference, a significant difference. That did matter to Nick. But what he wanted, really wanted, was so much more than that. He wanted the athlete to come to him ready, as Eve had, as a few others since her had, though none so gloriously, to come to him with all the tools, needing only his guidance. Nick knew now that he'd wanted that gold medal more badly than Eve ever had.

Now he was stuck wondering how trying to shove American history through such reluctant brains had anything to do with running. Why couldn't he have a real job? Programming computers. Fighting fires. Planning city development. Or at least make real money. His sister was making a killing selling real estate. Real grown-ups worked in offices with secretaries.

Tonight was his night with Eve, but he could never say all this to her, never talk about his fears of being worse than mediocre, because his failure and disappointment were linked to her. He was the coach and she was the athlete. Though, of course, that had all changed years ago. Now she was the coach, the life coach for thousands of people. The guru, he liked to tease her. Still, together they had failed to medal. And nothing had ever mattered anywhere near as much, at least not for Nick. Yet, sometimes, he could vault over that horse, sometimes he could retrieve that ancient place inside him that knew the ideal form was there, whether it materialized or not. She was his *David*.

A note was taped to the small windowpane of his classroom. Unlocking the door, he tore off the note, wondering how it could have gotten there over the weekend. Some kid who stayed late on Friday? He dropped his briefcase, pulled out the pile of history papers, and stacked them on top of his desk. *My grandpa was a colonel in the Pacific,* the first one began. *One time they were bombed by a Japanese submarine.* Nick wrote *F, See me,* at the top of the paper. The kid was middle-class, with all the advantages in the world, and he wrote like a fucking second grader. He took a deep breath, erased the grade, forced himself to read the rest of the paper. It didn't improve. He rewrote the *F, See me.* He couldn't stand people not living up to their potential, their minimum potential. Unable to face the next paper, he strolled to the faculty room for coffee. On the way down the hall, he read the note that had been taped outside his classroom. "Nick Capelli," it began. "Great to see you're still teaching and coaching. Good for you! Would like to come by and see you soon. I'm working on a story for the *New York Times* about Marianne and her new book. Her publisher says you're still managing her! I understand she's going to be on Miranda's show this week. Regards, Joan Ehrhart."

Nick stopped and leaned against a locker. Why did the reporter call Eve "Marianne"? She hadn't gone by that name in twenty-five years. The hallway seemed to shrink, making Nick feel grotesque, like Alice, like this one note was a rabbit hole plunging him deep into his history. Nick Capelli. Marianne Wade. Nick was still here, at Kennedy High School, and nothing—except Marianne's name—had changed. The feeling almost choked him.

But that wasn't true. That wasn't true at all. A lot had changed. He had sent Eve to the Olympics. She had written a successful book, even, briefly, a best seller, and now a new one, which was destined for the top of the list. He and Eve had maintained a friendship for all these years. Who could claim a lifelong friendship with his first wife?

And more. Nick had met a woman that he wanted to spend his life with. He had Judith now. He had learned, was learning, to bridge that current that had always flowed between his dream of perfection and himself. With relief, he remembered how much he loved her, actually loved her. It was real. He did love Judith. A real person who cried, talked, played, read the newspaper with him, made meals, did dishes, a real life, a life. Judith had an overweight best friend who wore too much jewelry and perfume, who laughed too loudly. Judith had little tantrums and occasionally threw harmless objects. She worked hard at her job, railed against her supervisor, ate ice cream from the carton, twirled her hair with her index finger, read novels, slept poorly, and sometimes woke with blue half moons under her eyes. Judith didn't expect him to be much more than he was, which had always bothered him in a woman but now was a relief. He was, in fact, much more than Judith thought he was and he enjoyed trying to prove that to her.

Oh, a lot had happened. In spite of these walls. In spite of the gray green chill of the high school. Who was this Joan Ehrhart? The name was vaguely familiar. He'd probably read articles by her. Nick crumpled the note and pushed it to the bottom of his coat pocket.

Cathy Jacobsen with her white blond hair and pink skin and talcum powder scent was in the faculty room already, sipping tea and grading biology tests. Nick was grateful to see her, and after making a pot of coffee, sat across from her, wishing he had brought his own papers into the faculty room. Her pink skin was lovely this morning, like the first moments of dawn, fragile and light and nearly transparent. He had never found Cathy Jacobsen attractive, let alone sexy, but now he felt a yearning, as if her very pinkness were innocence he could swallow.

She took a sip of her chamomile tea and said, "Good morning, Nick. How are you?" The epitome of kindness.

"I was just having a moment of feeling old."

She smiled, as if she knew what that was, though she was not much over thirty.

"These halls, they felt like—" He was going to say "prison

walls," but that was such a cliché and not exactly right anyway. "Like some kind of time tunnel."

"You've been here a long time."

"Twenty-five years." The words themselves sounded like crumbling bricks, like decay itself. Not even a principal, not even a vice principal.

He wished the day were over and he were going to his dinner with Eve.

Cathy Jacobsen had never touched Nick before but now she reached out, from the ratty old armchair where she sat to the Salvation Army castaway where Nick sat across from her, and placed the middle three fingers of her right hand on his knee. "You're a sensational teacher, Nick. You're exactly where you belong."

Nick was much more grateful for her touch than he should have been. He placed his hand over her fingers on his knee and said, "Thank you, Cathy. I better get to my history papers." He stood, feeling almost shaky, and walked back down the hallway, glaring with fluorescent brightness now that the janitor had arrived, to his classroom. He dug the note from the reporter out of his pocket and read it a second time, then tossed it in his desk drawer.

Later that day, while he was trying to give his juniors a half-hour history of Southeast Asia as a context for their unit on the United States' involvement in the Vietnam War, the last unit of the year, his phone buzzed. He ignored it. What could be important enough to not wait until the end of the day? Five minutes later, a student who worked in the office barged into his classroom and handed him a note, which read, "A reporter for the *New York Times* called. Joan @ 244-8760."

Nick finished his lecture, promised his students their papers the next day, and dismissed the class. He read two more World War II papers, and then, on a whim, popped his head into Cathy Jacobsen's biology lab. "Have a great evening," he told her. She looked up from her desk, a look of pink surprise on her lips. Even from this distance, a faint waft of talcum scent reached Nick. She flipped her white blond hair and said, "Oh!" and that was all.

"Cathy Jacobsen," Nick mumbled to himself on his way to track practice.

George Winston had long ago retired and Nick now had the entire track-and-field team under his command. He had in fact guided them to eight city and two state championships, and probably could have found a university coaching job if he had tried. Maybe he really did like high school kids. At least the ones on his track team. As he approached the field, something inside him loosened and smiled. His hurdlers, Douglas and Ralph, were already stretching. His high jumper, Andrea, was running a slow lap. These were the kids who listened eagerly to Nick, who drank down the recipe for success in Eve's first book. DIG: discipline, integrity, guts. It was a fine recipe, too, something to live by, and not a lot of crock like so much of the advice in self-help books. Nick didn't really even think of Eve as a part of that phony movement, and it bothered him a bit, the way her excellent book had grown to become a set of CDs, workshops, lectures, the way Eve's wisdom was getting dispensed like medicine, the way what had been theirs alone now belonged to a growing contingent of fans. DIG worked, that set Eve apart, and Nick didn't like to see her book on the bookstore shelves alongside titles like, *Helping Yourself, Who Else Will?* or *Achieving Your Dreams: The 12-Month Plan* or, worst of all, Walter Spinnaker's *Ten Steps to a Joyous Life*. Even Judith, who was very discerning about literature, liked Eve's book, though she had laughed at the title of the new one.

Nick began running his own warm-up laps around the track, clapping encouragement and shouting instructions to his athletes as he passed them. He felt good now, a warm expansiveness in his chest. This was the very track on which he had met Eve, and tonight he would have dinner with her. That continuity, that loyalty, struck Nick as success, as the greatest success one could hope for in life. To celebrate, after he'd run a mile, he gathered his team and ordered a fartlek day. Nothing took discipline, integrity, and guts like doing good speed work, and his team groaned at the prospect of the next two hours. Nick ran every single sprint and crossed every single hurdle alongside his athletes, killing himself to make a decent showing against the sixteen-year-olds. He made it one of the most difficult workouts he could to prove that he was willing to work every bit as hard as he expected his athletes to work.

The light changed over the course of the afternoon. It started out crystalline, bright rainbow prisms hidden in the corners of the landscape, the sun hard and not too warm, but dutiful. By five-thirty, the sky relaxed to a soft gray, not willing to even hint at summer yet, but still no longer winter. Nick told his athletes to go to bed at 9:00 P.M., with a book if they didn't think they could sleep that early, and to show up for the bus tomorrow afternoon by 3:15. They had a meet at Lincoln High. It would be an easy win, so he expected each athlete to use the competition to work toward a personal best. The Douglases, Ralphs, and Andreas shook their heads solemnly, while the others, the time-wasters, fidgeted, craved junk food, scowled at the thought of missing their late-night television shows, which, Nick knew, they wouldn't skip anyway. The team was dismissed.

At home he showered and pulled on freshly laundered jeans and his long-sleeve burgundy sweater. He looked at himself in the mirror as he pushed up his sleeves, then let them down again. Sitting on the bathroom counter, right next to his razor and comb, was a picture of them, the evening after her race in Montreal, 1976, a couple of hours before the first time they made love. He'd left the picture out the first time Judith had stayed over to serve as further proof of his honesty in claiming to be Eve's husband. Then, as he and Judith got closer, Nick thought it best to stow the picture in a drawer. But Judith noticed its disappearance and told him it was ridiculous to hide meaningful artifacts from his life. So here it was. Eve wore her blond hair loose around her thin shoulders, and her body was hidden in a long, hot-pink parka. Though only nineteen years old, the expression on her face was anything but childlike. Her eyes reached out over the Olympic Village, beyond the borders of Canada, out into the grab bag of her life. If the world was anyone's oyster, it was hers that night. And Nick, he stood beside her, goofy with his black, bristly hair rounded into a big Italian Afro. He wore a wide tie and a brown corduroy sports jacket, the dressiest he could do back then, and his head was tipped back slightly, to make room for the joy burning in his chest and throat. Who would have predicted Moscow and the following years of confusion?

Nick combed his hair, which was still jet black but now trimmed close to his head, and pulled off the burgundy sweater for a quick shave. He didn't look bad for forty-eight. He'd never been masculinely chiseled, not with his full cheeks, but he was friendly looking and, he liked to think, not unsexy. Women liked his thick lashes and good smile. As a kid, before he realized he didn't have a prayer as a competitive runner, he had wished for another couple of inches in height, but even that was unimportant now.

Nick arrived at the restaurant before Eve. This week she had chosen a new upscale place. Seared fishes. Greens that used to be weeds. Antique beans. He ordered sparkling water and, for the hell of it, a bottle of Syrah.

There she was. He could see her on the sidewalk through the window, a bit rushed, some new passion heightening her skin color, exaggerating her movement. She paused once inside the door, calmed herself, didn't look around for him, waited for the maître d' to approach her. Then one of her delighted smiles. First for the maître d', and then for him.

"How's Judith?" It was Eve's first sentence every single week, delivered in a breathy flurry of activity as she shoved her big leather handbag in the booth, scooted in herself, shrugged off her coat, got comfortable. For gigs Eve always looked impeccably natural, not shellacked like most motivational speakers, but for Nick, her hair was usually disheveled and, if she wore any makeup at all, it was smeared. Tonight he reached across the table and pushed her hair out of her eyes, tucking it behind her ears, then took a napkin, moistened it with saliva, and scrubbed off the bit of mascara on her cheekbone. She grabbed his hands, pulled them to her, and bit two of his knuckles. "Well? How is she?"

"She's fine." Nick was touched that Eve cared about his relationship with Judith, and yet the intensity of her interest was a bit annoying.

"The sadness?"

Judith's husband had died four years ago in a freak accident involving a chainsaw and a power line. Though as far as Nick could tell she and Roger had been particularly unsuited for one another, the trauma of his death was like a toxic spill from which she might never recover. Eve called it her sadness. Nick believed that one day, if she ran enough miles, if she experienced enough years of his kindness, she might burn it off. "Comes and goes," he told Eve now.

"You must be very tender with her. I know you are."

Nick nodded impatiently. "We have a lot to talk about. Namely, *Miranda*."

"Okay. I know. But Nick, an extraordinary thing has happened." She paused while running her eyes over the menu. "Let's order lots of courses. I'm starving. Look, you ordered wine! What kind of workout did you have today? Can we eat a lot?"

"Fartlek with my team. Very intensive."

"Good!" She clapped her hands, and the wind blew her menu into the candle flame where a corner caught fire. "Oh! Oh, my god!"

Nick grabbed the menu and blew, but since the paper was so thin, it only blazed more. "Jesus." He rolled the end of the menu that wasn't yet burning and dunked the fire in his water glass.

The waiter rushed over, whisked away the wet, burnt menu and the water glass, which now had bits of charred paper floating in it.

Wiping away laughter tears, Eve said, "I'm having soup and the medallions of beef and then dessert, but I'll decide which dessert later. So Nick, I was at that writers' conference last weekend. It was a mistake—or would have been a mistake—for me to be there because it was so snooty. Poets and literary essayists, novelists. I thought I'd get some tips on promotion, but those people act like promoting one's work is akin to prostituting one's child. What's the point of doing work if you don't want it to have an effect on people's lives? Anyway, it *would* have been a waste of my time except that I met the most extraordinary person. A poet. Audrey Boucher."

"I thought you were just bad-mouthing poets."

"I was. They're a silly lot. But not *really,* of course. Poets are the spokespersons of the gods." Eve stopped, her water glass poised halfway to her mouth. "Hold on a minute." She dug a pad and pen out of her big leather bag and took a note. A moment later, her attention was riveted back on Nick. "Can we stop at the bookstore after dinner? I want to get her books. Her words are lovely, Nick. She lives in Maine, right on the coast, apparently on a piece of land that in the spring is covered with wildflowers and in the fall—"

"Eve, I don't have a lot of time tonight. We need to talk about the show on Thursday."

"Sure. Okay. But wait, first, tell me how you are. You haven't told me anything." Eve's skin was still flawless and her blond hair had only a few strands of gray in it. Nick liked that at least she wasn't getting any younger. He liked how much she needed him. But he resented that she was becoming other people's golden moment, too—not in the way she had been his, but through her CDs she was supplying thousands of people with life direction. The whole world was discovering Eve Glass. It was good he had found Judith. He had found her just in time.

"I'm fine," he said. "This weekend I was making a list of the mistakes I've made in my life."

"Oh, Nick."

"No, I wasn't being morbid or excessively negative. It was interesting. I was calculating."

"Was I on the list?"

Nick leaned over the candle flame and kissed her cheek. "You know you weren't."

"Yes, but there was some kind of big mistake in there, wasn't there? Some mistake we made?"

"What do you mean?" It was the closest they'd ever come, together anyway, of discussing their shared aborted mission.

"Oh, I don't mean anything about the Olympics, Nick." She saw his face and jumped to, "And *definitely* nothing about you and me. We did that perfectly, don't you think?" She waited for him to nod assurance. "Something else. Something a bit more, oh, hidden. I think maybe we missed something."

How could Eve feel that way? Certainly *he* had missed something, but what could she have missed? "Perhaps. But listen, we have a lot to talk about."

"Okay. Santa Fe."

"No! Santa Fe isn't until May. *Miranda* is Thursday, in three days."

"But have you given thought to Santa Fe? You will come,

won't you? How could you possibly say no? I have a suite in the hotel right on the plaza. We'll have a marvelous time, Nick. I get so little time with you these days. Don't think I don't know how serious you are about Judith. Undoubtedly she resents our Monday-night dinners. You've never been in a hurry before, as you seem to be tonight, and I bet it's because Judith wants you home. Am I right?"

"Judith hasn't said anything."

"But she will."

Talking about Judith to Eve made Nick feel vaguely unfaithful. "I have thirty-five World War II papers to grade, that's all. So. *Miranda* on Thursday. Have you thought about what exactly you want to say?"

"She'll ask questions. I'll answer them."

"Yes, but you don't have to answer the questions she asks. You'll have a few ten-second slots. You know the drill. We need to figure out the three most important points to make about your new book. Eve." Nick reached across and shook her fingers. "You're not listening."

"I *am* listening. The three most important points to make about my new book."

"Good. What are they?"

"Everyone can achieve grace."

"Good. What else?"

"Achieving grace is like any other goal. One takes steps to get there."

"Good. And three?"

"Oh, Nick, it'll just flow."

"What about the definition of grace?"

Eve's face lit. "That's what I'll ask Audrey Boucher! Perfect. I wanted an excuse to call her. I bet she'll have an answer, too."

"Eve. Forget the poet in Maine. What do you say in the book?"

"Oh, I don't really *define* grace."

"Sure you do. You tell dozens of stories about grace. That run where you and I got stuck on the ledge in the lightning storm. Um . . . and the time we were snorkeling in Akumal and saw the giant turtle."

"Stories. Not definitions."

"Okay, but mightn't Miranda ask that? You have to be prepared. You can't say, 'I don't know.' You have to have something to say."

Eve clapped her hands. "I'll tell a story."

"You might not have a lot of time."

"A short one!" Eve laughed and then looked puzzled. "Nick, honey, I've talked to the press before."

"But this is *Miranda,* a major network talk show. Big-deal television."

"I'll be brilliant. Reporters love me."

That reminded Nick. "I got a note and call at work today from some reporter for the *New York Times* who knows your original name. She called you 'Marianne'."

"Oh, this is yummy," Eve said, closing her eyes briefly to shut out all sensory input but the chilled fava bean soup sliding across her taste buds.

"Who did we know way back then who'd be a reporter for the *Times* now?"

"I don't want to talk to her. I'm too busy."

"It was strange, the way the note was taped to my classroom door. Why would she come to school?"

"Oh, you know reporters. They love to think of themselves as sleuths. Even if you're perfectly accessible, it heightens their sense of adventure and feelings of accomplishment if they think they've tracked you down. Just ignore her. Try this soup. It's divine."

Nick opened his mouth and let Eve spoon-feed him a bite. "Ignore the *New York Times*?"

"Yes."

Nick felt he should argue. It would be in Eve's best interest to do the interview. But her refusal pleased him. Enough is enough. He'd wanted to throw the note away when he got it. "Okay, then. Fine. Back to Thursday. Miranda isn't always nice to her guests."

"But she'll love me."

"I just want you to be prepared."

Eve gave Nick a look of mock severity. "I stand warned. You're right. She can be a bit edgy. That's what makes her show good. But Nick, why do you suppose she chose me instead of Walter Spinnaker? He's never been on her show, and he's a lot bigger than me."

"Because Spinnaker is peaking, I would even say *has* peaked, which makes him old news. You're on the way up. You're the next big thing. You're onto something a little new and different."

"I am, aren't I?" Eve put down her soup spoon and looked at Nick intently over the bread basket.

Nick nodded.

"People get sick of 'ten steps' to anything. It only takes about a week to find out they don't work."

"Right." Nick liked when she started spelling out her attributes as a motivational speaker. She could work herself into a pitch of focus and passion, blowing off her distractions like wind dispersing litter. He relaxed. She would be brilliant on *Miranda*.

"Besides, Walter Spinnaker has no sense of humor, none."

"He hasn't *done* anything, either. So he's a psychologist. Big deal. You've practiced what you preach. You've achieved amazing goals."

Eve leveled him a smirk.

"You have."

"Maybe. Years ago."

"You're doing it right now. You're changing people's lives. Do I need to read you more of the letters?"

"Can we? Can we do that next week?"

"I'll bring some." Nick collected Eve's mail from the post office box each week. He screened the requests for engagements, tossed out the occasional crank letter, and passed on the pile of fan mail. The very best ones he saved to read out loud to her. "I want you to focus on the show on Thursday, okay? That's all you need to do between now and then."

"You're right. I am scattered, aren't I? What would I do without you?"

"God only knows."

"But Nick. Don't you think it'd be a good idea if I called Audrey Boucher and asked her what grace was?"

"She's the poet?"

"Mm."

What could it hurt? "Okay. Call the poet. But other than that, run, rest, and please try to write out a few smart responses to questions Miranda might ask."

"Can we stop by the bookstore?"

Audrey Boucher had three volumes of poetry. The books

were lovely to hold, made with high-quality paper. The image on the cover of one was an abstract of forest, living greens. The other showed a single shell on sand, taupe and dusty rose. The last one an abandoned cabin in a field, black and white. Eve bought all three, declined the bag, and held them between her breasts like something precious. She could be so focused—except when she got distracted.

On the street, Eve kissed Nick on the lips. "You'll watch, won't you, you and Judith?"

"Of course. You'll be wonderful. Don't forget: stay focused on the book."

"Will Judith watch with you?"

"She said she would."

"Nick? If she calls again, tell the *Times* reporter I can't do the interview."

"Fine."

"What would I do without you?"

Nick smiled. "Don't humor me."

"Good night, darling." She kissed him again, this time on the cheek.

On Thursday, Nick wanted to watch the show live. It was Eve's first major network appearance, and *Miranda* was a big deal. He wanted to let his last class out early, cancel track practice, and rush home. But if he did, he'd have to fake watching the show again with Judith, because they'd agreed to record and watch it together. He wasn't going to lie to Judith, especially not since she seemed like an easy person to lie to. Not because she was so trusting, but because she didn't notice details. She was a big-picture kind of woman, lost in her grief at Roger's death four years ago or absorbed in the future of one of her patients. She wouldn't notice if he watched the show live, then pretended to not have seen it when he watched it with her. But Nick wouldn't do that. He'd wait.

Except for maybe a quick sneak peek at the beginning.

At five after three, Nick dismissed his last class and hustled to the faculty room. There was a small, ancient television there that, if you held the antennae by the hand, would get a dizzying picture. The room was, thankfully, empty. Nick pulled the "on" button and waited for the picture to materialize. He heard Miranda's laugh, heard her preview the day's guests, and then, Eve! She was already sitting in the big easy chair next to Miranda's desk, which looked like a barricade, like a medieval line of defense. Nick didn't trust Miranda. Ah, but there she was, introducing Eve and sounding gracious. In fact, both women looked relaxed, convivial. Warmth and smiles and mutual exclamations of admiration. Nick was relieved. It would be fine. Miranda wouldn't try to skewer Eve. He shut off the television and walked slowly down to the track.

Nick arrived at Judith's house at six o'clock with Hunan bean curd, kung pao chicken, black mushrooms with Chinese broccoli, and steamed rice. Seeming to be as excited as he was about seeing Eve on television, Judith had already set out plates and flatware. They filled the plates and pulled the coffee table up to the couch.

There was Miranda again, brassy auburn hair, lipstick, fiery eyes. A little too intellectual for Eve's book, a little too much edge. Fingernails like precision tools, a mouth that looked made for verbal plunder. It was hard to imagine that mouth kissing, or even simply eating. Miranda was a talker.

It didn't help Nick's nerves any that Judith, chewing her broccoli loudly beside him, might share a bit of Miranda's edge. How to endure, how to achieve—Judith could accept the topics of Eve's first book, but grace, she had asked this morning as they were rushing to get ready for work, wasn't writing about grace a bit worse than claiming to know God?

There was the introduction again, going well, friendly, relaxed. What if that was only bait, though? What if Miranda was only petting Eve into submission so she could come in for the kill after a couple sets of commercials?

"She's perfect," Judith said, meaning Eve. "She knows exactly when to smile, how to make her eyes sparkle, the whole thing."

She did look good. Her blond hair was tucked behind her ears, still slightly tousled, but lovely. Her smile was big and easy, the girl next door. The highlights in her tawny irises became brighter on television, transcended the medium altogether, almost disturbing in how they reached out and zapped the viewers, like a sting of grace, a tiny sample. But it wasn't, as Judith implied, an act. It was sincere.

Judith was trying, though. He put a hand in Judith's hair and massaged her scalp. "I love you," he said, and she turned, her thin neck slightly stretched, her eyes wide open, reading him, reading him carefully, no smile, definitely not a smile. "I love you because you're *not* perfect. Imagine being married to that." Nick nodded his head toward the television. Finally, a smile, a small one. Nick leaned in to kiss her but she had turned back to the screen. She seemed as eager not to miss a word as he was. His kiss landed on the summit of her cheekbone.

The audience applause after the introduction was full, though not extended, and the camera didn't linger on the audience's faces, as it did with bigger celebrities. A few people looked expectant and eager, but most looked blank. They hadn't heard of Eve Glass. Not yet.

Miranda launched into the meat. "Eve Glass. Olympic darling in Montreal. Olympic *tragedy* four years later when Jimmy Carter ordered the American boycott for Moscow. And your book, *Going the Distance: Endurance for Achievers,* about those glories and disappointments. Welcome, Eve."

"What a pleasure to be here."

Miranda was a rocky cliff. Eve was the ocean at her feet.

"I loved your first book. It was *genuine* and *heartfelt* and packed full of *stories.* Very different from most motivational self-help books that are formulaic, so often making one feel inadequate for being unable to achieve what the author apparently achieved so effortlessly."

Eve nodded at Miranda's praise, knew enough to not beam, to keep her expression intelligent.

"There's a lot of wisdom in that book. And yet—" Miranda's eyes widened, ever so slightly, as she sank back in her big, queenly talk show chair. She paused after the "and yet," enjoying her cold tease. "And yet, it might be said that you *didn't* go the distance. We never saw you in Los Angeles in 1984. Do you still run?"

She didn't even wait until after one commercial to bring out the switchblade.

"Jeez!" Judith said.

Eve's face still matched the word *wisdom*. She held it, that former praise, in her mouth, relaxed, sensuous, as if she were sucking on a caramel. She knew how to use a pause, too, and did now. Though Eve's pause wasn't so much calculated as it was instinctual, letting the audience absorb Miranda's bitchiness, bonding Eve with the viewers, as if together they were waiting for Miranda to say something more insightful.

"Good, honey," Nick whispered. Judith glanced at him, a look of tiny alarm on her face. He gestured at the television, didn't want to miss an ear twitch.

"Do I still run?" she finally said, too dreamily. "Is that the question? Of course I do."

That caramel in her mouth, perhaps it wasn't about Miranda's previous praise at all. It was something else, some other distraction. Nick snapped his fingers at the television.

Miranda leaned forward. "Let me ask the question another way. Just after Jimmy Carter's announcement about boycotting the Moscow Olympics, you said, and it was quoted very widely in the press: 'I'm going the distance. One track meet, what does that mean for someone who's going the *whole* distance?'"

Eve smiled.

"In fact, you used that quote for the title of your book. We all expected to see you in Los Angeles in 1984. What happened?"

Close-up of an audience member narrowing her eyes, siding with Miranda, waiting for proof of genuineness. *What happened?* mirrored on the faces of several more audience close-ups.

"What is this?" Nick cried. "Why is she digging around a billion years ago? Why isn't she asking about the new book?"

"She's going for the dirt," Judith said sympathetically. "She must have found out some stuff."

Nick had told Judith all about those years after Moscow, when Eve was supposed to be getting her degrees and training for Los Angeles. Those years of parties, too much cocaine and liquor. Had Miranda gone so far as to discover the shoplifting conviction?

"Miranda," Eve began slowly, a vague smile on her lips, as if she weren't on a national network at all, but having a dreamy afternoon cup of tea with a friend. Nick found himself snapping his fingers again, as if he could wake her up. "I learned in those years, and remember, we're talking about my twenties, *young* twenties, nearly childhood, right?" she asked the audience and the camera panned a few women nodding, understanding. "I learned that there are a lot of different kinds of distances. That's exactly what my book is about. Running is a metaphor, Miranda, not an end in itself."

"In your book, you have what you call a recipe, a crucial trio of ingredients for 'going the distance.' You call the recipe DIG, and the ingredients are discipline, integrity, and guts. Are you a disciplined person?"

"No!" Eve cried out with her big, open-mouthed smile, not the public one, not the one she should be using on *Miranda,* but the too-big one she used when she was truly delighted. Nick could practically see the back of her throat before the camera quickly pulled away. "I'm not disciplined at all! That's why it needs to be part of the recipe for me, and for most people. You see, that's why so many self-help books, if I may use a tired expression, are so useless. They're all talk. The authors tell you that you need only their formula, and snappo, presto, you're a fully conceived, perfectly functioning person. I'm not about magic. I'm not about miracles. I'm about point A to point B. You are in one place and you want to get to another: *how exactly can you do that?* That's what *Going the Distance* tells its readers."

"It's true," Judith said, solidly coming to Eve's defense. "She doesn't give you that bullshit about how if you just did what the book said, you'd realize your every dream."

Miranda squinted her eyes. "You have a PhD in psychology?"

"My new book, *If Grace Is the Goal,* coming out next month, is about something very different," Eve said, sidestepping the question. "Point B is grace. Most people assume that grace can't be a goal."

Good, she ignored the bitchy question and turned the corner to her new book.

"Does she?" Judith asked.

"What?"

"Have a PhD?"

Nick nodded. "In phys ed."

"You're kidding?" Not only one of Judith's rare smiles, but a big one.

"That's funny?"

"I'm sorry," she said. "It just struck me as funny. I mean, she uses the title 'doctor' on the covers of her books. Dr. Eve Glass. Which is sort of funny when the doctorate is in phys ed. Don't you think?"

"She busted her butt for that degree."

"I busted my butt in nursing school and nobody calls me doctor, I can assure you."

"I know," Nick said, trying to disguise his impatience with a comforting tone. It pissed him off, though, that he had to defend Eve to Judith when she was also under attack from Miranda.

Luckily, the talk show host had no choice but to accept Eve's refusal to answer about the PhD. She would look petty if she pushed it, and if she knew the degree was actually in physical education, she couldn't publicly air that now, since she had feigned ignorance.

"Mm," Miranda said, either mocking Eve's sensuality or unconsciously copying it. "Tell us a little more about your new book. To me the concept of grace has always been in sharp contrast to goal setting."

"Exactly. And yet, time and again, my greatest gifts of grace have come when I was striving toward a goal. Think of Buddhist monks who apply strenuous discipline to their lives on their paths toward enlightenment. Or think of poetry! You know, I believe that poets are the spokespersons of the gods. Within the restrictions of language, they create . . . beauty, truth, grace. Think of haiku. Or a sonnet. These forms are quite restrictive, and yet, the results from the hands of true poets, is . . . again . . . grace. My new book is about exactly that: undoing the false contradiction between grace and goals."

Nick should have known. That damn poet in Maine. That's why she was so spacey today.

"I like that," Judith said, "poets being the spokespersons of the gods."

"*Yes*," Miranda said, warming up.

Well, okay, if both Judith and Miranda liked it, Nick figured he could relax. Miranda continued, "In *If Grace Is the Goal* you once again illustrate your points with gripping stories from your own life. The time, for instance, when you and your husband nearly lost your lives in a place called—"

"Hope Valley, yes."

"Will you tell us that story now?"

"Surely."

Judith shifted out from under Nick's arm. "She never says *ex*-husband."

"Ex-husband sounds bad," Nick said.

"First, though, let's take a little break, and we'll be back in a minute." Miranda leaned toward Eve, sister to sister, an intimate comment for the last second of the camera until the screen filled with a young woman bouncing her diaper-clad baby.

Unfortunately, after the commercials, Miranda allowed Eve only about twenty seconds to tell the Hope Valley story, thanked her for being on the show, and introduced the next guest, a hunk starring in a new soap. The camera captured about ten women in the audience seeming to orgasm at the sight of this guy in the flesh. Nick groaned and snapped off the television. Miranda hadn't been interested in the new book at all. Eve had been a sacrificial lamb that the talk show hostess had hoped to slaughter on stage, giving the viewers the satisfaction of seeing an expert on success fail. That had been Miranda's game plan, to direct the fall of someone she assumed was going to be arrogant. Eve's genuineness had disarmed her. Miranda was the one who had failed in her little hunt. That was why the segment was cut short, and the soap hunk would get the extra minutes.

All that made Nick mad. But he was even more bothered by something he saw in Eve, something entirely apart from what Miranda had been trying to do. It was a lack of focus, almost a disregard, a lackadaisicalness. Her new book would hit the bookstores this week. That meant she had to gear up, not slide into a slump. The look on her face reminded him of how she'd looked after Moscow, after the press quit calling, just when she was going to have to dig into her own resources, buckle under, and work for *four years* in order to make it to the Los Angeles Olympics. Then, too, she had looked as if she were smiling inwardly at herself, a look that was the antithesis of discipline.

Nick told all of this to Judith, who listened carefully; but when he was finished, she said, "Nick, she's not your responsibility. It's her career, not yours."

A couple of weeks later, to celebrate the end of the school year, as well as Bart and Roberta's return from their Club Med honeymoon, the two couples had dinner together. Judith had a small Craftsman bungalow in northwest Portland with a flagstone patio she'd surrounded with pots of blooming lobelia and Shasta daisies. It was an unusually warm evening for the beginning of May, and if you stood in the very back corner of her lot, you could see part of Mount Hood, shell pink against the paling sky. The smoking barbecue made Nick cough, but he dutifully turned the grilling vegetables as Judith painted her chipotle sauce on four pieces of fresh halibut. She carefully laid these on the grill, where they hissed and sizzled.

Nick and Judith had run ten miles that morning. He had had only juice and toast after that, and he was very hungry, but it was a pleasant kind of hunger, not urgent, rather full-bodied and soft. He licked some salt off the rim of his margarita glass, took a small taste of the tequila and lime. Judith looked stunning in a black, white, and gray batik skirt with a black tank top. She, who rarely finished a whole drink, had already polished off one margarita and had accepted another from Bart's blender. Celebrating or dousing? Nick wondered. On mile eight this morning, he had suggested that they get married. She had tripped on a root, a tiny root, and nearly fallen. "Get married?" she choked, after recovering from the stumble. "Where would we live?" As if Nick were after her house, not her.

She had sold the house she'd shared with Roger shortly after his death. She'd bought this one and had wanted, she told Nick on their first run, more than anything else, to make it into a home. Roger had been a climber who was more often in the Himalayas or Andes than in Portland. When he was home, so too were his climbing buddies, and their house had been like one big base camp. Roger liked to live that way, using sleeping bags instead of sheets and blankets, eating straight from the pot, even straight from the garden. He was a passionate man, wildly handsome, according to Judith, and he would have hated knowing that he'd died by power saw and electric line rather than on the face of a mountain. Judith never knew, even when he was alive, whether he was worth it, giving over her whole life, as she had. She did know that she wouldn't do it again. This Craftsman bungalow, which she had turned into a *home* home, was her statement of both independence and self. Where *would* they live?

As the shadow from the fence filled in the last pocket of light on the patio, Judith lit the candles on the picnic table, which was already set with four blue plates. Bart was comfortably camped in one of the Adirondack chairs, carrying on about the day he and Roberta had rented a car and ventured out the gates of Club Med into a couple of Mexican villages. He spoke of the men emerging from the jungle, stepping onto the road with their machetes as if they were revolutionaries, as if they were doing something terribly more exciting than keeping the paths from their homes to the road clear. Roberta shouted her comments, laughed at his jokes, and made fun of his naïveté. Nick sat in the butterfly chair, warm and hungry and happy, watching Judith at the grill, laughing at Bart with Roberta, licking the salt off his glass, tasting the lime and tequila. It was a beautiful cycle of tiny feasts for his skin, eyes, ears, tongue. Judith transferred the grilled halibut onto a blue serving platter and pronged the vegetables around the fish.

The phone rang. "Excuse me," Judith said, giving her beautiful smile, which was not quite so rare these days. A moment later, she was back, a quizzical expression on her face. "For you, Nick. It's Eve."

"Excuse me," Nick said, getting to his feet.

"Oh, Nick," Eve said. "I'm sorry."

"What happened?"

"I've gotten into a little bit of trouble."

"What kind of trouble?"

"I'm at Fred Meyer's. The Burlingame one."

"Eve!"

"I know," emphatically. Then quietly, "I know."

"Your book just came out."

"I know. It's awful timing."

Nick glanced out the open sliding-glass patio door. The candles were flickering. Bart was now entertaining with stories about the other couples they had met at Club Med. Roberta's gold jewelry clanked as she laughed. Judith stood within view, turned sideways, listening, he knew, probably perplexed as to why Eve was calling now, on a Saturday night, and here, at Judith's house. He saw her let Bart refill her margarita glass. She wasn't smiling at Bart's story. She wasn't attending to the dinner cooling on the table. She was listening.

Eve also listened, to Nick's silence, and knew he was deliberating. "I know it's the worst thing I could do to you right now, Nick. It's Saturday night. You're trying to have a romantic evening with Judith—"

"We have company."

"My book just came out. It's an awful time for bad publicity. The sooner I get out of here, the better. Please. Just this one last time. Please."

"No." For the first time in his life, Nick hung up on Eve. He immediately felt overwhelming guilt. He was, after all, her manager. When the phone rang again a second later, he picked it up.

"Just this last time. Please. Otherwise they'll put me in jail."

When Nick made his announcement on the patio, Judith said nothing at all. Bart walked him to his car.

"The tables have turned," he said in a voice husky with tequila. "It's time you listened to me now, buddy. You live too much in the past. You want everything to be this big wild adventure, this pure beautiful thing. You can't have it both ways, buddy, and frankly, you aren't getting any younger. Judith is a find."

"I know that."

"Then why the hell are you chasing around town after your ex-wife?"

"She's in trouble."

"*You're* in trouble, buddy. It's time you took some advice from me, for a change. Me and Roberta? We're solid. Sure, there are more beautiful women. Sure, there are more exciting lives. But hey, Club Med, friends like you two, a good job—"

Nick placed a hand on his friend's chest. "Keep it, Bart. I understand the stakes. I'm going to help out Eve. I'll talk to you later."

Dusk was over. It was dark now, but still warm in that green, wet way that early summer in Portland can be. Nick drove with the window rolled down, his elbow out, wondering. He often felt drawn backward, as if he were about to be sucked into a prior life. Maybe that's just what loyalty was, and what, after all, was one stupid dinner party compared to loyalty? What the fuck did Bart know, anyway? Nick had failed in so much of his life, but he had succeeded at always remembering that feeling he'd had on the track that day, watching Eve, who was then Marianne, run for the first time. That feeling of pure joy, of hope.

Not that the hope hadn't been challenged. The first time she had been picked up was the most heartbreaking. That was the only word for it. Track season had just ended, and Nick was having a barbecue for the team, boys and girls. Even George Winston showed up with his nerve-racked wife. But Marianne didn't show up. Which was impossible. Totally not predictable. She was his star runner, his protégée. Nick flipped hamburgers while Mrs. Winston twitched and supervised. Coach Winston paced the small yard, hands on his hips, uncomfortable in the social setting and with the fact that Nick, not he, the head coach, had organized the event. That alone would have been enough to unglue Nick. He had been teaching only one year. He had to constantly remind himself that he was an authority figure. Like the time when he left the grill to Mrs. Winston so he could go into the house to change the shirt he'd slopped barbecue sauce on and found, in his own bedroom, on his own bed, his worst long jumper making out with Winston's best shot putter. He'd almost backed out of the room, shutting the door quietly, as he would have done at a party in college, but then remembered he was in charge, responsible, that any resulting pregnancy or STD would be credited against his authority. Later, after the Winstons left and the kids started throwing food, Nick sent them all home, ostensibly because of the food fight, but actually because he was worried sick about where Marianne might be. Finally, late that afternoon, she called. Her voice was small, childlike, and very scared.

Perhaps because of her age, or her beauty, the Nordstrom detective hadn't turned her over to the police. But he had held her for extensive questioning, to scare her, and then insisted on calling her parents. Later Marianne told Nick that she had given the detective a made-up number and fortunately nobody ever answered that number all day. Meanwhile, she begged the detective to let her call her coach. At the end of his shift, when he just wanted to go home and didn't want to take her to the police, he relented. Nick arrived to find Marianne sitting in the tiny office that housed three different closed-circuit televisions that spied on women looking at bras, women sniffing perfumes, women trying on party dresses. Marianne, just seventeen years old, sat on the edge of a small bench, leaning forward, her feet tucked underneath her, her hands placed on either side of her thighs, gripping the bench. Her face was wet with tears. The detective took one last look at her, checked his watch, and said, "Take her."

This time Eve looked calm sitting in the small dingy waiting room of Fred Meyer's management offices, reading *People.* She had convinced them, yet again, to not take her down to the police station, but security had insisted that she come up with a responsible party to whom they would release her. The guard sat at a table in the next room, within sight through an open door, eating a Hostess cupcake and drinking coffee from a plastic cup.

"My husband is here," Eve called to him.

The guard stood and wiped his mouth, smearing the chocolate on his lips. "You Mr. Capelli?"

"Yes," Nick said, trying for a look of humility to make up for Eve's bold calm.

"Your wife tried to walk out the front door with an entire bag of groceries." The guard looked her over, from her sixty-dollar haircut to her two-hundred-dollar shoes. He shook his head in disgust, as if he regretted that he wasn't pressing charges.

"I'm sure it was a mistake," Nick said. "She can be so spacey."

"Get out of here."

"The lines were so long," Eve explained to Nick once they were in his car.

He started the engine. "A bag of groceries."

"It just seemed so silly to stand in that long line. I didn't think anyone would notice."

He wanted to tell her she wasn't going to be able to get by on her looks much longer, but he couldn't make himself say it.

"This is exactly why," Eve said, arranging her bag in the car and fastening her seat belt, "I need you to come to Santa Fe with me next month."

"To keep you from shoplifting? To count the towels in the hotel room at the beginning of the weekend and then again at the end? You know I can't go to Santa Fe."

"Why? School is finished. It's all paid for. They said I could bring a companion."

"Eve. I asked Judith to marry me today."

"Nick! Oh, *Nick,* honey, that is *fabulous!* Do I *ever* get to meet her? Then that settles it. You *have* to come to Santa Fe with me. Marriage makes women much more possessive."

"Judith's not possessive."

"Of course not. I'm just saying that marriage—"

"No woman would like her husband going off on a long weekend with his—" Nick forced himself to use the term they never used. "Ex-wife."

"But I need you."

"Eve, please."

"I feel shaky."

Her face, luminously bluish from the passing street lights, appeared truly frightened. She clasped her hands in her lap.

"I feel lonely," Eve said. "I *always* feel lonely. Remember the poet I told you about, Audrey Boucher? Well, I never called her. Instead, I wrote her. Twice. She hasn't answered my letters. Should I write a third one? To her I'm just some psychology junkie, hawking cheap emotional fix-its, making money off of people's desperation. Maybe it's true. Do you think that's true, Nick?"

"No."

"Why won't she answer my letters?"

Probably because Eve's letters were too intense. Probably because she asked for too much. Probably because the poet with her piece of land on the Maine coast coveted her privacy. "I don't know why, Eve, but you need to focus on the launch of your new book."

"How can I, when Audrey Boucher won't answer my letters?"

Nick closed his eyes, even though he was driving. When he opened them, he was still between the solid white line on his right and the spaced yellow one on his left. Eve Glass was still in the passenger seat, her head thrown back against the headrest, her arms splayed open at her sides, like she'd give herself over to the next bidder, whatever the offer. He knew he had to do *something* about her, but what?

A few weeks later, Nick lay in bed with Judith. Her second-story bedroom was like a tree house, surrounded with windows, so that lying on his back, he looked out on blue sky and cedar branches. He felt light and happy, floating in the feathers of the down comforter, imagining that heaven would be a blue field of color, no texture, just pure blue. The color itself. He pictured himself dead, floating in this ethereal blue, his cells porous, the blue flowing right through him, as if he were a hologram.

He rolled over on his side, thinking that now, after making love, might be a good time to ask Judith her thoughts on the marriage idea. He touched the wisps of her bangs, tracing the pale blue vein in her temple. Her eyes were open and she seemed to be following the movement of something out the window. Nick turned to look for the bird or butterfly but saw only the blue.

Judith began speaking while he was looking away. "I've been wanting to ask you."

She waited for Nick to say, "What?"

"It's about Eve."

He knew she wouldn't go on without an auditory signal that he was listening. "Yeah?"

"At O'Brien's. That night with Bart. You had said you wanted some advice about her."

"Oh baby, I was so smashed that night. You *know* that. Can't we both just agree that that night never happened?"

"What was the advice you wanted?"

"How the hell am I supposed to know? I'd had about twelve Irish coffees."

"I think you do know."

Nick sighed deeply to express his displeasure. When she simply waited, he said, "I feel responsible for her. Look. She had a really hard beginning. I don't even know what all her life was like before I met her. We don't and didn't talk about it. But I do know her dad was this crackpot traveling preacher of some kind. When she moved to Portland in '73, he'd rented some storefront in southeast Portland and started a church. I got the impression it wasn't the first church he'd started and that it probably wasn't all that legitimate. He had a different girlfriend—Eve called them 'stepmoms'—with every church. The thing was, Judith—" Nick heard himself almost shouting and he calmed down his voice. "She wasn't only an extraordinary runner. She was really smart. And in spite of her upbringing, or lack thereof, she possessed, has *always* possessed, this inner, I don't know, power or something. You know what I mean. You've felt it. At sixteen she looked like she knew more than most sixty-year-olds know about life. Do you know what I'm saying? About her *specialness?"*

Nick turned to look at Judith lying beside him on the bed and she nodded.

"Okay. So there's that. And I admit, she represented my hopes as a coach. Obviously. So Maddie Fisher—she was the Advanced Placement English teacher at the time—Maddie Fisher and I came up with a plan to give her a chance. Her dad and current stepmom were moving on again, leaving Portland, and we arranged for Eve to stay so she could finish high school in one place." He paused, waited for Judith to somehow correct his presentation of motives, but she didn't. "Eve lived with a friend of Maddie's. It worked out quite well. The father seemed relieved to have her taken off his hands, which, you have to admit, is sort of sad."

"What was the advice you wanted," Judith asked, "at O'Brien's?"

"Okay," Nick said quietly. "Even though Eve is smart, talented, all that, she's very vulnerable. I don't think you understand that. If I hadn't gone and picked her up at Fred Meyer's the other night, she'd have ended up in jail."

"Well, she *did* shoplift."

"I guess I feel like I took the responsibility for her when she was sixteen. And that responsibility continues. I can't just cut her off."

"She's forty-something."

"I know that."

"So you *still* haven't told me the advice you wanted."

"Well, obviously Eve's a problem. I don't know what to do about her."

"Maybe she's her own problem now."

"Can we talk about this another time?"

"Regina suggested—" Judith often quoted her therapist as if she were God, a voice without a body that must be obeyed. The pause was for Nick to digest that the upcoming request was going to be serious. "She suggested that I ask you to discontinue your weekly date with Eve."

Nick sat up, then laid back down again. "Jeez," was all he could get out.

"The point is, Eve has moved on, Nick. She's a successful author. She has her own business. You're the one who hasn't moved on. Maybe you need her to need you more than she does."

"It's not like I haven't thought of that. I wish it were true." If Judith could have seen the look on Eve's face in the car driving home from Fred Meyer, maybe she'd understand better. "Eve depends on me."

Judith shrugged as if to say, even if she believed that to be true, she didn't care.

The ether of blue in which Nick had been basking shrank down to a pinprick of light. He rolled away from Judith. "Look, is this jealousy? I haven't had sex with Eve in over two decades. That part of our relationship only lasted a couple of years, anyway."

"You manage her life."

Nick longed to go for a run. He got up, drank a glass of water in the bathroom, came back and sat down on the bed. "I wish it wasn't a problem."

"You just said yourself that she's a problem." Judith touched his back, then withdrew her hand quickly. She ran her fingers through the front of her short hair so that it stood up in little peaks for a moment before flopping back into place. He softened. He loved her slightly asymmetrical mouth, warm brown eyes, and easy bone structure, neither sculpted nor round, just friendly. Her body had the same friendliness. She thought she was too fat, and she *was* a bit rounder than most people who ran as many miles as she did, but the extra flesh was like an allowed margin of error, a statement of generosity.

"I hate feeling jealous," she said. "It makes me feel bitter and small."

Nick wasn't great at psychology, but maybe this one was obvious. Losing Roger had given Judith a pretty tight grip.

"You're not bitter and small," he said. "You have a very big heart. And I'm not going anywhere, sweetie. It's just dinner on Monday nights. I'm usually home by eight o'clock. You like time by yourself. You're always asking for it. So what's wrong with a couple of hours on Monday night?"

"It's not the time. It's your relationship with her."

"I don't understand," Nick said.

Judith shook her head. "Sometimes I think she's still the primary relationship in your life. You could have a regular friendship with her if she hired a manager. The way it is now—"

Nick got out of bed and searched for his sweats, found them, and hopped around on one foot trying to get them on. The irony was almost too much. As if Eve were the threat. How he'd love a night of surprises, a night of having no idea what the outcome might be, that feeling of discovering a person, of touching her body for the first time, the thrill of trust when you shouldn't trust. Judith had no idea that she was the only woman in his entire life to whom he'd been faithful, including Eve, including when they had been married.

"Let me think about it," Nick said, tying on running shoes.

"I just don't see us getting married when you are still so bonded with your ex-wife."

Nick stopped in the bedroom door and looked at Judith lying in the bed with the covers pulled up to her chin. He knew he was forty-eight years old. He knew his chances at glory had been reduced to nil. She knew it, too. So why strip him of his youth? His fifteen minutes. His *memory* of the fifteen minutes. Why didn't she know that if she took away his Monday-night dinners with Eve, his connection to that pact he had made with life, there would be nothing there for Judith to have? Without Eve, Nick was nothing more than an old guy who taught high school social studies.

And yet, two weeks later, sitting on the airplane, Nick realized that he was making the mother of all mistakes. He couldn't believe he had done it. For what? To listen to Eve argue with the flight attendant about the availability of lemon slices for her bubbly water?

"I bet if you peeked up in first class, there would be a lemon slice. Would you please? Just one little slice for my water. It makes such a difference."

"I'll check," the flight attendant answered tightly.

Nick downed his cranberry juice. Why had Judith tied his hands like that? She was a smart woman. She knew it would make him crazy, didn't she? Even so, Nick wasn't going to Santa Fe to make a statement or to be rebellious. Going to Santa Fe was more like struggling to the surface of a deep blue pool for air. Now, though, on the plane, he felt foolish. He loved Judith. This was a big adjustment, being faithful, staying home most evenings, sleeping with the same woman night after night. Still, he was ready for that. He could do it. Not just ready, not just willing, he wanted to. That was the real miracle. But Judith didn't know that, how could she?

"Oh, you are wonderful. Thank you," Eve said, accepting the small teacup filled with lemon slices. "These will last me the entire flight." Turning to Nick, "Isn't this fabulous! Look, *five* lemon slices." She squeezed one into her sparkling water and sat back in her seat, smiling. "Do you want to see the letter?"

He shook his head.

"Oh come on. Nick, you're being such a grouch."

She dragged her big leather bag out from under the seat in front of her and started rummaging. Once she found the envelope, she pulled out the yellow lined sheet and smiled.

"I'm not going to let you read it, but look, yellow lined paper. Isn't that, oh, I don't know, but *intimate* somehow?"

Nick closed his eyes, pretending to be dozing.

"Grouch," Eve said.

He awoke as the plane descended into the Albuquerque airport. The flight attendant was asking Eve, apparently not for the first time, to put her tray table in the upright, locked position. "One moment," she said, writing furiously.

"Now," the flight attendant said, reaching across Nick to lift the tray table herself. Eve yanked her notebook off the surface, steadied it on her knees, and continued writing.

"What are you doing?"

"Working on my talk."

"You finished it last week."

"Revisions."

"It's too late for that. You're delivering it in four hours."

She ignored him and continued to write feverishly. Ever since the *San Francisco Chronicle* ran a review blasting Walter Spinnaker's phoniness compared to her authenticity, she'd been in this pitched mood. What more could a motivational author hope for in a review than a declaration of authenticity?

Nick massaged his face and wondered if he could call Judith from the airport. No, better to wait until he got to the hotel. She liked focus. Anything on the fly made her feel cheap, as if she were a side thought.

"Did I tell you . . .," Eve said a few minutes later, as she handed her suitcase to the taxi driver. She paused to climb into the backseat. When Nick was seated beside her, she continued, ". . . that she's going to be there this afternoon?"

"Who?"

"Audrey."

"The poet? *Here*? In Santa Fe?"

"Mm."

"No, you did not tell me." So that explained the mania, the rewriting.

"She is. Not because of me, of course. She had a reading in the bookstore last night. She said she would come to my interactive lecture. I hope to have a chance to visit with her."

"We'll see."

"She's staying at some lovely place in the country for a couple of days. I'd like to go see it. Do you think that'd be possible?"

"Did she invite us?"

Eve paused. Then, reservedly, "Yes."

Not *us* then, *her.* He had come to Santa Fe, possibly losing Judith, for Eve, because she was family, because she said she needed him, because she begged, and she wondered now if she could get rid of him for just a few short hours for a rendezvous with some poet from Maine. "No."

"Oh, Nick."

"What?"

"You sound almost jealous."

"No, Eve, I'm not jealous. I'm thinking about *you*. Your book is getting great reviews. It's already scheduled for a second printing. You're reaching a new level. This is not the time to drift off on some fairy tale idea of . . . of . . ." Nick realized he was spitting. "All I'm trying to say is, this afternoon you'll have the biggest audience you've ever had. The hall seats seven hundred. They said it was nearly sold out. You have to focus on speaking to each and every person in that hall."

"Did I tell you why she hadn't written?"

"Yes, you did. She was traveling. She hadn't gotten your letters."

Nick felt claustrophobic the moment he set foot in the lobby of La Fonda, a huge historic hotel touting itself as the inn at the end of the Santa Fe Trail, claiming to have been in business since the beginning of the seventeenth century. Every square foot of the building was trying to scream, "Santa Fe!" The problem was, "Santa Fe" is not singular, so that every square foot had pueblo detail, Spanish detail, a little cowboy, a little Indian, a little old world, a little new world. The turquoise and terra-cotta color scheme, taken to an extreme, assaulted his hopes for a relaxing weekend.

"Tacky," Eve laughed, "but it could be fun. Come *on,* Nick. Lighten up. Look at this place. It's like Disneyland!"

The concierge himself led them to their suite, unlocked the door, and swept through the rooms like a breeze, straightening pictures, opening the balcony doors, jabbering away about how to use the adobe fireplace. Nick found a fiver in his pocket and handed it to the guy with a wink and nod toward the door, as if he and Eve were newlyweds. The concierge gave him a sarcastic know-all look and left.

Eve explored the rooms, calling out, "There's a whirlpool in the bathroom! And, oh, look! A spread of snacks! Yummy. Oh, I *love* this."

Nick stepped out on the balcony overlooking the Sangre de Cristo Mountains, burnt red and dry, a sharp contrast with the blue music of Eve's voice coming through the French doors. "Okay, okay, okay," he told himself. "I'm here. Okay. I'll be home tomorrow night."

"Thank you for coming, Nick." Eve fell back onto one of the two king-size beds, arms and legs spread-eagle.

He sat on the bed beside her, intending to use the phone to call Judith, but instead placed a hand on her stomach as if she were a hot-air balloon he could keep grounded. "You're welcome, baby."

"Baby?" Eve laughed her big-mouthed laugh. "*Baby*?"

"Sure," Nick smiled. "Baby." He tickled her belly with his fingertips.

"Oh, Nick, honey, I'm so glad you've found Judith. You deserve the very best." She ran her hand up his arm and squeezed his triceps, and then moved his hand away.

This tacky room, the hot ugly colors, his own skin airplane-sticky, her face slack with a desire that he knew wasn't for him, and still, it all combusted. He brushed her hair from her face, leaned down, and kissed her on the lips.

"Oh my," Eve said, raising one eyebrow.

Nick kissed her again, his tongue testing, remembering her faint gardenia scent, remembering her lean kind of hunger, not aching like Judith, not robust like he liked it best, but a slender kind of desire, focused and direct. His own desire took on a guilty impetus: he'd come at her request, insistence, he deserved something in return. He held her wrist against the pillow and looked for her tongue.

"Nick, *don't.*" She pushed him off of her just as someone pounded on the door. They both jumped as if they were teenagers getting caught.

"Yeah? Who is it?" Nick called toward the door.

"What the hell were you doing?" Eve asked, getting off the bed.

Nick walked slowly to the door and yanked it open. The same concierge smiled ingratiatingly as he held out a small white envelope. "A message for you, sir."

Nick plucked the envelope out of the guy's hand and shut the door without offering another tip.

"It's must be from Audrey! Let me have it."

Nick opened the envelope and pulled out a square of white paper.

"Nick! Give it!"

"It's not from Audrey." He folded the note and put it in his pocket.

Eve slumped back onto the pillow, disappointed. Then

turned her head with a sly smile and said, "It's from Judith, isn't it? Tell me what she says! Is it mushy?"

Nick let her think what she wanted. He dropped into one of the terra-cotta-colored armchairs, feeling heavily fatigued. "You're on in less than two hours. Let's eat lunch."

"Oh, yes, let's!"

The La Fonda Hotel ballroom, with its hand-painted thick wooden ceiling beams and hammered-tin chandeliers, was packed that afternoon. Two pyramids of Eve's new book, *If Grace Is the Goal,* sat on either side of the podium. The event, billed as an "interactive lecture," which Eve's Web site described as a cross between a speech and a workshop, was nearly sold out. Almost seven hundred participants! Eve appeared particularly poised as she took the podium and waited for the applause to subside.

"I won't ask you to live in the present moment," Eve began. "Nor am I going to tell you how to 'create a miracle mind-set.' I'm not about miracles. I won't say that I don't believe in them, but let's just say I don't experience them on a daily basis. And I *need* daily basis."

Eve growled *need* like the word was a perversion, and the audience laughed.

"I'm talking about practical steps. Steps, that's all, to get what you want. To have moments of—" Now she stopped, breathed, projected her body loosening so subtly the front row didn't even see the quiver, but so powerfully the back row felt their own releases. Her cadence slowed to awe. "To have moments of blessedness."

The audience sighed. They settled in for the afternoon.

"Living consciously," Eve told them. "Well, of *course* we'd all like to do that. What, is someone out there advocating the coma state? Of course not. But to tell you to live consciously is a bit like telling you that people need to eat food to stay alive. It's not news. What *is* news, what might help, are techniques for doing it. Every self-actualization book I read tells you that you should live in the moment, be conscious, practice compassion. No-brainers. What I'm about is point A to point B. If it sounds mathematical, well, it nearly is. And I'm going to give you the math.

"First, though, I want to find out about you. You, the lovely lady in the lavender blouse. Tell me . . ."

Eve was on. She wasn't using her speech script, not the original nor the version rewritten on the airplane. She had dramatically flapped it at the audience a few moments ago, then dropped it at her feet, saying, "You know what I'm going to do? I'm going to forget what I've prepared. I want to talk to you all eye to eye. I want to give you the frankest version of what I have learned. Let's just talk. Let's get to the bottom of this together."

It wasn't the first time she'd tossed her speech. Audiences loved it. They felt special, as if *they* were Eve's inspiration. In fact, they were. As they laughed at her jokes, moaned at her tales of woe, held their collective breath at her hints of grace, Eve absorbed their love for her. She had the brightest, most vibrant aura of anyone Nick had ever seen. It had been there like a full-body halo that first day on the track, and it was there now, gradually filling the room, growing with each smile and round of applause that reached her. It was like her aura had tendrils of blue light that swirled into the room, filling the crevices of longing.

Nick paced in the back of the hall, listening not so much to Eve's speech as to the whole ocean of sounds, as if he were an animal that didn't understand language—the quiet roar of audience rustlings, startling vocalizations that were laughter, Eve's lyrical voice. He was uneasy. This felt too much like the crest after Montreal, when she was the darling of the press, when they were on their way to Moscow.

After running her 1,500 meters in Montreal, he had been frustratingly separated from her for over an hour. Only the Olympic coaches were allowed on the track, but he was outside waiting, and so was the press, when she finally left the arena and ran, literally, into his arms. The nineteen-year-old wonder girl with her boy coach, only twenty-four years old himself. She wasn't a winner, not really even close, but she was definitely the prettiest, frothiest, most delightful girl on the track in that heat, especially compared to those communist speedsters, including the ultimate Soviet gold medalist, Tatyana Kazankina, whom the American press liked to portray as butch as they could. Marianne, as she was still known, leaped onto Nick, wrapped her legs around his waist, and planted her mouth on his. He had no choice but to hold her up by the buttocks, and the media pointed their lenses at the two kids. With her legs still wrapped around Nick, Marianne opened up to the reporters, one arm looped around his neck, the other waving, all while she sobbed, sobbed like a child who wanted to win more badly than any mortal could imagine. "She wanted it," a columnist for the *Post* reported, "she wanted it like no athlete has ever wanted it." Nick eased her onto the ground and watched his golden girl with the tear-streaked face answer questions with a poise as natural to her as running. Marianne Wade made great American press, and she knew it.

That night, after they had made love for the first time, Marianne sat up and said, "I'm going to be famous, you know."

"Yep, baby, you are. It's the gold in Moscow."

"I need a famous name, Nick. I want to get married, too."

"Okay," Nick propped up on an elbow. "When?"

"Soon. Right away. I've chosen my new name. Eve Glass."

"What's wrong with Marianne Capelli?"

She shook her head. "No. Eve Glass. Genesis and clarity."

"I don't know, sweetheart." Nick felt both touched and alarmed by her need to reach for an identity. But the Bible? A window pane? "Besides, the press already knows you as Marianne Wade."

Those next four years happened so fast Nick didn't know what hit him. They were like one blissful long-distance run. The perfect marathon. Eve Glass was a nobody, just some pretty girl from Oregon who ran in the Olympics and didn't even make it to the finals, but the press responded to her like a prophecy. The buzz was that she was going to do something amazing in Moscow. Especially if the slender, honey-blond girl whose personality was innocence incarnate got a little support. After all, she had been only nineteen in Montreal. She had two more Olympics in her for sure. It was worth it to the athletic-gear companies to endorse her, a four-year investment, anything to bring this girl to the top. It wasn't like she was getting the perks of a Chris Evert or Mark Spitz, but a mid-industry sneaker company kept her in running shoes and a manufacturer of sports drinks kept her hydrated.

No one was putting her on Wheaties boxes yet, but in those four years between Montreal and Moscow, there was no doubt in either of their minds that they would. Eve Glass, as she became known, had a reputation as an incredibly hard worker. She ran well in the Pan American Games, and even took second at the nationals. She was young, very young, and still getting faster. They planned on a medal in Moscow, but Los Angeles in 1984 was a good backup. They couldn't fail.

But they did. President Carter canceled Moscow, and Eve quit competing. For ten years, Nick tried. Even if she wasn't going to compete herself, he had dreams of the two of them coaching together, starting a club, shepherding a new generation to the Olympics. They had great ideas for coaching and training, which she wrote into her PhD thesis, and then eventually expanded into her first book, *Going the Distance: Endurance for Achievers.* But it was a very long eventually, during which time Nick taught social studies and coached high school track and field, dragged Eve home from parties, begged her to get serious, threatened to leave her, paid off at least four different department store security guards.

He did almost leave her once.

The Los Angeles Olympics had come and gone, and Eve's partying had become a calling more than a pastime. One Sunday she phoned Nick at three in the morning, said she was in trouble and needed him to come get her. A few minutes later, he pulled up in front of the southeast Portland address she had given him and double-parked in front of two motorcycles which looked menacing with their polished chrome and the way they leaned into their kickstands. Four women sat on the big porch of the house, the dark cylinders of beer going up and down like pistons. Nick approached cautiously until he was noticed, then stopped for appraisal.

"Anyone know this guy?" a woman shouted uselessly into the house. The disco was pumped and Nick could see bodies dancing inside. A skinny woman on the porch asked, not unkindly, "Whatta ya looking for?"

He knew enough to not say, *my wife*. "Eve Glass."

"I'll go tell her someone's here to see her. She know you're coming?"

Nick nodded.

"Anyone want another beer?" Everyone said they did. "You?" she said into the darkness beyond the porch.

"Sure," Nick said. Someone on the porch snorted.

Nick sat on the front lawn, his legs crossed. Fifteen minutes passed. The skinny woman hadn't returned, but someone stumbled off the porch and offered him a joint. He pretended to take a hit and handed it back.

"Eve's a fox," the woman said. "Total babe."

"Hm," Nick offered, noncommittal.

"You her boyfriend?"

"Mm," he said again.

"Want me to look for her for you? I don't think Val is coming back."

"If you wouldn't mind, please."

When that woman didn't return, either, Nick told the two remaining women on the porch, "Excuse me," and went in the front door. He expected someone to protest his entrance to the house, but no one even looked at him as he pushed his way into the blare of disco. There was a mirror ball hanging from the ceiling, slowly pirouetting, the chips of light like flying shards of glass. Only three couples were left, dancing in a rhapsody of sweat. He walked through the front room and reached a kitchen.

There a woman asked, "Hey, who is this guy?"

Another woman, "What do you want?"

"I'm looking for Eve Glass."

"She's in the bedroom."

Nick made his way to the back of the house. Pushed in one door and found a small group of women, but not Eve, huddled over a pile of coke. Pushed in another door and found the bathroom, empty. He locked the door behind him, peed, then went searching for Eve again. He finally found her, in the far reaches of the backyard, lying in a hammock between two other women.

"Oh, it's you," she said, squinting, as if she didn't quite recognize him.

She was bombed, and he was furious. "You called me."

"Yeah," she giggled, "but that was before I met Nancy and Olivia."

Nick walked slowly back across the yard to the house, through the kitchen, and then under the mirror ball and out the front door. That was it. That was absolutely the last time he would ever rescue her again. Fuck her thesis. Fuck their plans to be a coaching team. Fuck the whole damn thing.

"Nick." She was behind him as he descended the stairs of the porch, grabbing his hand, holding it tightly.

"Bye, Eve, honey," sang the woman on the porch who had called her a fox, a total babe.

Eve didn't answer, just clung to Nick like a recalcitrant child, until he deposited her in the front seat of his car. "Thank you," she said when he slid into the driver's seat. "I was getting in over my head. I've had too much."

"Too much what?"

"Everything. Too much everything." More chuckling.

"We're not kids anymore, Eve. You're thirty-three."

"A granny."

"I'm thirty-eight. We don't have a lot of time for fucking around."

"No more partying," she said, leaning over until her head landed on his right shoulder. "That's it for me. Nose to the mill. I'm finishing my thesis."

He told himself he'd give her six months, that was it. He didn't know what he'd do then, what exactly he would enforce at the deadline, but the amazing thing was that she'd done it. Not only completed her thesis, got her PhD, but found an agent who sold her thesis as a book. That was the thing about Eve. She did dink around. But sometimes, miraculously, she came through, and in a big way.

Now this. As if none of those years had mattered at all. As if Eve had known all along she could party her brains out and still rise from the ashes. Watching her now, reveling in the crowd's adoration, Nick admitted what he had never admitted to himself before: Eve had never cared about running even half as much as he had. Or even as much as Judith did now. For Eve, running had been a way to be loved. She was every bit as happy getting that kind of attention from being an author.

Which was exactly why he felt nervous now. This moment

in Eve's life resembled too closely the time after Montreal, before her fall. But the ante had been upped. Instead of people expecting her to win a gold medal for running fast, they now expected her to give them grace. The swarm of people wanting things from her was growing exponentially. This time Nick couldn't help her. He didn't know diddly about being a guru. Judith was right. It was time for him to let go.

Nick cracked the ballroom door and stepped quickly out into the lobby, easing the door shut behind him. He took a deep breath of the candy-bright decor, then pulled out his phone to try reaching Judith again.

"Mr. Capelli."

A woman stepped out of the ballroom behind him. She held out a hand, and when he hesitated, she laughed.

Nick smiled tentatively. The woman was sexy in a jaunty, tight-blue-jeans, white-T-shirt-and-black-leather-jacket kind of way. Big brown eyes and a friendly mop of curls contrasted with her challenging smile. "You don't remember me, do you?"

"I'm sorry. You look familiar."

"Man, you look just the same. I was on your track team—briefly, *very* briefly—at Kennedy High School twenty-five years ago."

Nick felt lost, as if he had wandered into a whole wilderness of former students, but to move things along, he said, "Oh, yeah, sure, I remember you now. How the hell you doing?"

"Good. Real good."

Nick nodded. "Running at all?"

She laughed as if he'd asked something absurd. "No, I'm not running at all."

"Yeah, I know, it's hard to find the time. Well, it's nice to see you. I'd better get back in there."

"Sure, sure. But Mr. Capelli. Listen. Did you get the note I sent to your room?"

"You're Joan Ehrhart." The face together with the name. He knew who she was. He knew exactly who she was.

A big smile. "Yep. I'm the *Times* reporter. I've tried reaching you a dozen times. It's gonna be a big story, Mr. Capelli. Great for Marianne. But I do need an interview."

"I'm sorry, but Eve's very busy. We're leaving right after the interactive lecture. Maybe another time."

"I thought you were staying until morning. How about breakfast? Seven at the café here in the hotel?"

She cocked her head, and Nick was sure she was mocking him. He wanted to tell her that she was pathetic to use her career to get revenge for something that had happened so long ago. But the truth was, she could do damage. He needed to go easy. He backed up a couple of steps.

"A lot has changed, Mr. Capelli. Hasn't it?" She looked like she was having fun.

"I'll speak with Eve and get back to you."

As he turned away, she said, "'Eve Glass' is more elegant, I suppose, but I would have stuck with 'Marianne Wade.' Sounds more trustworthy. But maybe that was the point."

Nick slipped back into the dark ballroom and eased his way up the aisle to the front, as close as he could get to Eve without being on stage. She glanced at him and he smiled reassuringly. An hour later, Nick made sure he was at the podium the moment Eve finished speaking. He stood with a hand at the small of her back while she greeted the crush of fans. The hotel had promised security, but neither of the two guys at the door looked a day under eighty, and they seemed to think their job was to make sure no one walked out with any hotel chairs rather than to protect Eve.

Nick whispered, "Come on. Back to the room. No lingering with the fans today."

Eve ignored him. She enjoyed signing books, shaking hands, listening to the personal testimonies about how her books had changed people's lives. A short woman wearing a multicolored hand-woven vest was describing, in tremendous detail, a hike in the desert, a hike that had been very difficult for her and which she had used DIG to complete. Eve clasped her hand, listening, and would have continued like this with her fans for another two hours if the poet hadn't shown up.

Nick had noticed the woman standing off to the side, away from the crowd, leaning against a wall and reading a book—not Eve's. She looked like a bird that had lighted in an unlikely place, just temporarily, and was resting before taking flight again.

A crow, not a sparrow, a crow wanting to escape. When Eve spied her and cried, "Audrey!" the woman lowered her book, removed her black-rimmed glasses, and smiled. She had piercing gray eyes, thin lips, and dark eyebrows. She wore a white, oversize man's button-down shirt, untucked, over teal jeans, and Birkenstocks with rag-wool socks. Her gray hair was short and tousled. If she were a high school teacher, Nick thought, she'd be a very strict grader.

"Thank you so much," Eve told the desert hiker. She squeezed the woman's hand. "You've made my day by telling me your story. Congratulations. You completed the hike and I know it is only the first of many journeys, journeys of all kinds, to come." The woman seemed to be satisfied with this and left smiling. Nick told the rest of the crowd that Eve would not be able to personally greet anyone else today. Then he kept his body between Eve and her fans as she skipped over to the boldly frowsy poet.

Audrey smiled again, surprisingly shyly, as she tucked her glasses and book into her bag. On closer inspection, Nick thought the poet looked more nervous than severe, as if she didn't know what to do with herself in the presence of Eve. The two women did not embrace. Nor did Audrey Boucher compliment Eve on her interactive lecture, or even mention it. She studied Eve's face intently, as if reading a poem, then blinked down to look at her own feet, whether in shyness or dismissal, Nick couldn't tell. Eve seemed even more nervous than the poet.

"I want you to meet my ex-husband, Nick. And this is Audrey, whom I've told you about."

The poet had a firm handshake.

"Nick, Audrey's invited me out to Galisteo for dinner. Would you mind terribly?"

Nick stared at Eve. So they'd already spoken? When did that happen? Did he mind? He felt as if she had whacked the back of his knees.

Nick was speechless with anger. He looked around for Joan Ehrhart, a wolf to whom he could toss Eve. He didn't see her, but the thought of her brought him back to his senses. He'd risked everything to protect Eve, and he needed to finish the job. Being whisked off to Galisteo was the best thing for her. Besides, it dawned on him how well this development would sit with Judith. Tomorrow, they would be on an early flight home.

"Fine," he said. "You have a car?"

Audrey nodded, looking again at Eve with a cautious curiosity.

Nick escorted Eve to the room where she grabbed her things, and then he walked the two women to Audrey's rental car.

"Get some rest," Eve said, patting his hand, as if she were leaving for his benefit.

He watched them drive away and then hurried back to the suite to call Judith. After letting the phone ring twenty times, he hung up. Not only was she not picking up, she had turned off her answering service. Nick went back down to the lobby, sat at the bar, and ordered a Coke.

"Are you Eve Glass's bodyguard or husband?" asked a woman sitting at the other end of the bar.

"Both."

The woman raised an eyebrow. Nick squared himself to the bar and propped up his elbows, making a personal barricade, but he could see the woman in the bar mirror. A real bimbo with big hair. She was forty-plus, and she filled her plus-size blue capri pants to the point of seam-stretch. Her breasts bulged out of the V of her white V-neck T-shirt.

"My name's Angel."

Nick laughed. "Right," he said. "But you know, I'm just having a Coke. I'm not really interested in conversation."

"Right," she said. "What's your name?"

"Max. I'm a truck driver."

The bimbo laughed. "Liar."

Nick shrugged.

"All right, I'll tell you my real name if you'll tell me yours. I'm Carleen. That's the truth."

"Nick. Nice to meet you, Carleen." He drained his Coke. "Gotta make a phone call. Excuse me."

Nick returned to his room and tried Judith again. Still no answer. He called Bart, and Roberta answered.

"Nick," she said coldly. "Hold on. I'll get Bart."

"Wait! Roberta!" But she'd slammed the phone down on her Formica kitchen table. Nick heard her yelling for Bart. Heard his friend tromp across the kitchen floor, fumble the receiver, then shout, "What do ya want, asshole?"

"Fuck off, Bart. I've been your friend a whole helluva lot longer than you've known Judith. Just because—"

"Which is exactly why I'm telling you straight. You shouldna gone to Santa Fe. You shouldn't be there now. You should leave your ex-wife to fend for herself, which believe you me she is perfectly capable of doing, and get your idiot butt home. If it's not too late."

"Okay, what if you needed me to accompany you somewhere, Bart. What if I went away for *one night* with you, say, on a camping trip. Would that be such a big fucking deal?"

"No, because we ain't gay, dickbrain. We'd be like two friends going on a camping trip, which people do. People do *not* go off overnight to luxury hotels with their ex-wives."

"Look," Nick said. "You're over my head. The point is, I love Judith. I'll be home tomorrow. But I want to talk to her tonight and she's unplugged the phone *and* turned off her answering service."

"Take a hint, then."

"Do me a favor, Bart. As my old friend. Drive over there. Tell her I'll give up managing Eve. Okay? Will you do that for me? Tell her she's right and I'm wrong."

"Tell her yourself." Bart hung up.

"Okay. All right, Bart, buddy. I'll talk to you later," Nick said to the dial tone. He set down the receiver very, very gently to counter his need to break it.

Nick splashed water on his face, then rode the plummeting elevator back down to the La Fonda lobby.

The bimbo was still there, sipping a martini. He began to sit down at the other end of the bar, but when he glanced in her direction, she smiled. "What'll you have?" she asked. "It's on me."

"I'll have what you're having."

"Two more Tanqueray martinis," she told the bartender. "Up with two olives."

Nick moved over to sit on the stool next to her. She looked like she wanted the standard script. His mouth already felt stale from the sentences he would speak to Carleen, so he took a lemon wedge from the bartender's cache and bit into it. The sour tang fired his glands and he shook his head. He'd never chatted up a groupie. "So, what did you think of Eve's talk?"

"I wasn't there. Sorry."

"Oh. So what are you doing in town?"

The woman laughed. "Surprised someone might come to Santa Fe this weekend for something other than a Personal Search for Grace?"

Nick met eyes with Carleen and didn't smile.

"Relax. I'm just messing with you. Sure I was at your wife's gig." She reached deep into the bag at her feet and pulled up a copy of *If Grace Is the Goal* and waved it in front of Nick's face as proof. "She's a smart woman. I admire her speaking talent. Where is she now?"

"Having dinner with a friend."

"Oh?" She raised her eyebrow suggestively, again, another stock gesture, and Nick began to have the uncomfortable sense that she was mocking her own image, that perhaps she wasn't as dumb and available as he had thought.

"So what do you do?" he asked.

"I'm an attorney for a nonprofit human rights organization."

"You are not."

She knocked a cigarette out of the pack on the bar and put it between her full lips. Nick opened his mouth to say that he would not be able to remain at the bar with her while she smoked, but instead he watched her cup the flame of her lighter and inhale. She turned her head and blew the smoke out into the room, a blue genie. She studied his face. "So are you two close?"

"Eve and me?"

She smiled faintly, smoked, nodded.

"Yes."

More nodding, then she crushed out her cigarette. "I'm sorry. I know you're the healthy type. My husband and I are separated. We are *not* close. I love him, but he's a jerk. And I'm unfaithful. He doesn't know that, but he senses it because I've become too patient with him, not desperate enough, not like I used to be before I started fooling around."

"Why don't you get divorced?"

She reached for the cigarettes again, but only pushed the pack down the bar. Licked her lips. Rubbed her nervous hands on her hips. Shook her head. Finally, "I just don't know."

Nick laughed. It was as good an answer as any.

On their second martini, Nick asked, "You really are a human rights attorney, aren't you?"

"Yes, darlin'. I even know what grace is. Maybe not as well as your wife, but I have an inkling."

"Are you making fun of Eve?"

"No, I'm not. I told you I have a lot of respect for her. In fact, although you think I'm trying to pick you up, I am not, and the reason I am not, is precisely because of the respect I have for your wife."

Nick stared at her.

"Why is it that men in these hip Western towns assume that women with big hair are idiots?"

"So where are you from where men have more respect for women with big hair?"

Carleen lit another cigarette. "Louisiana. And I didn't say more respect. I said they didn't assume dumb."

Carleen would be robust. He didn't need the two martinis to know that.

He swept his gaze around the bar, hoping the jarring colors and blocky architecture would alter this pleasant dizziness into an unpleasant one. In the far corner, sitting at a small round table that held a laptop, was Joan Ehrhart. She smiled and raised a tumbler, like a toast, then brought it to her mouth. Suddenly, Carleen felt like a safe harbor. Nick made firm eye contact with her. "I'm gonna tell you something."

"What's that, doll?"

"Eve and I haven't been involved in over twenty years."

"But you're married."

"Technically. But we both date. We're good friends, and we just haven't bothered to divorce."

Carleen shook her head. "Nice try, but I don't buy it."

"It's actually the truth. She's with a romantic interest right now."

Carleen turned up her lie detector radar and scanned Nick from the top of his frizzy head to the soles of his Italian loafers.

He said, "This bar is stuffy."

She nodded, slowly, still assessing.

"I've got this incredible view of the Sangre de Cristo Mountains. Let's go sit on my balcony."

"What I don't need is the wrath of the best-selling expert on grace. No thanks."

"I'm not bullshitting you, Carleen. Come on. Let's order dinner in the room."

The look on her face tenderized every muscle in Nick's body. He loved that moment when a woman's masks fell away. Carleen dropped the mock-bimbo one, the really-a-human-rights-attorney one, even the truly-a-ripe-luscious-woman mask. For a moment Carleen was simple, raw Carleen, hungry. Nick loved that moment when two people, face to face, are stripped down to their cores of desire.

She slid off her bar stool. "I'll do dinner. I kinda like talking with you. But don't try any crazy shit."

"You call the shots, baby. Whatever you want. But hold on one second. I have to confirm something with that reporter over there."

Nick strode over to Joan Ehrhart's table and stuck out his hand, pleased to startle her. She did not offer her own hand back. "Gotta take a rain check on that interview tomorrow morning," he told her. "Maybe another time. Nice to see you again, though."

"Has anyone ever told you you're an asshole?"

"Just leave Eve alone."

Carleen waited for him by the bar and Nick made for her in earnest now, wanting to dive under the fake bimboness of her as if she were a thick down comforter. Even before they reached the elevators, he'd forgotten what he needed to forget. Just smelling Carleen, the horizon of his mind expanded.

In the morning, someone unbolted the door and came in. Nick leaped up, shouting, "Who is it?"

"Nick, honey, it's just me." Eve sat on the edge of the bed. "*Shh.*"

He tore back the bedcover, as if Carleen were hiding at the foot. When did she leave? He tried to grab the clock, but it was bolted to the bedside table. "What time is it?"

"Don't be mad at me. I'm sorry I didn't call. That was so irresponsible of me. It just seemed like it didn't make any sense to come all the way back out here in the dark."

Nick groaned. How had Carleen left without waking him? He didn't even have her phone number. He swung his legs over the side of the bed, picked up the phone, and ordered coffee and rolls. "What time is it?" he asked again.

"Ten-thirty."

"Shit. We should be leaving for the airport now." She might still be in the hotel, but he didn't know her room number, or even her last name.

"You weren't worried?" Eve looked curious.

"Of course I was worried," Nick said, grabbing his pants from the floor by the bed. He saw Eve notice the rest of his clothes, which were scattered about the room. "But I just figured it was, you know, like you said. Get your stuff together. We're going to miss our flight."

Eve was thankfully quiet while packing, and on the flight home. At the Portland airport, they even took separate taxis. Nick sprawled in the backseat of his, glad to be finally alone. He needed more sleep. He needed to see Judith. He needed a very long run.

At home he checked for messages from Judith, none of course, and then dressed for a run. Before tossing his jeans in the laundry, he looked in the pockets and discovered a piece of La Fonda stationery, folded into a crumpled origami crane. When he unfolded it, he found Carleen's phone number and e-mail address. He sat down, reading and rereading. No message, no thank you, just contact information. That simplicity touched him. Her handwriting touched him. He was looking around for a place to keep the paper crane when the phone rang. Judith. He grabbed some matches that were sitting by a blue stubby candle next to his bed and lit the note. As the phone rang, he watched Carleen's phone number and address crinkle to black. He grabbed the phone as he walked the last flaming wing of the crane to the bathroom and dropped it in the toilet.

"Hello?"

The caller hung up.

Nick watched the toilet water swirl and gurgle out of sight, along with the last of Carleen. He thought of trying

Judith's number again, but even if that had been her, she wouldn't pick up.

He looked out the window at the pouring rain and lost heart for his run. He was an idiot. He couldn't believe he'd gone to Santa Fe. He couldn't believe he had slept with Carleen. He grabbed a water bottle and took off anyway, in spite of the rain. He would use the run as penance. He pushed his pace, reaching the foot of Terwilliger in record time, then ran up the hill, glad that the dense cloud cover and pelting rain would prevent him from seeing the Willamette River, the city, Mount Hood. Rain splashed against the hot tears on his face, and he pushed his pace still harder. He was an idiot. He'd lost Carleen. He'd lost Judith. Eve, the real Eve, was long gone.

He was an idiot! That one moment he had lived for, two and a half decades ago, like some kind of lighthouse in the past, a reverse beacon, his only hope, luring him forever backward. His life one big long stumble. And no wonder, because within his golden moment was imbedded an injustice, like a spot of rot in a juicy fruit, and that rot was growing now. Moments of failure and moments of grace. They add up to make a life. But when one moment is both . . .

Everything was slipping from his grasp. He pushed his pace still harder, but felt as if he were moving backward. Even so, he knew he would never get back to Eve. He also knew that somehow, one way or another, Joan Ehrhart *would* get to her. Oh yeah, he remembered who she was. He remembered her perfectly. Portland was blue with rain and cloud, and Nick wheeled his arms as if he were swimming through the cold moisture. He longed for Carleen's breasts. He longed for Judith's voice. He longed for the light.

# *A Glimpse:*
## *Joan*

The woods were gone. Even the creek was gone, although Joan found a big drain, at the base of a driveway, where a gurgling, even on this hot summer evening, suggested that water still moved through the ravine. Instead of evergreens there were a half dozen newer houses, painted in pale shades of apricot, green, and tan.

On the afternoon of the kiss and everything that followed, Joan had walked Marianne home, taking the path through this ravine, next to the creek, under the cover of tall, black-green trees. In the privacy of that dark canopy, Marianne had been solemn and quiet in a way that Joan had never seen her before. At first Joan chattered nervously, worried about Marianne's retreat, and then grew quiet herself. The small trickling creek seemed to roar.

Marianne veered off the trail and sat on the creek's bank. She patted the mud. "Sit."

Joan sat beside her.

Scooting forward, and then rocking onto her haunches, Marianne used her hands to scoop up some water from the creek. She splashed this onto Joan's head. "There," she said. "You're pure."

"Pure?"

"Do me."

So Joan did. Cupping her hands and filling them to capacity, she carefully lifted the bowl above Marianne's head and opened her hands. The water slid down her hair and face, and as it did, a white light glowed from the places where the water touched her. Joan saw it. Could have measured it. A glow several inches thick, coming off of Marianne where the water touched her.

Frightened, Joan stood up and took several steps away. Marianne remained seated in the mud, by the little creek, with her eyes closed. Joan backed up slowly, silently, from the glow of her. With her eyes still closed, Marianne said, "Don't go."

Joan tried to stay. She watched Marianne, who didn't budge, wouldn't open her eyes, wouldn't end her vigil by the creek. But the woods were too dark. The trees too tall. The water's gurgle almost a laugh now, too persistent.

"Marianne," Joan said.

"Shh."

"Get up."

Marianne only drew her knees against her chest with her arms, holding herself tight, her face pressed into the fronts of her thighs. The glow just a blush now, but even so, Joan couldn't bear the voltage of the moment. She turned and ran.

For years Joan wondered if that had been a test she had failed. Maybe if she had had the fortitude to stay, if she had been able to endure the glow of Marianne there in the woods by the creek, then maybe the rest wouldn't have happened. Maybe Marianne wouldn't have quit talking to her. Maybe she wouldn't have hooked up with the track coach. Maybe the meetings with the principal wouldn't have happened.

Now, standing in what she guessed to be the same place, although at present it was someone's manicured side yard, with unnaturally green grass and a border of pink and white impatiens, Joan knew that she'd tortured herself unnecessarily all those years. Marianne had been a disturbed girl, that was all, a very disturbed girl, and Joan had been a green sixteen-year-old.

Why then was it so hard for Joan to find compassion in her heart for either of them?

Worse, she couldn't shake that little zing of predation brought on by her editor's braying laughter, the lure of playing a little cat and mouse. She'd called it curiosity, at first. What *had* happened to the athletic duo? What *did* Marianne, aka Dr. Eve Glass, expert on grace, have by way of a "gift"? But watching Mr. Capelli—she couldn't call him Nick—squirm in her presence was irritating. His discomfort drove her curiosity to anger. As if her life hadn't moved beyond any little destruction he had wrought. As if anyone, anyone at all, cared about his obscure little world. She had to laugh at the way in Santa Fe he'd said, "Just leave Eve alone." Like he was in a Western or something. But that was part of the problem, his taking her so seriously, the way his fear stimulated the cat in her. It made her feel so, well, powerful.

But she could let go of that feeling. She wasn't a psychopath. She might enjoy batting his ego around a bit, but she had better things to do than spend much time on some twerp's oversize sense of importance. If it were just him, she could move on.

But Marianne. The way she looked right through Joan in the lobby of the La Fonda Hotel in Santa Fe, as if she had no idea who she was. Joan was angry with herself for feeling a moment of openheartedness, of feeling actually *glad* to see her, for considering the possibility that Marianne had grown up. Somehow she'd thought that maybe they could laugh together about that silly spring two and a half decades ago. She hadn't expected tears and apologies, for Christ's sake. But the blank stare. It reminded her so precisely of how she'd felt then.

The second meeting with the principal had been a brief one, and it did not include Mr. Capelli or Marianne, but it had included Joan's parents. Mr. Ubik's accusations were all implied, couched in references to "unwanted attentions," "unnatural attachments," and the "need for treatment." No one even mentioned Marianne's name. Joan's father had been so incensed he'd wanted to sue Mr. Ubik, the school district, the City of Portland. Her mother had convinced him that making any kind of scene at all would only damn Joan more. No one ever asked Joan whether any of the accusations were true. They spoke at home as if they were all lies, which only made it worse. Her parents got her transferred to another high school, and never in her life had she felt as alone as she did that year and a half before graduation. Even though no one at the new school knew about her, the shame was like a suffocating stink she could never leave behind.

All this from the woman who advertised herself as delivering grace to the planet. It was the irony, the lie, that was so hard to turn her back on now. It was Marianne's blank face drawing Joan across a line. She didn't think she could stop.

Joan dug out her cell phone and called Meredith.

"Yeah?" Meredith answered.

"Hey. Just checking in. Have time for dinner tonight?"

A long sigh. "Wish I did."

"I need to work, too."

"Where are you?"

Joan hadn't spoken to her girlfriend about the *Times* piece on Eve Glass again. Meredith, if she even remembered the conversation about it, probably assumed she'd told her editor that she couldn't do it. She rarely asked anymore what Joan was working on. Joan could have an entire life on the side, despite the fact that they lived together, and Meredith wouldn't have a clue. "At the library," she said.

"I better run." Meredith smacked a kiss into the phone. "See you later?"

Joan walked from the neighborhood that used to be woods to the high school. The space under the bleachers, where for a few weeks Marianne and Joan had smoked packs of cigarettes, looked exactly as it had then. The pavement was littered with the discarded butts of other crazed adolescents, along with candy bar wrappers, even a condom. Joan sat down and drew her knees up to her chest.

It was absurd to still be asking the "what if." But she did: What if she hadn't run that day by the creek? What if Marianne had felt deserted? There had been that glow, an essence Joan had never seen since in another person. And she'd run from it.

## *Part Two*

# Alissa's Edge

Alissa sat in her red Jaguar outside the house she and Seth had bought a month ago in Portland Heights. The rain, which had stopped briefly in May but was back again with a vengeance, pummeled the windshield. The huge evergreens behind their house moaned and swayed in the summer storm, reminding her of an Isadora Duncan dance. June already, but still rain. Over-caffeinated from the two espressos she had had in an attempt to drug herself back to sanity, Alissa blasted Bach's concerto for two violins and worked the controls of her seat adjuster, so that she was rocking, sliding, rising, and falling, as if her car seat were an amusement park ride. Even over the cranked Bach, she could hear the rain splat and echo off the Jag's hood. Sometimes she felt as if she just couldn't load her senses enough, as if she had such a large capacity for processing sensory data that she couldn't keep enough of it pumping through her body. Sometimes it felt like no matter how hard she pushed, she'd never find the edge.

Seth would not understand what she had just done. *She* didn't understand what she had just done. Three hours ago, she'd had absolutely no idea she would do it. She had responded to the ad in the newspaper, and then gone on to the interview not so much on a lark but as a joke, an elaborate joke, a story to tell Seth at dinner, to entertain friends, if they ever made any here in Portland, coming in as they had with all her new California money and picking up prime real estate with their loose change. Surely they would make friends. But now that she thought of it, her story of being interviewed by self-help icon Eve Glass might not be that interesting, or even funny, to Portlanders who probably already knew, and were tired of, the inside scoop on the woman.

But the lack of a good story to tell was the least of Alissa's problems right now. She had taken the job.

Struck with the desire to call her parents, Alissa adjusted her seat so that she could get out, turned off the stereo, and stepped into the rain, her raincoat folded over her arm. She walked slowly, letting the sky's tears drench her black Armani suit. What was she doing here? Why couldn't they have moved to Chicago? Now *there* was a town with a challenge. She'd find the mob's headquarters and get herself hired to rework the town fathers' images. Alissa laughed out loud at the picture of herself, thirty years old, Yale graduate, just barely pretty in that plain, Ivy League kind of way, freshness made beautiful by a gutsy confidence, a kind of "can't fail" face, which in her case was entirely homemade, in a meeting with a bunch of godfather types. The thing was, the picture wasn't that outlandish. Alissa understood deciding what you wanted and taking it. She hadn't been born with her gifts, like Seth. She'd made them from scratch, which was what she was good at, had done for a handful of Silicon Valley executives with extraordinary success. Of course that's what she should do now, what Seth had been expecting her to do in Portland, start her own public relations firm. She could do it. She didn't need to make any more money, but she could, probably lots. She looked, and was, young, and she looked, but wasn't, green. Seth said she was absolutely perfect for Portland, where freshness counted, where cynicism was not yet the virus it was in the bigger urban centers.

Her own firm. It sounded too easy. Too obvious. Too the-next-step.

Besides, Alissa hadn't come to Portland for the easy family connections, as Seth had. Nor had she come to follow Seth. Even he knew that. He assumed she'd come for the new market, the she'd-be-perfect-in-Portland part, and because they were both sick to death of Silicon Valley, that dry basin of computer madness, and the long commute necessary if you wanted to live anywhere other than in your office. Portland, Seth had been telling her, ever since they started dating their freshman year in New Haven, was the ideal place to live.

But this *rain*. Alissa mentally tapped the "play" button in her brain and began, from memory, to listen to the Bach CD she'd just shut off in the car, seeing how far she could get through the first piece, the double concerto for violin and oboe, by heart. She paused on the flagstone path leading to the arched front door, wooden with weathered-to-green brass braces, which looked embarrassingly like the front door to a castle. As the rain fell, she stood still on the flagstone path and turned up the virtual volume in her head, playing the music until she made it all the way through the first movement of the double concerto. But how did the second movement begin? It was the pretty one. *Adagio.* Those first notes, though . . . By now the rain had flattened her hair to her head and worked its way in the front of her blouse and suit jacket so that a stream flowed down between her breasts, pooling in the base of her bra. But why fight the rain? In fact, she figured it out. She had come to Portland for exactly this. The rain. The dense green days. The grayness. It was almost like she wanted to self-induce a depression to see what it was like. Maybe Oregon would subdue her, be like a nap in her life. It certainly wasn't that she liked nature, because she didn't. But these enormous trees, right here in the hills above the city, the relationship they had with the wind, the way they pitched and shuddered together, that was something to see. It reminded her of tornadoes back home in Missouri, the way they leveled houses and tore holes in fields. Real power. Power you couldn't control. Silicon Valley had been so literally sterile. The money, the long, flat, dry corridors of freeway. The unchanging weather, hot sun and colorless sky. Even the people could be played like musical instruments. Except that, if Silicon Valley were a symphony, it would have no dynamics, would be one long, flat sound. Seth was right to urge them to leave.

Happily becoming drenched, she wended her way around the side of the house, through the giant ferns and calla lilies planted years ago by the previous owner, until she came to the backyard, which was a thick stand of Douglas firs, the reason Seth wanted the house. His own forest. Near the back of the property, running across one corner, was even a small stream, undoubtedly swelling by the moment with all this rain. Alissa was hesitant to go inside. High above her head, two stories up, was the great room with its stone fireplace. A shadow, Seth's, passed across the ceiling. If he looked out, he wouldn't be able to see her. He would see only the wash of rain and a wet darkness.

Alissa stripped off her Armani suit. She also pulled off the silk chartreuse blouse, tearing a button, and kicked away her pumps. Finally her bra and panties were tossed on the fir needles that had accumulated on the forest soil, and she stood completely naked in her own backyard. She had never done anything like this before. Yet, she didn't feel deranged or even particularly rattled, though maybe a bit zippy from the espressos. Instead, she felt dead center on target, as if this were a homecoming ritual she performed daily. She wanted to shout, "More rain!" It was the only thing she could think of to ask for more of. Everything else she had or could buy. But rain, that was something she couldn't stop, so why not demand more? Soon Alissa trembled with cold, but she forced herself to stay another few moments, indulging herself in early stages of hypothermia, until she felt the chill reach her very core. Yeah, there was something spooky about Oregon. She quickly got dressed in her wet chartreuse blouse and black Armani suit, sans the panties and bra, which she shoved under an enormous rhododendron bush, ghostlike with its rotted pale pink blooms, like some kind of serial killer too deep in madness to carefully hide the evidence, and walked in the basement door. Restripping, she stepped into the guest suite shower and, a few minutes later, wrapped hot and steamy in a fluffy white towel, ascended the stairs to greet Seth.

She found him sitting in the great room, his tie loosened around his neck, the stock page open on the Oriental rug at his feet, entertaining his parents. Arthur and Nancy drank Scotch, he in the big armchair and she standing at the picture window with a hand at her throat, gazing at the storm, while Seth chugged a Coke on the couch.

"Where'd you come from?" Seth asked, reaching for the stock page lying on the floor between him and his father. He folded it neatly and tucked it into the magazine rack, as if he could tell, just by looking at her, that today she was more interested in rain than money.

"Alissa, dear." That was Nancy, her voice always approaching disapproval. Well, this was her own home, and she had the right to appear in a bath towel, with wet hair, in her own great room, did she not?

Arthur only cleared his throat and looked away as if she were in fact stark naked.

Seth smiled at her. "How'd you come in?"

"The basement. I was soaked, so I thought I'd not spoil the floors." It was an absurd answer. There were mats, and anyway, she could have removed her shoes.

He smiled again. Seth was gorgeous. His imperfect posture worked almost like a beauty mark, calling attention to his broad shoulders and hard chest and stomach, obvious even in a suit and tie. His light hair was baby soft and would undoubtedly begin wisping away toward partial baldness, even before he turned forty, but his square jaw and dead-sure, opaque brown eyes could carry any failure on the part of his hair. He gave her his sexiest smile now, insinuating his way inside her steamy bath towel, hoping to seduce away her vexation at a surprise visit with his parents.

"Well," Alissa said, unseduced, feeling like one of those trees surging in the storm. "You didn't tell me your parents were visiting this evening, or I would have made myself a bit more presentable." She felt unaccountably furious. While she had been having her woodland-nymph moment in the back-yard, which she had every right to have, her unofficial in-laws were drinking Scotch in the great room, infringing psychically on her neo-Shakespearean moment. Of course, they hadn't seen her. She really should control her anger. Arthur's friends would make up an important client base for the public relations firm that, standing now before Seth and his parents, she knew she would start.

"We were waiting for you," Seth said softly. "We thought we'd go down to get a bite at Aubergine."

"Lovely," Alissa said, gaining control of herself, already annoyed that she had lost it momentarily. What was happening to her? Control was her middle name. "I'm so sorry to have kept you waiting. I'll be ready in a jif."

*In a jif.* She was already talking like Nancy. *In a jif!*

Once seated at Aubergine, Arthur ordered an Oregon pinot gris, drank half his first glass, then leaned back and asked Alissa, "Don't you think this is the perfect time to start a family? You have your nest egg. Seth is gainfully employed. You're not getting any younger."

"Stop it, Arthur." Nancy, who was often in a daze, snapped to at the topic of marriage.

"Damn it, Nan, I want grandchildren." Arthur drained that glass and poured another for himself.

"In due time, Pops. Hey, what do you think of Roscoe?"

"You give it some thought, Alissa, my dear," Arthur said before he and Seth discussed a young recruit they had just hired. Nancy, relieved to leave the topic of Seth's marriage, pretended to be fascinated with the shoptalk.

Mozart tinkled into the room, but so faintly that Alissa could only hear, not feel, the music. She longed to turn up the volume, let the music fill the room, pulse into her limbs, especially after her second glass of pinot gris. She also longed to tell Seth about Nick Capelli and Eve Glass, to see his reaction to what she had done. Because in the end, even though Alissa had made much more money than he had and even though she was smarter, if college grades and test scores meant anything, she turned to him for final assessments of all her decisions. In the end, Seth could put his finger on the right thing faster than Alissa could.

Even down to the way she dressed. She needed that help.

Alissa had a studied elegance, a beauty that she had worked for rather than been born with. Her brown hair tended toward lank, her eyes were a bit too small, and rather than the high, prominent cheekbones she'd like to have, she had a prominent jaw, like her daddy's. One of the first things she learned at Yale, though, was that a certain amount of beauty could be assumed, not unlike the emperor's new clothes. I think (I'm beautiful), therefore I am. Simplicity, Alissa had learned, was key. Makeup announced a girl's insecurities, highlighted flaws. Too much embellishment implied a need to cover up. Tonight Alissa had stepped into a plain black dress and sandals and put diamond studs in her ears. When she reappeared in the great room, Seth's mom had looked at her with more approval than usual. Nancy seemed to be always looking for the Missouri in Alissa. Their new house, for example, was a bit too showy for Seth's mother, though at the same time, she enjoyed complaining about the children's ostentatiousness to her friends, knowing full well it advertised their delightfully shocking financial success. Alissa's own parents would marvel at the house as they would at an extraordinary fireworks display. If she had been dressing for them, Alissa might have added a lacy shawl and dangling earrings, rhinestone would have been fine. She would have painted her nails, fingers and toes, and probably put up her hair, the swirlier the better. Her mother often pushed her fingers through Alissa's thin, not quite chestnut brown hair, and said, "Oh, honey, let's get you a perm." God knew what she would look like today if she'd stayed in St. Louis. When she began school she had intended to return home after graduation, but unlike Seth, she could not bring herself to do what had always been expected of her. Why was it so easy for him?

Watching him talk with his father in the precious little French restaurant, she felt a mix of admiration and impatience with his easy acceptance of life, his willingness to not bother with choices. Why should he? Success, money, and a circle of important friends were guaranteed. But it wasn't the wealth that had attracted Alissa to him so fiercely, it had been his easiness, his absolute clarity about what he wanted. A quality she had always called, perhaps mistakenly, his Oregonness.

They met in the stairwell of a dorm in the first week of their freshman year. They were both leaving a party on the third floor. The party had bored Alissa, but the sight of Seth gave her hope.

"You look exactly like a Boy Scout," she told him. He wore a blue-and-green-plaid flannel shirt. His jeans were some off-brand, and hung a bit too far above his hiking boots. He was the dewiest boy she'd seen at Yale, and she couldn't believe that she hadn't noticed him before.

"I *am* a Boy Scout," he said with a confident smile. "Was."

Alissa wanted to say something cheeky, something that would lead them right to bed, but a hint of authenticity in him made her pause, consider giving him more lead. So she only nodded, smiled, continued on her way down the stairs.

"How'd you know?" he asked her back.

She turned. "That you're a Boy Scout? *Were,* that is. You look outdoorsy."

"I'm from Oregon."

"Logging family?"

Seth laughed. "Sort of. Where're you from?"

"Missouri."

"Really? Are you homesick?"

"No."

"I guess I am. Actually, I'm feeling really homesick."

Alissa didn't know what to say to that. She stared at his beauty, wishing she could soothe his poor Boy Scout heart.

"I could show you some pictures of things I bet you don't have in Missouri."

"Now?"

"Yeah."

So they went to his room after all, but she kept her distance while he took the stack of photographs off his desk and began regaling her with stories of his yearly fishing trips in the Cascade Mountains. Since he was a boy, a group of men and their sons had loaded up horses with canned beans, Dinty Moore beef stew, bottles of whiskey, fishing rods, and tackle boxes, and climbed up the sides of mountains to perched lakes with names like Sapphire and Crooked Man and Heart. Seth's favorite part was opening the tackle box at dawn each morning, and he mimed this now, with his beautiful, long-fingered hands. The first rays of sunlight would strike the shiny lures and gloriously colored flies, sprays of red, blue, and gold. Seth wouldn't touch fish cooked at home, but trout grilled over a campfire was food for the gods.

Seth was right, he showed her pictures of things she'd never seen in Missouri, like glaciers and rain forests and alpine meadows. It wasn't as if the boys in Missouri hadn't talked about fishing all the time, too, but they weren't fly-fishermen, and their stories were as muddy and flat as the rivers in her state. Seth's stories were white-water freshness, his history with the fish a kind of elusive beauty that was a part of his every gesture.

Moving to Oregon, finally, after twelve years together, was a little like moving into the heart of his character. Later this summer, Seth and Arthur would be going on their annual fishing trip. Already a couple of Seth's childhood friends had small boys of their own who would come along. The ladies,

Alissa learned, always had a lunch while the men were gone. It had been unclear when Nancy mentioned this whether unmarried partners were invited to the lunch, though Alissa suspected that the marital status of Seth and herself was the least of what worried the Kingsleys about the match. Which was not to say that Arthur and Nancy were unkind to her, because they were not. They seemed to be genuinely fond of Alissa, but there was a nervousness, a watchfulness for the tacky Missouri details that might crop up or, perhaps with time and aging, inch into her and Seth's lives like unsightly paunches. Alissa had been told that her accent crept in after a bit of wine. Seth once let on that his mother had asked who would take care of Duncan, Alissa's retarded brother, once her parents were gone. They seemed overly worried about these kinds of details, as if they were going to figure into the amount of dowry offered.

Alissa's parents, on the other hand, adored Seth. But then they would have loved a hog farmer, if that was who she fancied. The urge to call her family overwhelmed Alissa for the second time this evening—she had to tell *some*one about her interview today—but she was dining at Aubergine, not the type of restaurant where she could duck into the hallway to use her cell phone.

Arthur Kingsley was deep into a golfing story, something about the concurrence of the recent stock market plunge and a game he had had with a rival investor. Normally Alissa would have enjoyed the story. She knew how to smile sympathetically, show appreciation for a joke by laughing with her face open, admiring, silently begging for more of the story with her eyes. She even knew how to do those things without really listening at all. Tonight she struggled. The storm raged on outside the restaurant window, the Mozart played faintly in the background like an itch, and she wanted to be in them, the rain *and* the music, as if the combination of the two could steer her off of this crazy path she had started down this afternoon.

As if she knew anything at all about the motivational book industry!

Alissa had never read a self-help book in her life, until last night when she stayed up reading Eve Glass's *Going the Distance: Endurance for Achievers* and the new one, *If Grace Is the Goal,* in preparation for the interview. Alissa was intrigued that Glass seemed to be a self-made woman, though what she had begun as and what she had made herself into were both a bit vague. An "also-ran" Olympic athlete who peddles success and now grace. It was like a magic trick. She wasn't even a therapist, like many motivational writers and speakers, so she couldn't claim to have gathered her evidence and data from a caseload of clients. No, she just told stories from her own life, and Alissa had to admit, they were rather convincing stories.

It would be a hoot, she had thought, to meet this lady.

She'd been disappointed when it seemed, at first, that the entire interview would be conducted by the proprietary ex-husband. She wouldn't call Nick Capelli handsome. He had close-cropped, frizzy, near-black hair and full cheeks. His gray eyes were admittedly lovely, with a trace of defeat tempered by some resolution toward appetite. He was a stocky guy and probably had a hairy chest. He wasn't a loser, but he could have been. He had the air of having saved himself from something dire. Perhaps he was a cancer survivor, or a recovering alcoholic, or had been orphaned at a young age. Though he seemed affable, and probably liked most people, he did not like Alissa. She couldn't help it: once she felt his antipathy for her, she started playing to win. Even though she thought she wouldn't take the job, she wanted to make him offer it to her.

"Eve is a very busy woman," Nick Capelli had explained. "The manager we hire will have to travel whenever she travels, and look after all the flight, hotel, and speaking-engagement details. I'm looking for someone who is not above running down to the lobby for a cup of coffee when Eve wants one. I need someone who can be both discreet and discriminating while reading her mail. You have to know the junk from the important stuff."

He made the job sound like half a notch above child care. As if Eve Glass were a puppet. And if she *was* a puppet, who would hold the strings, the new "manager" or Nick Capelli?

Alissa gave the ex-husband a lot of lead. She nodded, listened intently, did not speak. Let him run his course.

"Look," he said. "You have an impressive résumé. You've been working in Silicon Valley for two high-profile firms. You say that your job was to create the images of the top-level executives. What Eve does is very, very different from what those people do. Her work is about the human spirit. We don't care about the NASDAQ index. We are not a corporation. We don't need any big guns here."

Alissa laughed. "Do I look like a big gun?"

"Why would you want this job?"

The poor guy was suspicious. Alissa bet he was some kind

of salesman. Or maybe a schoolteacher. To him, anyone who made a lot of money, or wielded a bit of power, was highly suspect. The problem with this guy was that he didn't have any natural edge, rather it was the situation now making him edgy and that was always unattractive, situation-induced edge rather than personality-based edge. For anyone taking this job, Nick Capelli would be the biggest obstacle.

"I'll be frank with you," Alissa said in as reassuring a tone as she could muster, since her impulse was to make this Joe more nervous. "My boyfriend wanted to move to Portland, where he grew up, to work with his father. I agreed to come with him. I wanted a change, too. I'm tired of remaking men. I want to remake a woman."

You would think Alissa had offered him a goblet of poisoned wine. His full cheeks puffed, then sucked in, as if he were going to spit out her carcinogenic answer. "Eve doesn't need remaking. She needs managing."

"I see."

"Look." Nick rubbed his face. "I've been interviewing folks all week. There was the gay guy who joked about how safe Eve would be in *his* hands. There was the woman with an eight-page résumé who offered stress-relief acupuncture in addition to all her other skills. A man who claimed to run a hundred miles a week showed up with a page of notes on how Eve's first book could have been improved. I've seen a lot this week. Let me make myself clear. I am not looking for someone to improve Eve. I am looking for someone I can trust."

He spoke of his ex-wife like she was an exotic pet, one that needed special foods, two walks a day, loving grooming.

In her past public relations jobs, her specialty had been creating human images, and even the men she was handling knew that at least to her, they were product. She could order special foods and prescribe exercise, sure, but it wasn't love that made her do it. This Nick Capelli guy wasn't going to get anywhere with his quasi-guru ex-wife until he was willing to drop the mush and see the science of marketing.

"May I meet Dr. Glass? It seems to me that this job is a match between two people more than anything else. You mention trust. I understand that she must face some unusual situations and touchy circumstances. She needs someone who can smooth the path for her. Why don't she and I meet and go from there?"

Alissa didn't need this job. She wouldn't take it if it was offered. But if she were considering it seriously, this was exactly how she'd proceed, *around* Nick Capelli. If it weren't possible to work around him, then the job itself wouldn't be possible.

"Fine." Nick stood and left the room, returning a moment later with Eve Glass.

This was the part Alissa most wanted to tell Seth about. She glanced at him now, eating his strawberry tart in four huge bites. She could tell that he was ready to go home by the way his irritation was expressing itself in voraciousness. Gulping his coffee, saying "uh-huh" too often to his mother, who was catching him up on the careers of childhood friends, and trying in a variety of ways, including eye contact and footsie, to get Alissa's attention. She ignored him, and he knew he couldn't be too annoyed because of her captivity this evening, how she had never consented to the dinner at all. But she did want his attention. Alone. She wanted to tell him about Eve Glass. It would take time. He wouldn't understand at first. Marketing manager for a self-help writer! She would have to make him see that maybe she had found the new challenge she needed, longed for.

When Eve Glass had walked in the room, she'd felt like a sculptor must feel when first glimpsing a block of beautiful marble. Or a landscape artist gazing at a hillside, perfectly sloped and sunlit, covered only with wildflowers. She wanted more than anything, it was an intense energy she could feel rising from her ankles, rolling down from her shoulders, to get to work on this piece of art that was Eve Glass. She could make this woman. She could do wonders with her. It wouldn't be easy, human products never were, but she wouldn't be starting from scratch. All the ingredients were there: the woman was lovely, articulate, passionate, and she had a book just off the press, a book that was doing quite well, but could be doing sensationally. Everything about Eve Glass could be made much, much better.

That wasn't all. The best part was the way that Eve smiled at Alissa the second she walked in the room. She knew, too. Right away she knew that Alissa could spark her career like a wildfire. Even before shaking hands, the two women laughed, short horselike guffs, at the recognition of potential.

Nick had banked on Eve disliking her, and was obviously irked by the women's immediate compatibility.

*She's perfect,* Eve communicated to him with a big smile.

*She's hard, cold,* replied Nick with his folded arms, flaring nostrils.

*That pussycat? Relax.*

*Find someone else.*

*I want Alissa Smith.*

*She's going to want a lot of money.*

*Good. You get what you pay for.*

"Will you excuse us for a moment?" Nick asked. He took Eve's elbow. "I'd like to speak with my wife in private."

Now she's his wife, not ex-wife as she had been at the beginning of the interview. Alissa sat back and wondered, yet again, why she was here. It was her. That woman. The expert on grace. What fun it would be to track numbers of followers, to orchestrate a spiritual surge, to hone a guru's image! Alissa had done enough research to know already that the measuring rod, her main competitor, would be Walter Spinnaker and his *Ten Steps to a Joyful Life.* With focus and guidance, Eve Glass could outstrip him in six months.

While she waited for the two to confer, Alissa realized that she had decided to take the job. At least for now. She could call in the morning and decline. She used these few moments to calculate her terms.

When Nick and Eve returned, Alissa stood and spoke first. "I'm going to propose something to you. Eve's book has been out less than a month. It's doing well. I think, in fact, I know, that with the right publicity it could be doing much, much better. I could handle the details of Dr. Glass's career *and* get that book onto the best-seller lists. The same is true for her audio sets, workshops, and interactive lectures. I propose we organize Eve's enterprise into one entity, and there are several ways to do that, we can discuss the details later. The point now is this: I'm willing to take on Eve Glass as a client on the basis of a percentage of net, no salary. That way, it's a win-win situation if I succeed."

"Oooh, just a second," Nick said, glancing at Eve in the expectation that she too would see what a con this woman was pulling on them. "That book is going to soar to the top on its own merits, whether we hire you or not."

"I doubt it. But that, I suppose, could be seen as the risk: hiring someone for a job you don't need done. The point is, having these disparate pieces of Dr. Glass's career bringing in random incomes is silly. They're all intimately related. They could be organized as a for-profit corporation and be much more lucrative."

"We need a manager, not a publicity person and *not* a corporate executive. We're not looking for someone to take Eve on as a *client*—"

"A good manager *is* a publicity person. As for the business organization of Ms. Glass's projects, that's just good sense."

"We have different philosophies."

"Ah." Alissa hefted her attaché and smiled at Nick. "Then I suppose it won't work out."

Eve Glass tossed her arms in the air and jumped to her feet, too dramatically, too suddenly, reminding Alissa of the crasser moments in Beethoven's symphonies. "I *love* the idea. Nick, if the book were to do well on its own, so what? She'll still be doing the managing work. It'll all come out in the wash, anyway."

"Exactly," Alissa agreed, curbing her impulse to argue further.

She was crazy, of course. A motivational speaker would never be as lucrative as the startups she'd galvanized in

California. There would definitely be no stock options. But that was the point, wasn't it? She didn't need more money. She needed to find the edge of her power to construct a human product.

"We'll discuss it and get back to you," Nick had said, his voice actually wavering, as if entrusting his ex-wife to Alissa was akin to throwing her into a den of lions.

"You're hired," Eve said in a burst, and the two women shook hands.

Arthur was unstable when they finally pushed back their chairs at Aubergine. He draped an arm around Alissa and squeezed her shoulder. "I want grandchildren," he repeated. "Is that too much to ask? Just tell me that's the plan."

"I'd like children," Alissa said. "Someday."

"So is Seth the problem? Seth?" Arthur lurched over to his son and hooked an elbow around his neck. "Are you the problem here? What are you waiting for?"

"Come on, Pops. Give it a rest. We both like to work, that's all."

"Who said anything about not working?"

"Ha!" Nancy woke up from her walking stupor. "As if having children isn't work." She fished the keys out of Arthur's coat jacket and handed them to her son. "Go get the car, honey."

When they were finally alone at home, undressing, Alissa said, "I took a job today."

"What? When did you send out your résumé? What are you talking about?"

"You're not going to believe it."

Seth sat on the edge of the bed in his boxers. Though he had never lifted a single weight in his life, had never even belonged to a gym, his arms were hard and defined. Alissa wished she hadn't mentioned the job tonight. Why hadn't she waited until morning? For one, he would listen better in the morning, but mostly because he was probably seducible tonight, or had been, before she brought up the unromantic topic of her career. He opened his hands in front of his chest, impatiently gesturing for her to go on.

"Eve Glass is an Olympic athlete turned motivational speaker. Her first book is about achieving success through discipline, integrity, and guts." Oh, god, it sounded so hokey when she said it out loud, especially to Seth. "She's just written a new book. About meeting goals and finding grace. How the two aren't contradictory."

"Jeez, Alissa."

"I know. It's nuts, isn't it?"

"You've been offered a couple of great jobs, just by word of mouth, since you moved to Portland. Why would you . . . ? I mean, I thought you were going to start your own firm. This is nuts."

One phone call and she'd be out of it. Of course, that was exactly what she'd do in the morning, call Nick Capelli and tell him she'd decided against taking the job. Make his day. Why wasn't she presenting this as the joke she had intended?

"I guess you could say I *am* starting my own firm. Eve Glass is my first client."

Seth only stared.

"Listen, Seth. This woman made me feel something totally new. For one, she's, like, gorgeous. She's forty-three, has blond hair with a hint of gray. It's perfect hair, mid-length, bouncy, fresh. And she has these light brown eyes, almost copper, like a cat's with that sense that the irises are transparent. So that talking to her you feel as if you're seeing her insides, and that makes you trust her."

"You sound like you want to sleep with her."

"I knew you'd say that, you pervert. No, it's nothing at all like that. What she looks like is important, though, if I'm going to promote her as the vehicle to grace, and even more important is the trust she inspires. She's a perfect product. Lovely and compelling. Beautiful. Wise. Articulate."

"You were right. We should have moved somewhere hard and urban."

"I'd be bored silly working for any of your dad's cronies."

"You said you wanted to work a couple of years, then have kids."

"So?"

"This guru thing wasn't part of the plan."

Alissa shrugged.

"Come here," he said. "You looked hot tonight. Let's just start the kid thing now, if you're bored. I like that dress." Seth slid his hands under the fabric, resting them on her hips.

"Your mother seemed to approve."

"You told *her*?"

"Of the dress."

"She'd approve of anything."

"No, she wouldn't." That would be Seth's perspective. She did approve of anything *he* did. It was so all-encompassing, he had no awareness of how all that approval ended just beyond his skin. Nor was Seth aware of how much he enjoyed the warm bath of that approval. Was he serious about kids *now?* The desire she'd felt a moment ago curdled at the thought of fucking for kids. "Let me get my diaphragm."

"I'm serious," Seth said, holding her against him, nuzzling her upper thigh. "Let's just do it."

"No." She pushed back his shoulders and went to put in her diaphragm, brush her teeth, wash her face. When she returned to bed a few minutes later, he was nearly asleep, and Alissa didn't bother rousing him. This Portland thing frightened her. Would he really start a family because his parents pressured him to? Whose parents didn't pressure them to? Her parents asked every single time she talked to them on the telephone. That didn't mean she had to do it.

Rather than getting in bed, Alissa crossed the house to her study, still unfurnished except for the big oak desk and stereo system, and called home. "Sorry to call so late, Ma."

"Hi, sweetheart. It's not late. I was just watching Letterman. How are you?"

Alissa began to tell her mother about Eve Glass and Nick Capelli, making the story of the couple and their Olympic career as "*People* magazine" as she could for her mother's benefit.

"I know her!" her mother interrupted. "Why, she was on *Miranda* not long ago. Oh, it was tragic, just tragic, when the Russians ruined those Olympics. And she was such a nice girl, and she's still just lovely. Wait until I tell Daddy. Oh, honey, you're really making it big now."

"Mom, it's not that big a deal. She's just—"

"Besides, working for a woman is better," her mother continued. "She'll understand when you need time off for starting your family. I'm so mad at Daddy, by the way. Remember that gal Ruthie who does the books for him?"

"Sure."

"She's expecting."

"That's nice."

"Well."

So she wasn't married. "Well, *what,* Ma?"

"I don't know that it's all that nice she's that way, being on her own and all, but she *is* that way, and she plans on going ahead and having the baby, which she should of course, and since those are the facts, I think your father should give the girl some time off. At least hire her back when she's ready. God knows she'll have to support herself and the baby. He says she made her bed and has to lie in it."

"You know Daddy. He's all talk. He'll hire her back."

"Hmph."

"How's Duncan?"

"He drove the forklift into the warehouse door and broke the automatic opener, leaving the door stuck open. All the inventory is just sitting there for the taking. So your father hired guards to spend the night in the warehouse until he can get it fixed."

"Duncan shouldn't be driving the forklift."

"Tell that to John. He taught him."

Alissa's oldest brother refused to believe in Duncan's limitations. He had always railed against his mother for overprotectiveness and his father for not giving the younger boy a chance. How many times had Alissa tried to explain to John: Duncan is retarded.

"I'm glad he wasn't hurt, anyway."

"Someone might *get* hurt with these gorillas Daddy has hired. They're *armed*. Really, Alissa. He goes too far."

"Yeah," Alissa laughed. "Who's going to steal bags of fertilizer?"

"Daddy thinks everyone in Jefferson County has been waiting for this moment to loot his warehouse."

Alissa laughed again. "I better get to bed, Ma. You and Daddy figure out when you want to come visit. We have tons of room. Is Duncan up?"

"He's asleep. So's Daddy."

"Tell them I said, 'hi' and 'I love you.'"

Alissa hung up the phone and put on headphones and Brahms. She lay down on the hardwood floor for which she hadn't yet found a rug, and absorbed the violins until they reached that raw place inside her, a beautiful ache.

A memory of the buck-toothed orchestra teacher rose on a crescendo, like a genie with hands that closed around the neck of the music. Funny how often she thought of that lady and that strange afternoon abduction. She was twelve years old and playing in the middle school orchestra, which rehearsed the last period of the day. Alissa always rushed right off afterward to swim practice, but on that Thursday, the buck-toothed teacher—why couldn't Alissa ever remember her name?—firmly gripped her elbow, even before she had snapped shut her violin case, and said, "No swim team today. You're coming with me now."

The woman had stringy hair, going gray, the unfortunate protruding teeth, and a skin tone that wouldn't be so claylike if only she allowed herself a bit of sunshine, maybe some exercise. Yet she appeared quite happy. When Alissa would stop by the music room before school to deliver a note from her mother excusing her from the last period of the day in order to get to a swim meet on time, the orchestra teacher would be sitting in the middle of the room with music, often Vivaldi's *Le Humane Passioni,* turned up so loud that Alissa would hear it a good distance down the hall. The teacher wouldn't be smiling or swaying or anything crazy like that. She would be listening, sitting in the middle of the room simply listening. Music was the only nourishment she needed.

The thing was, Alissa liked the buck-toothed orchestra teacher. That devotion to a single interest reminded her of her brother Duncan, who loved machines, and only machines. He took great joy in standing before a newly painted thresher, first admiring its bright colors and shiny surface, then moving on to examining the enormous blades, touching, if he was allowed, their edges. Duncan lusted after the power of those rotating blades. If he had had a little more sense, he could have been a race car driver. The teacher, too, seemed to be admiring to the point of passion a power she did not have.

On that Thursday afternoon, though, Alissa was frightened of the woman as she ushered her out the school door to her ancient car, buckled her into the passenger seat, and drove her into downtown St. Louis. The whole way talking. "Alissa, you have a talent. You have a rare, rare talent. What I would have given to be born with what you were born with. Do you know what I wanted more than anything in the world? A career with the St. Louis Symphony. You could have that. You could have that soon."

The woman had arranged not an audition exactly, Alissa was far too young for that, but a hearing from the St. Louis Symphony director himself. It was an enormous coup on the part of the teacher. Her goal, which she accomplished, was to get a letter of recommendation, written that very afternoon, from that distinguished person confirming Alissa's talent. Alissa played for him, and he did concur that her talent was extraordinary for a twelve-year-old girl who had been playing only two years. He personally recommended she begin lessons with the violin virtuoso Mr. Oliver Ward. When the middle school orchestra teacher brought Alissa home that evening, she presented the letter to Mr. and Mrs. Smith, clearly believing this evidence of Alissa's musical genius would persuade them to hire Mr. Oliver Ward, the best violin teacher money could buy in St. Louis, and to have Alissa quit swimming.

Her parents took a more practical point of view. The idea of paying extraordinary fees for a special violin teacher, one for whom they would have to drive in to St. Louis, when the one right at school was free, even for a talented girl, was ridiculous. Furthermore, no one in the family, other than Alissa of course, liked the sound of the violin. When she practiced, Duncan covered his ears and scrunched up his face, as if the music caused him pain, and her mother became nervous. John called her Miss Maestro, taking every opportunity to mock the way she held her bow and instrument. Her father often said, "Let's get you a nice guitar." Even with all that, if the violin had been Alissa's only talent, perhaps they would have hired the expensive teacher. But Alissa was an exceptional student, and even more important, already winning blue ribbons at swim meets. Swimming, they all agreed, was a much more useful talent to cultivate, and so that is what they had done. In fact, swimming had won Alissa a free ride to Yale.

"Aren't you angry?" Seth had often asked, refusing to believe that she hadn't regretted giving up the violin.

No, she wasn't angry. It had made sense then and it made sense now.

"But you just gave it up? When you had all that talent?"

Well, yes, that is exactly what she had done.

"You could have kept playing, anyway. Just for fun."

"But I didn't."

"*Why*?"

It was obvious to Alissa why, but she had never been able to make Seth understand. She'd lived in Jefferson County, Missouri. Her brother was retarded. It was almost more than her mother could do to get him to his special school every day, let alone her to swim meets. Furthermore, John, the oldest and only child in the family who was not exceptional in either direction, would never get a scholarship to college, so all their savings had to go toward his education fund. Alissa had willingly given up the violin because she didn't want to be greedy. She thought she had enough.

But tonight, lying on the hardwood floor of her bare office, the Brahms flowing into her bloodstream like heroin, she knew that her agreement with her parents wasn't simply a lack of greed. It *was* that. But it was also a *kind* of greed. That buck-toothed teacher was Alissa's worst fear: to live out her life within the enclosure of a middle school classroom with Vivaldi her only sustenance. Even at twelve that had seemed possible for Alissa. Possible, and terrifying. She gave up the violin so that she could leave Missouri, leave the fertilizer company, leave the hard work of Duncan, and have *this.* This life that leaped beyond the very idea of enough.

When she opened her eyes, she saw Seth standing in the doorway of her office, still in his boxers, sleepy. He was speaking, but with the headphones on, she couldn't hear him. She just stared, as if he were Oregon wildlife, as he gestured for her to take off her headphones. She pretended she didn't understand, knowing he would not be so rude as to step over her and turn off the music himself. Finally, he gave her one long look, as if he too were assessing everything afresh, turned and left the doorway of her study. Alissa closed her eyes and let the Brahms surge through her once again.

What if the orchestra teacher had been right all along, not about whether she should be a violinist, but about whether this was all that really counted anyway? The music.

The following week, Alissa took her new client shopping. She loved that first moment when the elevator doors of the department store slid open. It was like lifting the lid off a trunk of shipwreck treasure. The store reeked of perfume and glared with mirrors. Pearls, gold, and rubies gleamed in the artificial light. Even the salespeople were delicious in their tight suits, designer glasses, and extreme hair. This first floor of the department store presented an almost perversely exciting bombardment of the senses.

"Why are we down here?" Eve asked.

"We start with accessories." Alissa hoped her client wasn't going to protest the materialism of department stores or the shallowness of appearances.

"Isn't that backwards?"

"No. Accessories make an image. Trust me."

Eve just laughed.

The men Alissa had worked with had been grateful for the help. They knew they needed an image and didn't have a clue how to go about getting one. Dressing those guys had been easy, putting them in one hundred percent cotton shirts, trousers that fit, reminding them to carry their wallets in their back, not front, pockets. They needed to look loose, brilliant, as if they understood the most micro part of the computer, and most of all, their image needed to excite people's greed. But Eve's image had to inspire confidence in her ability to produce a state of being. Her hair, clothes, shoes, even smile, needed to say, I'm a straight shot for nirvana.

While Alissa stopped to orient herself on the floor, surveying all of the accessory islands for the one most likely to have tasteful jewelry, her client headed straight for a pair of pearl and sapphire earrings that some Missourian debutante might wear.

"Too princessy," Alissa said.

"Then what about these?" Eve asked, moving to a case of Southwestern-style earrings, lots of turquoise and silver.

Alissa wished the man studying bracelets in the cabinet on the other side of the sales island were her client instead. She could do wonders with him in about thirty minutes. His suit was so stiff it looked like a coat of armor. He was probably shopping for a lover. If he were shopping for his wife, he would have chosen much more quickly, much less carefully. A man is so easy to counsel. But then that was why she wanted this job, wasn't it, to try working with a woman? Still, women required diplomacy rather than straight-out manipulation, and that was dicier, perhaps not Alissa's strong suit.

"No, not those, either, Eve. Some medium-size gold hoops. Simple but sturdy. Like these. You need something that will fly with a literary audience."

"But my audience might not be so literary. They might be

more like trailer trash." Eve laughed again, almost as if she were her own joke.

"We're taking a risk here, Eve. The 'trailer trash,' as you call them, will always follow you. We're going for a bigger audience, that's all. Trust me."

"You say 'Trust me' a lot."

"You need to, for us to get our work done."

"Nick said . . ." Eve paused and smiled faintly, as if she were suppressing a bigger smile. "He said that to you, I'm a human product."

Alissa bit back her impatience. No male executive would ever have made that comment. Of course Eve Glass was a product. That was the whole point.

"Eve," Alissa said slowly. "I've read your books. Your wisdom deeply affected me. I'm here to help you share that with a larger audience."

Eve leveled a long, appraising look at her, and Alissa began to fear she'd miscalculated the woman. She knew Eve was intelligent. That was obvious, even in the hokey books. But she hadn't counted on any part of her intelligence being renegade.

Alissa was about to try another pacifying comment when Eve's face loosened into a delighted smile. "Can't I have these *big* hoops? Look. Aren't they great on me?"

"Yes, but we're not going for gypsy seer. We're going for enlightened guidance counselor."

"I like you," Eve laughed. "You're funny. Why did you want this job? Really."

"It's just what I told your husband—"

"Ex-husband."

"Ex-husband, then. But wait. I don't get it. Are you divorced?"

"Not yet, but soon. We have to. He's getting married. But don't say anything around his fiancée! She doesn't know we never divorced."

"Is that why he, or you, hired me?"

"I think so. Of course, Nick has some long, involved rationale about my career growing beyond his expertise, blah, blah, blah. But I suspect Judith is jealous. Nick never said that. But I don't think it's a coincidence that he wanted to hire a manager at the same time he's getting married. Do you?"

While talking, Eve had found a case of rhinestone pendants. Her face softened as she admired them, her fingers gently resting on the glass. "Can we look at these?" She glanced around for a salesperson to help her.

"No," Alissa said. "Earrings."

"But you didn't answer. Why you wanted this job."

"You're a challenge to me, Eve. Selling a software image is one thing. Selling grace is another."

"Ha. Selling grace!"

"What I do is like theater. It's as if I'm a director of a play, and you're the star. What's exciting to me is seeing how many people I can get to buy tickets, and also, once the show is on, how much we can move them."

"Move them? You mean, emotionally?"

"Partly. Yes."

"What do you want them to feel?"

"Confidence in you. Confidence in your ability to show them something about finding grace in their lives."

"What about you?"

"What *about* me?" That businessman had worked his way around the display cases and now stood not four feet away. Up close, he didn't look like a businessman at all. Too hard around the edges.

"Grace. Do you know what it is?"

"Look, Eve. You're right. Nick's right. You *are* a product to me. You and your grace. What do I believe in? I believe in hard work. I believe in things I can see, smell, taste, and count."

"Like money."

"Yep. Isn't that what you really want from me, to help you make money?"

"I don't know."

"There's nothing wrong with wanting to make money. Women have such a problem admitting they want money as badly as men want it."

"Maybe not all women *do* want money as badly as men want it."

"Look. I've told you why I took the job. Why did you hire me?"

"Nick needed to hand me off. I liked you best of all the choices."

This was going to be difficult if that was the extent of Eve's motivation.

"You seem sad," Eve went on. "Like there's a giant symphony inside you that you're completely ignoring."

"I'm not *ignoring* it," Alissa started, and then caught herself. This woman was kind of spooky. "Look. Let's be real clear right now. I'm not looking for enlightenment. I'm doing a job. If you don't want me to do it, I need to know

now." The man in the dark suit was staring at them. "Put those earrings back. Try these."

"No, no, no," interfered an older saleslady. Her short hair was a metallic silver, and a strand of pearls held her half glasses around her neck. Her French accent was perfect for the jewelry counter, as were her long red nails. "Too bold on the lovely lady. Something much softer."

Eve opened her palm and showed the saleslady the pearl and sapphire earrings. "Oh, yes, darling, those would be lovely with your perfect skin."

"Perhaps. But we need something to go with a suit."

"I don't wear suits."

"No, of course not," murmured the busybody French saleslady. "Some lovely loose fabrics, silks and lacy camisoles."

Eve smiled at her. "Do you think?"

"Let's go upstairs and try some suits now," Alissa said. "We can come back for the earrings."

The militaristic businessman stepped closer, as if he wanted to smell the women.

Alissa took her client's elbow and pulled her toward the elevators.

"Soft!" the French accent called after the two women. "Something feminine, not too harsh."

Waiting in front of the elevators, Alissa felt frazzled. Usually she allowed herself to savor shopping sprees. Maybe they were in the wrong store. She didn't really know Portland yet. Finally, the middle elevator's door opened. As the two women stepped in, Alissa was startled by a strange flash of red light, as if the elevator were malfunctioning. She thought of getting off again, turned to ask Eve if she had seen the flash, and noticed, as the door slid shut, that the man in the dark suit had slipped up behind them and gotten on board. The elevator said *ding,* and began rising.

"Excuse me, ladies," the man said. "I'm Detective Wallenborg. I'd like to speak to you in our offices, please?"

Alissa felt the shaft of the elevator rise in her core, like some terrible symphonic swell, as Detective Wallenborg manipulated the elevator buttons, overriding her request to stop on the third floor, Ladies' Suits. Up they rose to the top floor and the offices of the department store managers.

When Alissa called Nick Capelli early the next morning, he agreed to meet willingly enough, but he tried to play the tough guy. He showed up at the Coffee Mill unshaven, unsmiling, though he wore a tie with his freshly ironed blue shirt and black jeans. A light sweat dampened his skin like distrust.

Alissa began as civilly as she could. "How are you, Nick?"

"What can I do for you?" he asked, playacting formality.

"For three weeks," Alissa said, shifting with impatience in the hard chair, "I've worked full-time on Eve. I've booked her thirteen speaking engagements, put together a superb press kit—"

"No one asked you—"

"Let me finish. And I've mailed out hundreds of press releases for *If Grace Is the Goal.* Eve has eight radio interviews and four newspaper interviews. I haven't made a red cent."

"Oh, now just a minute. That was the deal. That was the deal *you* proposed."

"That's right. That was the deal *I* proposed. In good faith. I'm not sure you held up your end of the good faith deal."

"Look, the problem between you and me is that I care a

lot more about Eve the person than I do about her career. With you, it's the opposite. I mean, why should you care about her? It's a job. But I wanted to hire a manager. Not . . . not some full-service corporate executive."

"You've been managing her career up until now, right?"

"More or less. She and I together."

"So why are you stopping now?" Alissa thought it might be illuminating to hear what he said.

The waitress brought Nick's huevos rancheros and Alissa's bowl of fresh fruit with dry toast. He used the side of his fork to cut one of the eggs, letting the yolk run out. "Two reasons. Her career's getting way bigger than I can handle anymore. And I'm getting married."

"Congratulations."

"Thank you." A nice smile, actually, when he relaxed. Great hands, too.

"If you don't mind my asking, what does getting married have to do with not managing Eve's career anymore?"

"Oh, well, it's a bit complicated. Judith, my fiancée—" He smiled again. "That sounds so funny to say, fiancée. The last time I got married was to Eve, decades ago. I didn't expect to do it again." A couple of big bites of runny egg, salsa, and beans. "As you know, Eve needs a lot of things, including someone to travel with her. Judith didn't like the time I was spending doing that. Understandably." He lowered his eyelashes, and Alissa thought it wasn't so understandable to him as he claimed. "Oh, hell." He set down his knife and fork. "The truth: she gave me an ultimatum. Hire someone to manage Eve's career or she wouldn't marry me."

"Most men don't respond well to ultimatums."

Now he looked at Alissa more intelligently. "No. But I love Judith."

"That's nice."

"Nice? *Nice?*"

"Nick, there is something else I need more clarity on."

He raised an eyebrow.

"I spent yesterday afternoon at the Justice Building."

He closed his eyes briefly, and when he reopened them, looked resigned. "Did they book her?"

"They sure did. She has a court date next week. How many priors does she have?"

"Surprisingly, just one."

"Surprisingly?"

"She's been caught a lot more times. She usually talks her way out of it."

"That's interesting, because yesterday she gave the impression of almost wanting to be arrested."

"Really? She didn't flirt? Ask the cop about his mother? Something like that?"

Alissa shook her head. "It was a store detective. She was quite passive. When he asked to see the contents of her purse, she reached right in and handed him the two pairs of earrings she had swiped."

"Shit."

"Exactly. There were two pairs of earrings she wanted, pearl and sapphire and some big gold hoops, that I vetoed. Wrong image. So she stole them. What am I supposed to do now? I've put three long hard weeks into this woman. I've set her up for an extraordinary boost in her career. If she's going to shoot me in the foot, I can't do this. I suppose I could have asked in the interview if she had a criminal record, but it didn't occur to me."

"I wouldn't exactly say 'criminal record.' Everyone has a couple of traffic tickets."

"Nick. Please."

He put down his fork, sat back in his chair.

"So, how long has she had this little kleptomania problem?"

"I don't think clinical terms are necessary. She just—"

"Kleptomania is hardly a clinical term. Don't try to gloss over this. I've just tied my career to Eve's, and I'll be perfectly honest with you. If you're hiding anything else from me, you'd better come clean now. I have to decide whether to continue."

"Yeah. Okay. I understand."

"So?"

Nick shook his head. "There's nothing else."

"Oh, really? Then what's this?" Alissa tossed the envelope on the table. "You and she both asked me to screen all of her mail. However, I felt somewhat out of line reading this particular letter from Maine. It's really none of my business, and yet it is. The contents could be damaging to a career that's dependent on a wide middle-class base. Who is Audrey?"

"Jesus. The poet?" Nick winced, though Alissa sensed the wince was more for show, as he reached for the envelope and extracted the three sheets of lined yellow paper.

Alissa crossed her arms. A bit of kleptomania, a woman lover, these were not big problems in the scheme of things, compared, say, to laundering drug money in the Cayman Islands or pedophilia. Still, both could prove significant obstacles to marketing grace. "The letter is rather incriminating."

Nick examined the envelope. "This came to her post office box. Why not directly to her home?"

"It mentions in the first line of the letter that Eve asked her to write to the P.O. box, not home."

"Why would she do that?"

"You tell me."

He read the whole letter, and then said, "You know, I don't think Eve's correspondences or personal relationships are our business."

Alissa laughed. "But you just read the whole letter."

Nick shrugged. "Yeah."

"Yeah. Right. Your ex-wife is not the ray of golden sunlight she at first appeared to be."

"Oh, she is! She really is. But flawless? Of course not. And who she . . . feels, you know, romantic about is her business."

"Wrong. Nick, it's my job to sell Eve Glass. To galvanize sales of her books. To swell the attendance of her workshops and interactive lectures. I can't do that if she gets bad press. Or even quirky press. The point is, we want press, lots of press, but Eve's got to be clean. 'Clean' as defined by Middle American standards. 'Clean' according to most people on the map. Do you understand? We're selling grace, not vacuum cleaners."

"So, you're quitting?" Nick placed both palms on the tabletop. You would think he was Eve's father for how defensive he was about her.

"No. I'm not quitting. We've gotten too far, too fast, for that. Eve is dynamite, and her share of the motivational-book market could be huge. But I'm going to need your help. She trusts you the most. I understand that your fiancée is not very interested in your being involved in Eve's career. But I don't have any sway over Eve emotionally, and you do. You need to make sure she does not shoplift, not even a candy bar, ever again. You have to make her understand that."

The absurdity of this situation, of the turn in her own career, poked Alissa in the ribs. A desire to laugh welled up in her throat. Nick saw it, and he laughed out loud. She'd been wrong about him. He did have edge. Not a sharp one, but sometimes a blunt edge can have a bigger impact.

Controlling her own laugh impulse, Alissa added, "Nor can she get wrapped up in anything lurid romantically. In fact, it would be best if she had no romantic attachments for the next six months."

"You're really a trip."

"What?"

"Like you think you can just tell a person to not have a romantic attachment."

"You're an engaged man. I assume that means you've made a commitment to be involved only with Judith. Am I right?"

Nick didn't nod, but Alissa assumed agreement.

"Some people make that commitment to their work."

"Is that what you've done?"

"We're not talking about me. We're talking about what I think Eve needs to do in order to succeed."

"I know. But I'm asking anyway: is your primary commitment to your work?"

"Yes."

"I thought you said you had a boyfriend."

"So?"

Nick lifted his hands and shrugged. "Your boyfriend

doesn't mind being Number Two, after whomever you're working for?"

"I don't number the parts of my life."

Nick rubbed the dark stubble on his full cheeks. "So it looks like I really do need you, doesn't it?"

"It looks like it." And it looked like she needed him as well.

"Are you still as red-hot confident as you were in the interview that you can, so-called, remake Eve?"

"Nick." Alissa leaned across the table. "I've created images for men with much more damaging proclivities than Eve's. Who have stolen whole fortunes, not just a pair of pearl and sapphire earrings. Eve Glass is a piece of cake. If."

"If?"

"If she wants to cooperate."

"She does. You won't find a stronger will than Eve's."

"Will is only so strong as the desire that accompanies it."

A queer look crossed Nick's face. Will, she suspected, was his weakness. But they weren't talking about him, so she pressed, "So then, what exactly are Eve's feelings for the poet in Maine?"

He rubbed his face again and closed his eyes for a moment. He admitted, "I don't know. I'm worried. And you're right. We need to keep Eve away from her. The woman is too . . . too . . . oh, you read the letter. She sounds so damn holy. Her perfectly crafted sentences. Her crashing surf. Her sniffing hounds. The whole thing is so honorable or pious or something."

"Does Eve love her?"

"God, I hope not."

"I couldn't quite figure out from the letter how *she* feels about Eve. There was a mention of some night in New Mexico. But she touches on it like whatever happened there might blow up in her face. It's like the whole letter tries to deny whatever it was that happened between them. And yet, she dangles it there."

"Exactly! It's like she's luring Eve with all that pretty language and at the same time, making it very clear that she isn't available."

"So why are you so worried? What harm could she do Eve?"

Nick only shook his head.

"Look, I'll talk to Eve about it. I'll ask her what's at stake."

"You'll *ask* her? How can you do that? She'll know you read the letter."

"Of course she'll know I read the letter. I'm supposed to open and read everything that comes to the P.O. box."

"Just throw it away. That would be better."

"Don't be ridiculous. We'll nip this one in the bud. Trust me."

She reached across the table and took his hand, surprising herself as much as she surprised him. She never touched people casually. But he looked so lost for a moment, as if giving up control of Eve was painful for him. She knew from Eve's books that the guy had been her husband/coach/manager since they were both kids.

"Eve's going to be just fine," she said. "I may be a marketing wizard, but I'm actually the same species as you: human. I love making success happen, but I won't let anyone hurt Eve in the process."

He clasped her hand as she tried to withdraw it. "You promise?"

"I promise."

How, Alissa wondered, had she ended up comforting Nick rather than threatening to quit as she had planned?

August in Portland is lovely. Being nearly a hundred miles inland, as well as a good distance north of the equator, the evenings are long and warm. Alissa wore a summer dress, short and loose, while Seth wore old denims and no shirt at all. They sat, for once alone and relaxed, in lounge chairs on the small patio in the backyard, more like a back forest, drinking the last of an apple-crisp sauvignon blanc. In the morning, Seth would leave for the father/son fishing trip, this year to a pedestrian-sounding destination, Fallen Log Lake, and Alissa would fly with Eve to Chicago for the Living Now Book Expo, but for the moment, the evening held Alissa and Seth in its pocket. Dusk haunted the forest with shafts of a reddish light coming through the Douglas firs. Alissa's favorite Bach concertos drifted out the open upstairs windows, too softly, much too softly, but at least Seth hadn't asked her to turn them off altogether.

"Eve thinks we should put in a hot tub back here." Actually, it was Nick who had said that when he visited her office earlier in the week. They had begun meeting regularly, during the day when Judith was at work, to talk over the details of everything from sales of the books to Eve's moods. Nick, as it turned out, was anything but an obstacle. He was the easiest route to Eve. The ex-couple was like a pair of fraternal twins, different in so many ways, but still entwined.

"I don't want to cut any trees," Seth said.

"No, of course not."

"You're obsessed with change, did you know that?"

"I didn't say *I* wanted a hot tub. I said Nick did."

"You said 'Eve.' Who's Nick?"

"You know who Nick is. Eve's husband. Ex-husband."

"Well, who said it?"

"Nick said it."

"When was Nick here?"

"Earlier this week. He stays very involved in all the details."

"I thought you said his fiancée forbade that." Seth laughed. "I thought you wanted total control over The Product.'"

"He helps. He has a lot of information that's useful."

Maybe *information* was the wrong word. When Alissa had pumped him for biographical details on her childhood, Nick had said, "Eve doesn't have a past. That's the *point* of her."

"Everyone has starting blocks," Alissa had said, purposely using the running metaphor, which made Nick laugh and loosen up enough to reveal, "Her dad was some kind of country preacher. I gather he was a pretty strange guy. Snake-handling. Sermons hollered in forest clearings. Weird shit. The dad moved every few months. He was always looking for a congregation. Her junior year, when I met her, they'd just moved to Portland from the other side of the Cascades. When the family moved on again in the spring, Eve stayed in Portland. She didn't stay in touch with him."

Alissa wanted to tell this much to Seth. Testing the waters, she said, "He's told me some interesting things about her childhood."

"Childhood is childhood. Most people's are pretty boring."

Alissa looked at Seth as if she had never seen him before. "Yours maybe."

"She's just a client, hon." He reached over to stroke her thigh.

"I know." Alissa softened with his touch. "But I admire the way she has built her character. I mean 'character' like in a novel. It's like she's built a person from scratch."

Seth's hand moved beneath the hem of her dress. His eyes were closed and his eyelids fluttered. "But what has she accomplished?"

He meant, what are two self-help books compared to Alissa's worth in seven digits? By way of answering, she said, "Do you know why I fell in love with you, Seth?"

He opened his eyes and smiled. "You said my Oregonness."

"Yeah. Those stories you told me about packhorses and trails barely cut into the sides of mountains and fishing lures and rainbow trout leaping out of streams. Even in New Haven, your skin smelled like wood smoke to me."

Still smiling, he moved his hand higher up her thigh. He had thought she was only changing the subject. He didn't realize she was trying to make a point. Alissa loved her work, making products out of human beings, and yet, this time, she felt profoundly frustrated to be denied access to the non-product part of her client. Even Eve only laughed when Alissa asked her questions about her life prior to the Olympics, as if the years simply didn't exist. And when Alissa had asked her, point-blank, if she was in love with Audrey Boucher, Eve had fixed her copper eyes on Alissa, startled, then looked away quickly, as if just saying the word *yes* would take everything away from her.

Seth said, "Come here."

The urge to cry, which she hadn't had in years, rose in Alissa's chest. She wanted to make love with Seth, she always did, and yet, just this once, on the eve of his annual fishing trip, she wanted even more for him to tell her how it felt to get a trout on his line, what he heard at night lying in his sleeping bag next to an alpine lake, or even what his dad's old cronies talked about around the campfire. Moving to Portland had robbed Seth of his easiness, or turned it bad somehow, transformed it into complacency. Not only was he satisfied, he was bored and didn't even care that he was bored. He would go on the fishing trip because it was expected of him, not because it gave him joy. She missed him, she missed the boy who wore his jeans too short and who admitted to being very homesick. Alissa got up from her own lounge chair and straddled him on his, her sundress hiking up as she did. He stirred beneath her. She touched the place where his pectorals met his collarbone, the place where he was perfect, then slid her palms down his chest, around his sides, until she could gently massage his lower back. That was risky. He might flip over and ask, instead, for a back rub. But he didn't. The stirring between their open bodies grew insistent, and she leaned in to kiss him. Seth was a good kisser, and a moment later, it was the trees, Bach, and Seth inside her. She hadn't forgotten her diaphragm, but if she had gone to get it, who knew if Seth would still be awake when she returned.

It was lovely, lovelier than it had been in a long time, and they lay together on the one lounge chair as the light shifted toward darkness, except for high in the trees, far above their heads, where the late rays of sunlight, red with dusk, lit the tips of the evergreens. Seth held her gently as he slept, and for a moment, just a brief moment, she felt that three-year-old kind of safety, as if she were in her mother's arms and did not know there was a stick that measured success, had never made a choice beyond reaching for a bite of food.

Alissa didn't sleep, and the feeling of utter contentment was really only a brief flush. She was considering getting up, and doing so slowly so that she didn't wake Seth. She thought of calling her mother. It was still early. Duncan and her father would be watching television, and her mom would be polishing kitchen counters or reviewing her household budget, making sure she could account for every single penny.

Alissa had just extracted herself from Seth's embrace, straightened her dress, and stood a moment to get her bearings in the dark backyard, now lit only by the squares of light from the windows of the great room, high above her head, when she heard a sound, as if an animal were in the calla lilies by the side of the house. Alissa was not fond of the raccoons that prowled around out here at night, and had moved to shake Seth awake when the shadowed shape of a person stepped around the side of the house.

"Who is it?" Alissa demanded.

Seth woke with a guttural cry.

"Oh, god, I'm sorry," the dark shape said, sounding as frightened as Alissa. "I'm so sorry. This was the address on the press kit. I'm a reporter for the *New York Times.* I'm looking for Alissa Smith, manager for Eve Glass."

A very silent moment wrapped the patio. Alissa straightened her dress again.

Seth rose to his feet. "For crap's sake, it's nine fucking o'clock." He grabbed the empty wine bottle and two glasses and went in the basement door, slamming it shut.

"I'm Alissa Smith," she said slowly, trying to clear her wine- and sex-soaked brain. "My office is in my home." The *Times.* This was big. She had to be gracious, no matter how rude the reporter.

"I'm sorry," repeated the voice from the dark. "I've been trying to reach Eve for a while now. I got your press kit today and since I was having dinner with a friend in the neighborhood, I thought I'd just leave a note off at your office. Anyway," the voice gained confidence, "I'm doing a big story on Eve. I've completed all my background research. I just need the interview."

The woman stepped out of the house's shadow and onto the patio, where the dim starlight revealed a black leather jacket, the sleeve zippers open, and tight jeans. The eyes were dark, not unlike the feared raccoon's, and the smile tense. The weak starlight caught the silver rings on the reporter's hand as she handed Alissa her card.

"Why don't I call you first thing in the morning," Alissa blurted, and then regretted the readiness of her tone. Shouldn't have said "first thing." Better for them to be hungrier than you.

"Good."

"Actually," Alissa said, "we're going to Chicago in the morning for the Living Now Book Expo. The interview will have to wait until after we return, but I shall call you. Good night."

The reporter passed a hand over her face, as if she were recovering from a bad moment, and then seemed to smile privately before stepping back into the darkness. Alissa waited, listening to her steps retreat down the path to the front of the house. Crazy reporters.

Traffic the next morning, on the way to the Portland International Airport, was horrid, but it didn't dampen Eve's excitement about the recent surge in sales of her book.

"Do you think," she asked Alissa, "that there is any way we could get statistics on how many of my followers have actually experienced grace as a result of the plan in the book? Wouldn't that be super? To be able to say, 'Eighty-four percent of Eve Glass's readers have achieved grace.'"

"You're my kind of client." Alissa wasn't sure if Eve was joking, but she laughed anyway. "I'll get right on it."

"But it's not really possible, is it?"

Alissa shrugged. "We have a decent-size mailing list. We could do a survey. It might be fun."

Alissa didn't mention the reporter. An in-depth profile in the *Times* could be good, even sensational, especially for their goal of attracting a more literary audience. But Alissa would have to establish clear parameters and make sure both the reporter *and* Eve understood what they were. Anyway, before scheduling anything, she had to talk to Nick. That had been his one nonnegotiable rule: no reporters that weren't cleared by him. His protectiveness was actually sort of sweet. Eventually she would make him understand that the few stains on Eve's reputation were nothing to worry about, as long as they were handled properly, and that was Alissa's expertise. *Her* one nonnegotiable rule was that she had to be kept informed. As long as he played by her rule, she'd play by his. She had planned on calling him from the airport this morning, to tell him about the *Times* interview, but that idea was being foiled by the traffic.

They arrived only twenty minutes before their flight. Eve said she'd be in the gift shop while Alissa stood in line to check their bags. "Get me the *New Yorker*," Alissa requested, "and meet me at the gate."

When they were seated in the lounge, waiting to board the plane, Eve opened her big leather bag, and a glint caught Alissa's eye. A glass object.

"What's that?"

"Just a gift for someone."

"Who?"

"Someone who likes seals."

"From the gift shop?"

"Mm-hm."

"Why isn't it in a bag?"

"I like to save trees."

She'd heisted it, that was why. Any moment airport security might descend, and if they did, Alissa was quitting. "Excuse me," she said.

"Where're you going? We're boarding in a minute."

"To make a phone call."

"Here. Use my cell phone."

"A private phone call. I'll be right back."

Once out of earshot, Alissa dug her own cell phone out of her bag, punched in his number, and waited for that husky voice. "Hi," she said.

"Hey. I thought you were on your way to Chicago."

"We are. I think Eve just stole something from the airport gift shop."

A long hesitation, then, "What am I supposed to say?"

"You're supposed to make sure she doesn't do that."

"What'd she take?"

"Why does it matter?"

"It might."

"A glass seal."

"See? It does matter. I bet it's for that poet. Remember that part in the letter about the rocky cliff and seals below it?"

"Oh, yeah. God, that woman is bad news. Eve calls her The Correspondent."

"Why?"

"Because letter writing is as close as she'll let Eve come."

"I guess that's good news, isn't it?"

"I guess. But the tension of that arm's length only heightens Eve's—"

"Desire?"

"Desire."

Why, lately, was Alissa so conscious of her little lies, the kind she had always told in the service of her work? Facades, images, stage sets, that was her job. She liked to think of it even as a kind of art. Words and money and accessories were her medium. Yet this summer she kept stumbling on these little constructions, as if they mattered. Just now she'd told Nick that Eve called Audrey Boucher The Correspondent. It was in fact Alissa who had coined the term, though when she had used it, Eve had howled with laughter and adopted it as her own term for Audrey Boucher. It was almost as if Alissa didn't want Nick to see her own arm's length, her ability to dress situations in sarcasm.

"What else?" Nick asked.

"Nothing." She shouldn't have called. The thing about the reporter could wait.

"You two going to be okay there in Chicago?"

"What if we weren't? Would you fly out?" Alissa wanted to kick herself in the silence that followed her cute reply.

"I just want the two of you to be safe, that's all," he said. "Just be cautious."

"Cautious of what? We're going to the Living Now Book Expo. The worst that could happen would be that I'd start meditating."

"That seems highly unlikely."

"Highly."

"Yeah. Okay. Don't let Eve out of your sight. Don't accept any impromptu interviews. All interviews have to be set up in advance. No exceptions."

"Okay, sure. Yeah, I know."

"Am I being too bossy?"

"No reason to stop now."

Nick laughed. "Okay, have a good trip. And hey, I got your e-mail about book sales. Congratulations. Is Eve happy?"

"Ecstatic."

"Good. See you later this week, okay?"

"Okay."

Neither of them hung up.

"Call me from Chicago if you need anything."

"I will."

"Or just to check in."

"I will."

"Okay, bye."

"Okay, bye."

When Alissa returned to the seating area, Eve said, "You called Nick to tell him I stole a seal. Here's the sales receipt."

Alissa wished she could simply trust that what Eve said

was true, but she couldn't stop herself from examining the sales receipt. It did indeed list "ornamental seal" and the dollar amount.

"You didn't believe me about the trees, did you?"

"No. I guess I didn't."

"I promised you."

"I'm sorry."

"They've already called our row."

Alissa stood up. "Anyway, I didn't call Nick about the seal. I called him about a *Times* reporter who wants to interview you."

Alissa was surprised Eve didn't jump to her feet and clap her hands the way she did when she was pleased. Instead, she rustled in her bag, acting as if she hadn't even heard.

"Isn't that exciting?"

Eve still ignored her. Alissa had seen this before. People who had a threshold for fame. They devoured the attention until a certain level was reached, and then anxiety devoured them. Alissa's job now was to help Eve over this threshold. She wouldn't mention the *Times* reporter again until they returned from Chicago.

"Come on," she said gently. "Let's go do Chicago."

Eve had insisted on a window seat. Alissa wanted the aisle. They were lucky enough to have no one between them. Eve pushed her big bag under the seat in front of her, loosely fastened her seat belt, took a swig of Evian, and placed the bottle in the seat pocket. Then she handed *People* to Alissa and opened the *New Yorker,* as if the magazines were interchangeable.

"Could we trade mag—"

"Oh, my god," Eve whispered. "Oh, my god. She has a poem in here."

"Who does?"

"The Correspondent."

Alissa leaned over to look at the table of contents, and sure enough, there was The Correspondent's name.

Eve turned the pages of the magazine slowly, as if she were pulling back the papers covering a box of chocolates, until she reached the poem. Perhaps it was the sun coming in the small port window, but a faint, shimmery light surrounded Eve as her eyes landed on the poem. Then the light shifted, flashed red, and disappeared. Eve placed a finger by the title of the poem. She pulled the magazine closer to her face, still holding the place of the title, as if she couldn't get past that. A silence swallowed up the next few moments. Alissa looked away, figuring that Eve wanted to be alone with the words. When she finally looked back, the magazine was lying in the empty seat, and Eve was looking out the window, her hand on her cheek.

"What is it, Eve? Was the poem nice?"

"I don't think so," she whispered, her voice feathery with tears.

Alissa picked up the magazine and found the page with the poem. It was entitled, "The Gracemonger." It was not flattering. The lady who hawks grace like shellfish in the lane. As if inspiration can be wrapped in newspaper and handed out for a tuppence. The lady who sings in the streets, city by city, peddling her soul, alive, alive-o. Cockles and mussels, the poem echoed the folk song that Alissa remembered, the one her kindergarten teacher used to sing in her high, wavering voice.

"What a bitch," Alissa said, but even as she said it, she thought that maybe this was a good thing. Maybe Eve would give up The Correspondent and get on with the business of selling books and grace. "This was a really, really bitchy thing to do." Alissa took the hand that Eve still pressed to her cheekbone and tried to get her to look at her.

Just then, a woman with hair that had lived through far too much product and whose eyes were a blue not found in nature leaned over Alissa and said, "You're Eve Glass! Oh, I just *love* your books. They've saved my life, they really have. May I have your autograph?"

"Can't you see that I'm in the middle of a complete breakdown?"

The woman recoiled as if she had been kicked. For a moment she looked sorry, but as she turned back down the aisle, she blasted, "Well, ex*cuse* me."

"I'm going to Maine," Eve said, standing up, as if she could get off the airplane now.

"Sit down. Buckle your seat belt. We're taking off momentarily."

"It's not what you think. I love her."

"You can't love her. You're a public figure."

Eve looked at Alissa as if she were as emotionally clueless as a computer.

"This is a big gig. There will be thousands of people there."

"I don't care. Don't you realize that yet? *I—don't—care.* Look at this poem."

"I read it. I know. That must hurt. But look, Eve, it's a sign that you're important enough, big enough, to come under attack." It was a line that often worked with Alissa's Silicon Valley clients.

"Bullshit. She used me. She thought it'd be cute to sleep with a trashy motivational speaker and then to write about it."

"Eve, keep your voice down."

"Ma'am, I'll have to ask you to take your seat, please." A flight attendant blocked Eve's attempt to slide past Alissa's knees and into the aisle.

"I have to get off this plane."

"That's not possible now. Please sit down."

"It's a medical emergency."

The flight attendant's face paled.

"It is not," Alissa said emphatically. "My client is just a bit frightened of flying."

A second flight attendant arrived to back up his colleague. They waited until Eve had reseated herself and buckled her seat belt. A moment later, they were off the ground.

Eve sat back in her seat, her hands placed on the tops of her thighs, and stared at the head directly in front of her. She took long, measured breaths.

"Eve?"

"What?"

"I see sparks coming off of you."

"That happens," Eve answered distractedly, as if Alissa had merely pointed out an eyelash on her cheek. Eve abandoned the breathing, pulled out her cell phone, and punched a number.

Alissa snatched the phone out of Eve's hand. "You'll cause the plane to crash." She tucked the cell phone in her own bag as Eve yanked the airplane phone off the back of the middle seat in front of them.

"Give me a credit card number," she said to Alissa, who

ignored her. Eve hung up the phone and slumped against the window.

The plane soared skyward, and although the ascent pressed Alissa against her seat, she felt suspended in the air, as if the airplane weren't there at all. Her past clients had been circumspect and discreet about their love interests. The release of information had been tightly controlled, meaning that press conferences were called and only specific questions were answered. Spooky reporters didn't lurk around anyone's home. Conflicts were played out in the pages of newspapers and trade publications, even the personal ones were disguised as business ones, and not in literary magazines. Not one of her past clients, not a single one, had emanated anything other than flat, businessman energy. She was afraid to even touch Eve for fear of getting a shock. Alissa longed to be on the ground. The desire to call Nick persisted in her throat.

Eve remained silent, staring out the window, for the entire flight to Chicago. She didn't try to call Audrey Boucher again, nor did she try, when they reached O'Hare, to book a flight to Maine. She was pale but no longer teary. She appeared to be thinking deeply. In fact, she seemed to have thought herself into a completely different frame of mind by the time they reached the Park Plaza Hotel.

"Is there any mail for me?" she wanted to know while Alissa checked them in.

"No, I don't think so," the receptionist replied.

"But would you please look."

"It would come up on the computer as we check you in. There's nothing here."

"I'm sorry to be so insistent. But I know I was to receive a letter here. Please, there must be a place where the physical letters are kept. Would you go through them?"

"Surely, ma'am," the receptionist said in a dull tone. He clicked hard on the computer and then disappeared into a back room.

Alissa was amazed. How, in the passage of a four-hour flight, had Eve's justified fury at being publicly mocked by the person she claimed to love evolved into eagerness, once again, to hear from the woman?

"You were right, ma'am. There is a letter for you." He handed her the plain white envelope, hand addressed with green ink. Eve pressed the letter to her throat and tears welled in her eyes again. The receptionist also handed each of the women a key to her room and wished them a pleasant stay.

"I'm going to rest a bit," Alissa said, eyeing Eve's precious letter as if it were a bomb. "Want to meet for dinner in two hours?"

Eve nodded.

"Are you okay?"

She nodded again.

"Don't call The Correspondent."

Eve's smile was dismissive, as if the sooner she could get rid of her nosy manager the better.

"Trust me," Alissa said. "It won't work. Your thing with her is letters. I have a feeling she would feel violated if you called."

Eve laughed.

"Okay, intruded upon. I'm just saying it's a bad idea."

"And what would you say is a good idea?"

"The woman wrote a patronizing poem about you and published it in the *New Yorker.* You don't need someone in your life who would do that."

"I won't call her," Eve said. "I wasn't going to. Your concern is sweet."

"The first six months of a book's life are critical," Alissa said. "You have to hold it together for another three or so. Do that for me. Do that for Nick. Tomorrow's a big day. You need to conserve your energy."

Now Eve's smile was compassionate, as if Alissa were the one falling apart. She said, "I'll see you in two hours. Let's eat somewhere really nice. I'll ask the concierge about restaurants, okay?"

Alissa was relieved to reach her room and lock the door behind her. The utter privacy of a hotel room was luscious, and the cell phone in her handbag nearly purred. She dropped the bag on the bed and watched it, as if the phone might leap on its own out of the bag and into her hands. She reviewed the pieces of business she needed to go over with Nick, until something quite different from thought compelled her. She dug out the phone and her fingers punched the number.

Even when a woman answered, Alissa was not deterred. "What's Judith doing home in the middle of the afternoon?" she asked when Nick got on the line.

"What's up?" he asked.

Alissa ignored the caution in his voice and told him, "You should see what that poet wrote in the *New Yorker.*"

"The *New Yorker?*"

"Yep."

"About what?"

"About Eve."

"You're kidding. No, you're not. Is it bad?"

"Yes. Well. She doesn't ever *name* Eve. I mean, now that I think about it, hardly anyone would even know it's about her. It's just a poem."

Nick was silent and Alissa knew he couldn't talk freely. She said, "I'll call you back later."

"Will you?"

"Yes," she answered the wistfulness in his voice with her own. "I will."

Eve didn't have to speak the next day, only sit in her publisher's booth, greet fans and sign books, hundreds of them. Alissa sat at her side, passing her the opened books, massaging her hand when it cramped. All night long Alissa had worried that Eve would go AWOL, would have vacated her room by the morning, would refuse to sign for more than an hour, or, worst of all, would bark at her fans. But Eve was golden. She insisted on continuing, even when the publisher's rep suggested she stop. The line extended well into the exhibition hall, and Eve appeared intent on signing every last book.

In between two fans, Eve leaned over and said, "Audrey Boucher hasn't signed this many books in her lifetime, let alone in one sitting."

"You got that right."

"Let's go home tonight."

"We have a flight in the morning."

"What's your name, ma'am?" Eve glowed at a young white woman with dreads. "There you go. May the goddess bless you."

"The goddess?" Alissa said under her breath.

"She loved it. Couldn't you tell? I want to go home tonight."

"I'm not taking a redeye. Besides, you can't fix anything by going home tonight instead of tomorrow. It's already late in Maine."

A gentle-spoken man held Eve's hand for too long. She still smiled at him warmly before yanking it back and signing his book.

"Who said anything about Maine? I told you I wouldn't call her. You were absolutely right before. A phone call would be all wrong. Even e-mail is too immediate and intimate for Audrey."

Alissa laughed. "She'd rather communicate via national magazine."

"That wasn't communication meant for me. She never dreamed I'd see it. Eve Glass, motivational speaker and writer, reading the *New Yorker*? Wouldn't happen."

"It did happen. Eve, pay attention to your fans."

"That was a fluke. I bought the magazine for you. She was right, I don't read the *New Yorker*." There were tears in Eve's eyes.

"Come on," Alissa said, "you've signed enough. I'm going to tell your fans that you have to go."

Eve took the next fan's book. "What's your name?"

"Rosemary."

"Tell me your dream, Rosemary."

"To fly," the woman said.

"Ah, then, may you fly," Eve said, scratching her name in the book.

She turned her tear-streaked face back to Alissa. "Would

you mind if I went to the airport and caught a red-eye by myself?"

"Eve, get a grip. Wipe your . . . your tears."

"I can't wipe my tears with the back of my hand in front of all these people."

"Shit." Alissa dug through her purse but couldn't find a handkerchief. "You can't go home tonight. I promised Nick I wouldn't let you out of my sight. We're staying here at the Park Plaza tonight. We'll leave first thing in the morning."

"Hey. Marianne." A woman crouched down in front of the table so that she was eye level with Eve. "Long, long time. How're you doing?"

Eve quickly wiped away her tears using the back of her hand after all.

"Excuse me," Alissa said, stepping between Eve and the reporter. "Nice to see you again." She tried to hide the alarm she felt at seeing this reporter, who'd been in her backyard two nights before, here in Chicago. "But I'm afraid Eve is not available to the press today."

The reporter stood up and put her hands in the air. "No problem. Look, I'm not at Expo for Marianne. I'm doing a story on that self-styled guru who's just been busted for sleeping with his followers. Chad Dalton? Hear about him? A lot of his victims are here today and I'm getting interviews. When I saw Marianne was signing, I just wanted to stop by and say hi. Nothing formal."

Alissa glanced at Eve, who sat with her hands folded in her lap, staring at a spot on the table, looking mysteriously blank. She reached for a confident but friendly tone as she took the reporter's elbow and ushered her away from the booth. "Great. Nice of you to stop by. Eve appreciates the wonderful support she's received from the media. Let's talk soon." She looked over her shoulder at Eve again and then whispered, "The poor thing. She's exhausted. So many fans here today." She squeezed the woman's elbow and let go.

The reporter—what was her name again?—paused in the aisle, looking at Eve, before walking away.

"That's it," Alissa told the line of fans. "I'm sorry. Dr. Glass has another commitment. She wishes you all the best."

Alissa and the publisher's rep hurried Eve through the crowd, out of the exhibition hall, and into the hotel lobby. The rep asked Alissa if they'd be okay and quickly left to have drinks with a colleague.

In the elevator, riding up to their rooms, Alissa asked, "Why'd she call you 'Marianne'?"

Eve shrugged. "Confused reporter."

"She said, 'Long time,' like she knew you."

"I get that a lot. Maybe I *did* know her at some point in my life. She probably interviewed me years ago or something."

"The *Times* will be great press for you. I'll call her later this week and set up the interview."

"No," Eve said. "I don't want to do that one."

"It's the *Times.* You have to."

"Please." Eve shook her head and looked ready to cry again. Nick was right. Audrey Boucher was trouble. Her little literary sabotage had completely undone Eve. Maybe she could get Seth to call the poet, posing as a lawyer, and threaten libel.

Upon returning home from Chicago, Alissa had a few days alone before Seth returned from his fishing trip, and she enjoyed filling the house with music. The time alone made her feel righted, full, happy with herself. She did not call Nick, and he didn't call her. She would see him at Eve's gig at Powell's Books in two weeks, and a break seemed like a good idea. She cleaned the house for Seth. She hoped that he was steeping in his alpine glory, that the trip would jolt him back to his boyish self. She planned, for his first night home, dinner at their favorite restaurant.

Instead, they argued before he had even brought his backpack in off the porch.

She had only told him about the poem in the *New Yorker,* thinking that it would impress him, at least mildly, and she didn't mention the lurking reporter at all, afraid that he would find a way to insinuate that Alissa had opened up their lives to all kinds of weird things. He did anyway.

"Damn, 'Lissa, I read that freaky book on my trip."

"What freaky book?"

"Grace and goals."

Alissa tried to laugh, but Seth didn't even smile. He said, "What's any of this have to do with you? She writes like some kind of hick preacher, except with New Age rhetoric thrown in. It's like you're going back to your hillbilly roots. What's up, babe? I can't handle this."

"*What? Hillbilly*? I grew up outside St. Louis."

"Missouri."

"Yeah?"

"Outside St. Louis, Missouri."

"Yeah, that's where St. Louis is. You've been there. It's a city. You've met my family. They're not hillbillies."

"Arguable."

Alissa was silent, and Seth knew he'd gone too far. "I'm

just worried about you, 'Lissa. I can't hang with you becoming some kind of New Age circle-dancer."

She didn't need this tonight. She let another silence drop between them. This time he didn't move it out of the way.

"Will you listen to me for a minute?" she asked. Still, he was silent. "You know me. You know who I am. I graduated from Yale on a swimming scholarship. I majored in history of ideas *and* business. I understand hard work. I understand long distances. I don't believe in most of Eve's schlock. But you know, I don't much believe in your father's philosophy of success, either. There are two ways to get something in this life: inherit it or work your butt off. What Eve, my product, did, was work her butt off. She invented herself out of nothing. That fascinates me. The idea of creating an audience, a fan base, sales for *grace,* that interests me a lot."

"You don't even know what grace is."

"And you do?"

"Maybe."

She waited, truly hoping to hear his version, but all he could say was, "Don't get too cynical, Alissa."

"Don't tell me how to get."

"Look." He took both of her hands in his. "Babe, you've already made it. You have everything: money, looks, me." He tried to sound sheepish. At least conciliatory. "Seriously, you don't know when to stop."

"I'm thirty. My life isn't over. Why should I stop? Stop *what?"*

"Trying to prove yourself."

"I'm not trying to *prove* myself. I'm challenging myself. I've done suits and they were highly predictable. They wanted to win and the number of dollars gained determined if they had. Anyone with half a brain can make money in the stock market. This is a little trickier. When you're making a human product, you can't completely control the parameters."

"Then why bother trying? Why not just let humans be humans?"

Alissa had the feeling that Seth *had* rediscovered something about himself in the mountains, maybe something important, but that he wasn't inclined to share it with her, as if he didn't believe she could see the humanity in *him*.

"What was your trip like?" she asked, her words sounding as flat as Missouri.

"I need a shower," he said. "Man, I reek." He kissed her cheek, as if they hadn't argued, and left the room. It was worse than continuing the argument, this giving up. As if he knew something that he was sure she wouldn't get, no matter how hard he tried explaining. But that was just it. He hadn't tried.

The bookstore was dusty, nearly humming with the silent language of its volumes. The floors were cement, cracked in places, and the shelves reached to the tops of the high ceilings, many books gotten only by tall ladders. They were piled and stacked and properly upright, all ways, like a book lover's dream. If these books were music, this would be heaven for Alissa's buck-toothed middle school orchestra teacher, a chaos of felt message. More warehouse than bookstore, Powell's was a Portland landmark, a nationally recognized literary center. Most authors they hosted were poets, essayists, well-honored fiction writers. Convincing Joshua, the events coordinator, that Eve Glass belonged in his reading series was quite a coup, and a good start toward corralling a more discriminating audience. Perhaps not as discriminating as Seth, but there were plenty of high-brow readers who, when the right spin was put on a book, read anything. Eve's sage advice, backed by rich stories, was not unlike Anne Lamott's or even Pema Chödrön's. Alissa was confident her client would do well this evening at Powell's.

The timing was perfect, too. September. A time to burrow in. A time for all the bookish squirrels to come gather their literary nuts.

"Where are the chairs?" Alissa asked Joshua when he greeted her and Eve in the bookstore's foyer.

"We've set up in the Pearl Room," he said, leading the two women down short stairways, around corners into other rooms, and finally into the back of the store, where only a few dozen chairs were set up.

"You don't understand," Alissa said sharply. "We were at the Living Now Book Expo a couple of weeks ago where Eve Glass signed *hundreds* of books. This won't do."

"We've got some extra chairs in the back," Joshua said in a polite, soft voice. "If we need them, I can set them up real fast." He must have been some kind of poet himself. He had uncombed black hair and big black glasses, and wore polyester plaid pants. His once-white T-shirt was too small, and his arms were thin and pale.

"This is nice," Eve said mildly. "It'll be fine." She wandered off to touch the books.

Alissa consulted her watch. Fifteen minutes before showtime. Where was Nick? The restraint of having not spoken since Chicago, rather than feeling prudent, felt like an aphrodisiac. She missed him. She'd been foolish to talk to him as she had from Chicago.

Alissa turned in a circle, looking for him, looking for an audience, feeling almost frightened. This scarcity of chairs. This ambient wisdom, guaranteed by more books than she had ever seen in one place. This reckless collection of literature. Doubt has been described as a seed. As a worm. Alissa, who had experienced doubt maybe twice before in her life, and then at times when it had hardly mattered, experienced it now as a dull red tingling that began in her toes and rose up through her body in waves.

Joshua returned with two folding chairs under each arm. He set these up and went for more. But at twenty-five past seven, just five minutes before Eve was to begin, there were entire rows of empty chairs. Nick hadn't arrived yet, and probably wasn't coming. Or maybe he would come and bring the elusive fiancée. The thought of Judith, Judith of the short leash, irritated Alissa. When was their wedding, anyway? She wished there was time to get a latte. As if caffeine were what she needed. She should be trailing Eve, who had wandered over to the poetry section, undoubtedly to finger and linger over Audrey Boucher's books.

At seven-thirty, Joshua escorted Eve out of the poetry section and to the podium.

He introduced her a little too kindly, a little too apologetically, managing to make the point that Dr. Glass was a significant departure from the bookstore's usual reading series. Alissa stood, leaning against a bookcase to the side of the audience, such as it was, scowling, as the events coordinator turned the podium over to Eve.

A husky voice near her ear said, "Hey," startling her.

"Oh, Nick." He looked tense, too. "How are you?"

"Good."

"There's no one here," she whispered. "Two-thirds of the chairs are empty. I'm sorry."

"You take your work so seriously."

"You hired me to—"

"To look after Eve. You insist on forgetting that we have very different ideas of what your job is."

"My self-image is ruined if I have to think I've been hired as a babysitter."

Nick smiled, his full cheeks rounding and his gray eyes more intelligent than she remembered.

"How's she doing?" Nick whispered.

"She's okay. But she's lost her focus. I don't know what's wrong with her."

Nick nodded, watching Alissa carefully.

"What?"

"Nothing." He smiled again.

Alissa let her body fall back against the bookcase. She tried to think of something else to say about Eve. "I think it's that poem. It really hurt her. There's this reporter from the *Times* who keeps calling, wanting an interview. It could be a really big break. But Eve refuses to do the interview, says she can't handle anything right now."

"A reporter from the *Times?*"

"Yeah."

"Why didn't you tell me? You're supposed to tell me about all interview requests."

"Nick, relax. I just told you that Eve won't even do the interview. So what was there to tell you?"

The tension that sprang up between them was delicious.

Alissa took his sleeve and pulled him back into the stacks. "Are you mad?" she whispered. "I'm not keeping anything from you. We just haven't talked. In a couple of weeks."

With her back against the books, and her hand still holding his sleeve, he was close enough that she could feel the warmth of his breath. That doubt, no longer a tingling, more like a red field, kept him close to her.

Nick blinked. His long black lashes a kind of luxury. "I'm sorry."

"Sorry?"

"For involving you in this."

"What am I involved in?"

They both glanced out the end of the aisle of books that held them in place, together, almost alone, certainly out of Eve's line of vision. Then back at one another.

Nick shook his head, looking lost.

Alissa touched his temple, just in front of the ear, and felt the pulse there. Sometimes, with Seth, Alissa felt as if she had earned him with her own hard work and success, with her own looks. But just *barely* earned him, as if her success and her looks *just* crossed the line. She always had to reach for him. Nick was right here.

She removed her hand from the side of his face, dropped it to her side, then lifted it again to place on his sternum. She exerted a bit of pressure. She hadn't meant it as a push, but Nick stepped back, deeper into the shade of the stacks, and Alissa fell toward him, gently. He slowly tucked her hair behind one ear and then the other, as if he wanted nothing in the way. His lips were full and comfortable, supple. His hands reached down over her back, and she leaned into him. Kissing Nick was like a big blue wave that cooled the hot red field of doubt. She felt very sure.

Later, Alissa would remember that she heard a disruption in the audience, not a loud one, but a sound that spoke to some part of her brain roving outside the kiss. It was the silence, though, the cessation of Eve's voice, that finally pulled Nick and Alissa apart. They looked at one another as they listened. Eve had definitely stopped talking, and the audience was silent. The only sound was a burst of laughter, a rude snorting hilarity, fading into the adjoining room, like a train speeding away. Alissa and Nick stepped from the stacks into the audience and saw Eve leaving the podium, the pile of her books untouched, some notes in her hand, headed for the exit. They rushed to her, each taking an arm. Alissa knew she couldn't have seen, couldn't possibly have seen, and Eve only said that she was sick, that she needed to go home right away. Alissa went to the podium and spoke into the microphone, explaining to the small audience that Eve Glass was not well.

That's when she saw, sitting to the left of the podium, in the third row of chairs, the *Times* reporter. She smiled at Alissa and stood, as if to approach her. Talk about persistent. Alissa pretended she didn't recognize the reporter. She left the stack of Eve's books for Joshua to dismantle and rushed through the islands and cliffs of books until she reached the front of the store. She pushed through the doors and found Nick and Eve waiting for her on the wet pavement, huddled close to the windows of the bookstore's café. A light drizzle had begun falling. Alissa took one of Eve's arms and Nick took the other, and the trio walked two blocks to where the red Jaguar was parked. Nick helped Eve into the passenger seat and crawled into the back himself.

No one spoke as Alissa drove. She knew they should be cooing over Eve, asking what exactly hurt, what symptoms she had. Neither she nor Nick placed a hand on her forehead or offered her ibuprofen. Alissa refused to let go of that feeling she had had with Nick, that dead-center sureness she felt against him, not even for a moment, not even to inquire about how Eve felt. Three times she looked at Nick in the rearview mirror, not caring if Eve noticed. It wasn't a recklessness she felt, nearly the opposite, as if she were finally driving fast enough and the speed gave her control, perfect control.

Nick walked Eve to her door. Alissa assumed he would go inside with her, get home on his own, but she waited, and he returned moments later, climbing in the front seat.

"She's not well. I'll come over in the morning and check on her."

Alissa nodded and drove away from Eve's house, thrilled to have Nick alone in the dark of her car, as if she were kidnapping him. But of course she wasn't. Ten, maybe twelve precious minutes, she calculated, that's all she had until they reached the house he now shared with Judith. Only later would she remember that he hadn't given her driving directions. The memory mortified her, that he would know she'd scoped out his house, that she'd driven by, a few times in fact, to see where he lived. It was a cute Craftsman, nicely landscaped, though not as tidy as she would expect, given who Judith seemed to be.

Tonight she did not think about Judith.

She stopped the car under a weeping willow, half a block before the house, driving right into the curtain of branches that fell over the side of the road, so that they were enclosed in a dark willowy canopy. The place was like a tomb, or maybe a womb, of Wagner's most brooding symphonic moments. Alissa felt unaccountably sad, and yet it was a sadness permeated with potential. She turned off the engine so that she could listen better. She wished she could choose the exact Wagner movement. She wanted to hear that, and not Nick's words.

"None of this fits you," he said, smoothing his hand along the leather dashboard of her car.

"None of what?"

"The Jag. The power clothes."

"Bullshit. It all fits me."

"Maybe."

"You don't know me."

He shook his head no, then reached over and ran his fingers across her bottom lip.

Alissa closed her lips around his fingers.

He pulled them out slowly. "My car is at the bookstore."

"Oh!" Of course it was. How stupid of her.

"It doesn't matter. I'll get it tomorrow."

"I can take you back there."

"No. Listen. Alissa. I need to talk to you about Eve."

"What?"

"You promised me once you'd look after her. Promise me again."

"I will. I said so."

How ironic, since together they had just dumped her at her doorstep, sicker than either of them had ever seen her.

Nick said, "I'm afraid of the *Times* reporter."

"You've met her?"

"Yeah. She had contacted me about an interview a while ago, before I hired you. I thought she'd dropped it."

"But what do you mean 'afraid'? The chick is edgy, that's all."

"Actually, we know her. From a long time ago."

Alissa was still listening to her phantom Wagner symphony. She didn't want to talk about Eve or the media. She reached for Nick's hand, finding his knee instead.

"I'm serious, Alissa. It could be a problem. I sort of made a mistake, maybe a big mistake, a long time ago."

"What are you talking about?" Alissa withdrew her hand.

"Her name is Joan Ehrhart. She went to Kennedy High School. Tried out for my track team the same year Eve started."

"Did Eve go by 'Marianne' back then?"

"Yeah. It's her given name."

"The reporter called her 'Marianne' at the Living Now Book Expo."

"She was *there*? In Chicago? Shit."

"Yeah, but Eve said she didn't remember her."

"She might not. You know Eve. She's very focused. I'm sure she's forgotten all about it."

"About what?"

"I did something kind of unfair. First day of practice, I had the girls race. Joan won. She beat Eve. But I was so overwhelmed by Eve, I ignored Joan."

Alissa took his jaw in her hand. "Nick. A small injustice in *high school*? She probably doesn't even remember. Trust me. The woman is harmless. So she has a bit of bluster about her, like anyone who's trying to cover up insecurities. All writers are deeply insecure, even the successful ones. I promised you: I'll look after Eve. There's nothing to worry about." Alissa was touched by the depth of Nick's earnestness. Touched and annoyed. She wanted him to be overwhelmed by *her.*

He turned his face in her hand. "I have to go."

She ran her thumb across his jaw.

Nick fumbled for the door handle. "How do you get out of this thing?"

Alissa had the power, from the driver's seat, to keep all the doors locked. She should have, right then, unlocked his door for him. Instead she put a hand on the back of his neck and tried to draw him toward her. "Nick?"

"Yeah." His hand still groped the dark interior of the door.

"Will you kiss me again?"

He looked like a crumbling wall. He looked like truth itself. He didn't use his voice, only shook his head. Then again, shook it. Alissa found the will to unlock his door. He got out of the car, walked around the back of it, pushing through the draped willow branches, and leaned in her window, said, "Just this once more." He kissed her more gently than Alissa had ever been kissed, then pulled out of the car window, so that she couldn't even see his face, just his chest and waist, but she could hear his voice. "Good night."

So here at last was the fault line in her life, the place she had so successfully avoided all these years, where a little slippage could change the whole gestalt. She drove home slowly, through the winding streets of Portland, wondering what next. She reached behind her for the case of CDs and dragged them onto the seat still warm from Nick. Unzipping the case, she pulled out one and then another CD, tossing each into the backseat in frustration. Forget Mahler. Not Beethoven. Not even Bach. Wagner would now be unbearable. Something was wrong, very wrong. She couldn't settle on what she wanted to hear.

She felt like a bursting dam. She used words to plug the crack, quickly, desperately, knowing it would fail even as she tried. I graduated from Yale, she told herself. I lettered in swimming. I understand long distances. I understand commitment. I understand deconstruction. I understand the components of success. I believe they can be fitted together like Tinkertoys. I have tried to invent myself, like Eve did. But it's failing. I can tell that it is failing. None of the signs are visible yet. On the surface I still look like a million dollars, in every sense of the metaphor, as well as literally. But something is wrong in my core. Maybe it is biology. Maybe deconstruction and the subsequent construction of a human life are in fact an invention of the human imagination. Maybe biology is God. Maybe DNA is the bottom line that can never, never ever, be crossed. The idea of human choice is a mirage. Or maybe Eve Glass has been right all along. Maybe grace exists. Maybe it's all we can hope for, moments when it descends on our lives.

Finally Alissa's hand fell on Vivaldi's *L'Estro Armonico,* the composer's breakthrough composition. She slipped the CD into the player and turned up the volume as loud as her ears could stand. Instantly every detail of that nearly empty classroom came to her vividly, as if she were peering through the small glass window in the door. There was the blond wood of hardback chairs, the black stalks and open petals of music stands, the green chalkboard with the bass and treble staffs painted in white. There was the music teacher herself, ecstatically alone within the heart of her music.

When Alissa came in the front door, Seth sat in the great room, still wearing his white shirt and red tie, gray slacks, his jacket flung on the couch. He looked angry. He had something wadded in his fist and, as she came all the way into the room, he shook it out as if he were unfurling a small flag. A few Douglas fir needles fell to the ground. He held a pair of wet, earth-covered panties. On the couch lay her soiled bra. Seth asked, "What the hell is this? Exactly."

"Underwear," Alissa said.

She stood facing the man she'd been with for a dozen years. He was to her like a great continent. He had been the crucial ground beneath her feet for so much of her life. But Nick. Nick was like that first raft across the Bering Strait.

Here, then, was the edge.

# A Glimpse:
# Joan

Joan began to feel like a stalker. Who the hell was Dr. Eve Glass? The lady who hawks grace, as the poet wrote in the *New Yorker.* A woman who sparks bits of light, who inspires envy. She had gone to Santa Fe to attend Eve Glass's interactive lecture and, hopefully, to interview her. But she hadn't gone to Chicago for her. She wasn't lying about the Chad Dalton story, but Marianne's handler had made her feel as if she were. Which made her angry.

It was time to let Marianne go. Let her tell her own story however she wanted to tell it. A story, Joan had begun to realize, that had nothing to do with her. It had come as a surprise, but Joan finally saw the possibility of Marianne truly not recognizing her. Joan had been a moment in Marianne's history unworthy of memory. Joan knew she should move on.

That was the plan. To move on. To reconnect with Meredith. Both of them had become too obsessed with work.

So Joan decided to surprise her girlfriend, her overworked, deadline-crazed girlfriend, with dinner at the office. They'd spoken earlier, and Meredith had complained that she wouldn't even have time for takeout, that she'd be at work until at least 11:00, and that she was just too tired to even talk about it.

That evening Joan picked up fat burritos, driving across town to the place that had the salsa Meredith loved best, and then driving all the way out to Tigard, where the software company had its offices. She was feeling guilty for having worked so much herself lately, and also for keeping the Eve Glass story a secret from Meredith. As if she were still pursuing the woman or something. Joan would drop that assignment, and Meredith's new software would be out momentarily, and then they'd get their lives back together.

Most of the lights were off in the industrial complex, and a janitor pushed a big rag mop down the hallway. Meredith's office door was shut, and Joan smiled at the picture of Meredith at her computer, deep in concentration. It didn't occur to her to knock.

It was only 7:00, but the wine bottle was empty. The desk was littered with random chunks of uneaten baguette, and the room smelled of prosciutto and Brie. His tie and her shoes were off, and they sat facing one another in office chairs, her feet on his lap.

It was classic. With her boss, no less. Some last gasp of loyalty obscured the truth momentarily, and Joan thought Meredith could sue him for sexual harassment. He was rolling in dough. Of course, with her stock options, so was Meredith. They were apparently rolling in it together. No one, quite obviously, was harassing anyone.

Later Joan would wish she'd launched the foil-wrapped burritos like little silver torpedoes, one at his face and the other at hers. But she'd only backed out as quietly as she'd entered and carried her bag of chips and salsa and burritos back down the hallway, out the door, and across the parking lot to her car. Meredith did not come after her.

Joan drove straight to Powell's, where Marianne would be doing a reading from her new book.

# *Part Three*

# Eve's Apple

The air in Powell's was musty with old books. Eve looked for the oldest, most unusual volumes, and pulled them from the shelves to hold. They were comforting, a buffer against Alissa, who fluttered around nervously, giving orders to the events coordinator. Eve asked him where the poetry was kept and then went off to find Audrey. Unlike most bookstores, which carried maybe one copy of her most recent volume, Powell's had them all, several copies of each, taking up a good foot of the shelf.

She wanted to stay right there, with Audrey's books, but the nice young events coordinator gently gave her his arm, as if she were blind, and ushered her up to the podium. Eve smiled at her audience as he introduced her, but she couldn't quell a rising panic. Alissa was irritable. Nick was missing. Joan sat in the third row, vying for eye contact. Far too many chairs were empty.

And, even as she began her talk, she couldn't banish Audrey from her thoughts. She imagined, with intense prescience, Audrey's poem about her tucked snugly into a new book, one that didn't yet exist but that would someday, leaning gently against her other volumes. The poem that hailed Eve.

Focus. Reel in your audience, such as it is. Smile. Breathe. Slow down. Invest yourself with meaning. Access the light.

Ha! How long it'd been since Eve had felt her own luminescence. It was what everyone wanted, and she had given it willingly, that was her job. But the light had built itself a private study and, increasingly over the years, had shut itself inside, so that people glimpsed only the glow coming from under the door.

How, after a lifetime of developing yourself as a product, do you parse out the authentic from the manufactured? This was a question Audrey had asked her in New Mexico, and she hadn't meant it to be mean. She'd wanted to know. It was the best question anyone had ever asked Eve. The question had helped her choose Alissa, who saw *only* product when she looked at her. The honesty in this view refreshed Eve. It was as if Alissa, in one threshing, took what she needed and handed Eve back to herself. The authentic Eve. But who was that?

Eve took a deep breath, inhaling the fresh-cut-pine smell of the podium. She searched her audience for an anchor, a believer whose eye contact might remind her of her message. Then all at once it came. The light. Only this time it wasn't the soft glow emanating from her belly, or the hard wattage she'd occasionally felt flicking from her fingertips and toes.

This time it was a jagged halo of many colors pulsing around her soul, like the aura that precedes a migraine.

"'The future belongs to those who believe in their dreams,'" Eve quoted Eleanor Roosevelt. A balding man in the front row pulled out a tiny notepad and scribbled with the stub of a pencil he kept in his breast pocket. Eve smiled at him and he beamed back.

"'Imagination is the beginning of creation,'" Eve now quoted George Bernard Shaw. "'You imagine what you desire; you will what you imagine; and at last you create what you will.'"

The pulsing light was a warning. Eve tried to soften its edges, worried her audience could see the harshness, but the neon effect was beyond her control. She softened her voice instead, and continued on.

At last Nick appeared behind the rows of chairs. He looked agitated as he surveyed the scant audience, scowling at the empty chairs, until his eye caught Alissa leaning against a bookcase to Eve's right, not five rows back from the podium. He didn't even notice Joan sitting in the third row, on the other side of the room. As he headed for Alissa, his face sweetened.

Eve managed to keep speaking, miming joy as convincingly as she could for her audience, even as Nick and Alissa slipped into the corridor of books, out of her sight. The two people who were supposed to turn to her first, always, were hidden deep in that canyon of books doing who knew what, and had left her alone at the podium.

Eve's sudden loneliness loomed so large, she tripped on it. And she fell toward Joan. Why not? Eve's eyes grazed the woman sitting in the third row, looking astonishingly like the girl at sixteen, same curly hair, same ironic smile, same jaunty posture. She forced her eyes to keep moving, to sweep over Joan without pausing, without signaling recognition, even as she felt herself give in to the inevitability, eventually, of contact.

Nick and Alissa remained out of sight. Eve searched out the balding man's eyes again, trying to stabilize herself, but despite his obvious gratitude for her attention, she faltered. What was she doing here? Why was she peddling grace?

She must have been doing okay. There were nodding heads, hopeful countenances, even some eyes shining with tears. People loved quotes, and Eve used a lot of them. She even quoted Martin Luther. "Why," she asked her audience, "would I quote someone who lived five hundred years ago? Because grace is ancient. Every belief system ever developed has known grace one way or another, no matter how corrupt those institutions of faith may have become.

"In my first book, I talked about how to achieve goals, whether the goal was to get out of a bad relationship or to make more money, but maybe," and here she paused and visibly held her breath, waited, "maybe your goal is to experience grace just a bit more in your life. That's mine."

Someone snorted. Eve glanced quickly at Joan, but it wasn't her. It was one of two short-haired, glasses-wearing young women sitting directly behind her. The nonsnorting one elbowed the other, to quiet her, but then both of their faces convulsed with the need to laugh. They couldn't control it. The one snorted again, and then the other emitted sounds of laughter escaping from her chest in spite of trying to hold it in. The one sitting closest to the aisle grabbed her friend's arm and dragged her out of the audience, both of them bent over in the agony of trying to control their laughter.

They ran, clutching their stomachs, to the back of the bookstore. Eve heard, as everyone in the bookstore did, their explosion of glee when they reached the next room where they could free their mirth.

Normally, Eve could have handled the situation. If it hadn't been for the empty chairs. Or Joan's presence. Or Alissa and Nick's absence. If it hadn't been for Audrey's poem, flying around the bookstore like a bird looking for a book in which to nest. She might even have commented on the laughers' departure, smiled like a proud mother at the lightheartedness of her progeny, spoken about the act of laughing being sacred, healing. If someone scowled after the women, as her loyal and balding fan did now, she would have laughed herself and said, "Oh, laughter is never inappropriate."

Tonight, though, the laughter only fanned her panic. She looked for Nick. And for Alissa. By now they might be making love in the bathroom. Or risking a dark back aisle of the bookstore, in some lesser-used section, like the one holding books on entomology or Icelandic history.

Eve was alone.

That outburst of laughter was the sharpest knife. It sliced her open, and what she saw was ugly. She was a bullshitter. A fraud. A girl with a cart, yes, but of brightly colored vials of sugar water, which she sold to the people as medicine. A gracemonger. A hot, dry fever invaded her arms, legs, and then her head. Though she'd been speaking for only ten minutes, Eve leaned into the microphone and said, "Thank you so much for coming," as if she had made her full presentation.

She avoided the confused stares of her audience as she stepped away from the podium. It felt like a miracle when Nick, and, a second later, Alissa appeared at her side, after all. Even flooded with hormones that sang only one another's names, they wouldn't let her drown. They acted as if they'd been there all along.

"She looks incredibly pale," Alissa said once they were on the sidewalk, walking in the rain.

"I think I have a fever," Eve whispered.

"I'll take her home," Alissa said, gently, to Nick.

"Do you mind if I come, too?" he asked.

Eve kept her eyes on the glistening sidewalk cement while too long a moment passed before Alissa answered, and the moment was full of a tenderness she could not bear. She lifted her head to break her awareness of it, but as she did, she faced the plate glass window of the bookstore's coffeehouse. At a table directly in front of her, warming their hands on layered coffee drinks, were the two women who had laughed. They saw her now, with her two escorts holding her arms like she was some kind of fainting queen, and their faces busted open with more laughter that Eve could see, but not hear, through the glass. Their eyes seemed to roll like mad cows' eyes, and their pink tongues flapped in the big red cavities of their mouths. Their laughter was profane, a joyous release. Eve had made their day.

When they got to Eve's house, Nick didn't even stay for a minute. He came to the porch, watched her turn the key in the door, and then he returned to that ridiculous red car of Alissa's. Eve didn't look out the window at them. She let them drive away into the dangerous night to whatever joy or doom they would find together. Considering her tea cupboard, she tried to decide which tea would most closely match Audrey's scent. She chose the cinnamon spice, although that would be an exaggeration, especially the spice. Perhaps if one could sniff a live cinnamon tree in all its complexity of roots in soil, leaves in sky, not just the peeled, treated bark, the scent might approximate Audrey's. She carried the tea into her bedroom, where she changed into yellow flannel pajamas and crawled under the down comforter. Eve allowed the fever to addle her thoughts, as if it were a recreational drug that she was giving in to.

Death by laughter. What that possible?

Eve set down her teacup and reached for the phone. She called her poet who lived with three bloodhounds on the coast of Maine, in a house set back from a wave-battered cliff.

People answer the phone when it rings moments before midnight. They think someone has died. But when Audrey answered, her voice wasn't enough. Eve heard that "hello" and realized she needed more than words. So she placed the handset gently into the cradle of the phone.

The next morning Eve awoke to a lovely Saturday. The night rains had washed the sky clean, leaving only a transparent blue, and the sunlight coming in her bedroom was pure and brilliant. She could see the entire color spectrum in each ray. Eve's fever was gone, but it had left her feeling dry and empty. She got up and drank two glasses of water, and then lay in the stream of sunlight for a long time, as if it could recharge her.

Without the fever, without Nick and Alissa propping her up, without the need to sell grace, Eve thought of the two laughing women differently. She lay in bed trying to understand how. To say fondly would be misleading. Maybe jealously.

As if she wanted to ride the rapids of that laughter to somewhere entirely new, fresh, true.

A journey. That's what she needed. She would go to Audrey.

Eve leaped out of the bed. She yanked her suitcase off the top shelf of her closet and threw it on the tangled sheets, and then she started rifling through her clothes, looking for the perfect effect. Nothing. How do you dress for a poet who cares most about the beauty of language? All of Eve's clothes looked tacky, too lacy, too short, too *some*thing. She pulled on a low-cut white tank top, a purple miniskirt, and a pair of sandals, and grabbed her shoulder bag.

She went shopping. Eve wasn't supposed to be in the department store at all. Because of the earrings. She had gotten only a bit of community service and an order to stay away from the premises of the store for a year. Which made stepping through the glass doors when they opened at nine o'clock very exciting. She spent several hours trying on shoes and then leather coats, of which Audrey would never approve, and then admonished herself to get serious. Dressing to please someone else is a complicated business. You don't want to dress as they do, because people are rarely attracted to themselves, so you must dress how they would dress if they had thought of it. You have to be a step ahead of them. In the case of dressing for Audrey, she had to be casually elegant, but the elegant part had to be disguised because Eve doubted Audrey would want to acknowledge to herself that she liked elegant. Though she was quite sure she did. Her poetry, after all. Eve did find a beautiful white cotton shirt, classically cut, quite elegant actually, but one shirt did not make an outfit.

Eve supposed she wasn't trying hard enough. She shopped aimlessly, wandering among the racks, in and out of departments, as if she were a nomad hunting herbs. That very thought came to her while she rode the escalator down from the fourth to the third floor and she looked out over the merchandise, like a field of wildflowers, trying to figure which patch might yield the greatest harvest. She did, for a moment, truly believe herself to be in the out-of-doors, perhaps somewhere in southern Italy, perhaps a couple of thousand years ago, her eyes alighting on some bright green that might be just the herb for which she searched.

She returned to her real self somewhere among the dress blouses. The department was quiet, except for one woman who wanted a cream silk blouse to go with the chocolate brown wool slacks she was wearing. She seemed a bit urgent about the cream blouse, and had engaged a saleslady to help her. She wanted attention, lots of it, and that interested Eve in the woman. She did not want the saleslady to wander off to attend to other tasks. She wanted company as she pulled different blouses from the racks and held them against her thin chest. A nod or comment from the saleslady would send her to the mirror for further evaluation. Eve noticed that when she made these trips to the mirror, she left her purse on the floor by the rack from which the blouse came.

A thief has logic, just like anyone else. Eve had been banned from this place. Why? Because she had stolen from them and might again. She shouldn't have snuck into the department store, but knowing that she would not steal from them again, which was really the issue, not her presence itself, she didn't feel guilty being there. Now, her reasoning continued, if she took this *purse,* she wouldn't be stealing from the store. She would be stealing from that lady in the chocolate brown slacks who wanted a cream blouse. But the logic went deeper than that. What she was about to do didn't feel like stealing at all. It was more like asking someone out on a date, that vertigo from the dual chance of rejection and possibility. That purse pulsed like the cover of a good novel. Eve wanted to look inside.

So she hovered, watching the purse. The woman picked it up off the floor, slung it from her elbow as she moved to another rack of blouses. The purse seemed heavy, pulling on her arm, as she pushed blouse after blouse aside in her search. Then, an interesting blouse. The arm straightened and the purse slid to her wrist. She bent and let it rest on the carpet. She held the blouse against her chest and turned to get an opinion from the saleslady. But the saleslady had wandered back to her checkout island. Which annoyed the customer. Eve saw her frown, consider whether to call across to the saleslady, and then compose herself, and finally, with the blouse held out in front of her on the hanger, stride over to the checkout island.

Her purse remained on the carpet, beneath the hanging blouses.

That would have been Eve's moment. The customer's back was turned. She was absorbed in her pursuit of the saleslady's opinion. But Eve was torn. As much as she wanted to lift the purse, she was interested in what would happen now between the customer and the saleslady. She empathized with the customer. After all, there was no one else, other than Eve, and she wasn't asking for assistance, in the department. There was no reason the saleslady couldn't have remained in attendance.

"Too plain," Eve heard the saleslady say rather too sharply.

She dropped the pile of tissue she'd been arranging and bustled to a rack in the far corner of the department. The customer followed, still carrying her tailored cream blouse. Eve's opportunity was yet improved, but still she watched as the saleslady held up a cream blouse with a big ruffle down the entire row of buttons. Now Eve wasn't a professional fashion consultant, but even she could see that that woman in her chocolate brown slacks would no more wear those ruffles than she would wear spike heels.

If, for Eve, thievery were a kind a revenge, she would have found something to steal from the snooty saleslady, for whom her dislike was growing. But it didn't work like that. Again, the thief's logic. She wanted to give that poor woman who needed a blouse to go with her slacks a hug. Feeling close to her gave Eve a rather desperate urge to *know* her. Of course she couldn't give her a hug, or even introduce herself, so instead, she walked quietly over to the rack from which she had taken the blouse, which was still in her hand, and stood beside her purse on the floor.

It was that feeling at the top of a roller coaster, the moment before the descent of the biggest drop. She crested the rise, then swooped down and lifted the purse off the floor. She slung the long handles over her shoulder and walked slowly away. She even paused, one department over, to inspect a chartreuse jacket. This wasn't theater, she wasn't trying to look nonchalant and innocent, she was truly interested in the jacket, which was a nearly luminescent green, a color that floated off the fabric. Eve could have taken *that* instead, but she wasn't supposed to shoplift from the department store. So she continued on forward, trying to remember exactly where her car was parked. Once she rounded the escalator, she stopped to stuff the purse into her own big shoulder bag, as any woman might do after making a purchase, and kept walking. She remembered that she had come in through Men's Apparel, so that's where she exited. Once outside the department store doors, Eve turned her face toward the bright yellow sun and smiled, eyes slit to protect her corneas, and let the warmth shoot straight into her pores.

The purse in her bag was a like a piñata. Or a box of Crackerjacks. A blind date. A letter from Audrey. The contents were anyone's guess, but they might be richly rewarding. Eve sat in the front seat of her car, the vast parking lot surrounding her, the sun pouring in the window, and pulled the purse out of her shoulder bag. She let it sit in her lap for a moment. A supple, dark brown leather—to go with her wool slacks, of course—the kind that feels creamy to the touch. A simple zipper closed the one cavity and Eve pulled it slowly, like she was undressing The Correspondent. That thought made her pause, laugh. Yes, unzipping The Correspondent. The tiny *zzzzz* sound was lovely and satisfying. She reached her hand in before she let her eyes enter, remembering Halloween parties where peeled grapes were eyeballs and wet noodles were brains. Instead she felt a small packet of paper. Letters? A leather rectangle. The wallet probably, and it was fat. Loose coins, a pen, a tin of mints. She was about to open her eyes, going first to the letters, or what she supposed to be letters, when a shadow crossed her car. Two hairy hands clamped on the open sill of her window. The torso of a headless man, but not voiceless, for he said, "Ma'am, would you please step out of the car?"

"Sure." Eve tossed the purse in the passenger seat.

The detective's back was to the sun, and she was facing it, so she saw only a black cutout of a man. She imagined he looked like most department store detectives, including pocked skin, too much hair product, and a blocky body. She smiled at the sun, well aware that he would think she was smiling at him. Also well aware that, although she was forty-three, she wore a purple miniskirt and a sleeveless top, cut low enough to show the swell of her small breasts. That guy didn't know that she was a former Olympic runner. He didn't know that she was a national expert on grace. But he probably knew that she looked good.

Even Audrey had given her that. Cockles and mussels alive, alive-o. She claimed, not with words, oh, no, she wouldn't stoop to even talk about it, but with her entire being, she claimed to be unimpressed with the words *Olympic* and *best-selling.* What interested Audrey was the pretty waif girl with her shellfish cart. A poetic image. Hawking whatever she had. As if grace were just desperation turned inside out.

"What do you need?" Eve asked the detective, and asked it seductively, not because she wanted to get away with something, because even though she knew she looked good, she knew that looking good at her age can annoy men. No, she spoke to him seductively because she *wanted* to annoy him. Make him want to say, "Oh, don't think that'll work with *me,* sweetheart."

He asked to search her car, so she said, "Sure," as she reached in her bag for her cell phone. In her peripheral vision, she saw him lurch, and she smiled, realizing that he thought she might be reaching for a gun. Right, she thought, just call me Louise. Or was that Thelma who blew the guy away? But her moment's amusement passed quickly when, looking at the dial pad of her cell phone, Eve realized that there was no one, no one at all, that she could call.

An hour later, at the station, Eve closed her eyes as another man took both of her wrists in his one big hand. She looked for and found pleasure in the dry warmth of his skin. She concentrated on the softness of the pads on his fingertips and at the base of his palm, the way the bird bones in her own hands rested against these pillows of flesh. She even looked for the pleasure in the cold hard metal encircling each wrist now, the ache of its chill on her tender skin. A ratchety clank and the cuffs had her hands in the perfect position, behind her back, for the beginning of her yoga routine. She could bend now, reaching her connected wrists up behind herself, as she leaned forward, gravity flipping her hair over her head, her hamstrings stretching. But of course she didn't bend now. She searched for the next possible bit of pleasure, like looking for the next stone in the crossing of a swift cold creek. The best she could do, and this would be a slippery stone, was the face of the booking officer.

Not unpleasant. Not ruddy red or unnecessarily hard. In fact, he was a large, pudgy man, with fat cheeks, a broad nose, and overgrown eyebrows. A moment ago, before he'd cuffed her wrists together behind her back, she might have been able to run. While still looking up into his pleasant face, she laughed at the thought of herself in flight with a law enforcement officer in pursuit, and this, it turned out, was what he didn't appreciate.

"Lady, there ain't nothing funny about what's happening to you."

Just then another officer entered the booking room with a printout in his hand. He said, "Two priors."

"Huh," the big guy grunted his approval. "Nothing even remotely funny."

"I laugh when I'm nervous," Eve tried to explain.

She shouldn't have said "nervous" out loud. The word disturbed the air. Concentric circles of what felt like an electric current rolled off of her. The booking officer jerked, as if he'd been shocked.

"Sorry," she said.

He put a hand on the place between her shoulder blades and gently pushed. Eve closed her eyes again, not wanting to see where she was going. When she opened them, just five steps later, she was in a cell. The booking officer stood in the doorway, looking at her. She guessed he had been waiting for her to open her eyes. He said, "Booking vestibule. Someone will come get you for security and medical."

Then he shut and locked the door.

Eve looked for the pleasure.

This could be a locker room, she thought. A locker room found in an archeological dig, which would explain the absence of steamy showers, wooden benches, handy lockers, and, of course, human flesh. Unless this were an archeological site like Pompeii, in which case there might be a mummified woman, bent at the waist, standing where the showers had once been, her right arm stretched down to her ankle, her hand in the claw position. Would the archeologists ever have figured out that she had been shaving her legs when the volcano erupted? It was possible, after all, for a Pompeii to happen here and now. Mount Saint Helens blew, so Mount

Hood could blow, too. And if it did, this was where she, Eve Glass, former Olympic athlete and best-selling motivational author, would be immortalized. In the holding vestibule at the Multnomah County Jail. This was not a locker room, after all.

The cinder block walls of the vestibule, which were no more than four feet wide and six feet long, were painted white, semigloss. Eve lowered herself onto the cement bench and stared at the white cinder blocks. If this place were a black hole, one of those light-swallowing pits in the universe, she might be able to escape. The light that she was would be sucked through to the next universe. The beauty of black holes is that while no light can ever escape them, they are the birthplaces of stars. The end and the beginning all in one. But this place here, this holding vestibule, was a white hole, not a black hole, a place so brightly devoid of stimuli that all the energy coming from oneself ricocheted wildly off the walls, gathered, filled the room. No wormholes to the next universe. This room was like a blank slate, with nothing to absorb the energy, so there was only Eve looking at Eve. Maybe if she considered that shiny white cinder block wall a screen onto which she could project herself, she could watch herself like a movie. Stopping the random way her energy was glancing off the walls would help. These Multnomah County law-enforcement officers thought their jail, their handcuffs, the words "two priors," were the primary terror for prisoners, and perhaps to some they were, but the classic bare lightbulb would be what destroyed Eve.

Who she was now was not something she wanted to look at.

Eve asked herself what Nick would do in her situation. He'd look for the one mistake, the moment of divergence from the true path. He believed in absolutes: right, wrong, ultimate beauty, commitment to a goal. For so many years he'd managed to convince himself that she was the girl he mentored, raw talent and pure heart. He had so liked to think of her as entirely vulnerable, needing his protection. She had liked him to think of her that way, too, but she didn't want that anymore. She didn't want to be Nick's moment in the sun. She didn't want to be the star for Alissa's production. She wanted to be the director of her own story.

Eve had never *willed* a vision before, they had always come unbidden, but she did now. She stared so long and hard at the shiny white surface of those cinder blocks that her eyes became the lens of a movie projector and what she projected was the Eve that had been worth something.

Even then, in 1976, she lived for pleasure, but it was oh so easy to come by, and the forms it took were so rich and varied. Her mistakes, like setting her sights on making the Olympic team, rather than medaling in the Games, and therefore peaking at the trials and doing poorly at the Games, had meant nothing to Eve, because she thought she had years to correct them. In fact, it didn't even occur to her that peaking too soon had *been* a mistake until four years later, when Jimmy Carter canceled American participation in the Moscow Olympics. But that's a whole other home movie.

In this one, Eve did startlingly well at the nationals in Westwood, California, that June of 1976, which won her a lot of friends. She was the new girl wonder, only nineteen years old. The entire track-and-field community adopted her. Which made all the difference. She needed that support, but more, she fell in love with their generosity. It hurtled her into the Olympic trials a couple of weeks later, and she did it, she ran her best 1,500 meters ever and qualified.

By the time the American Olympic Team's plane landed in the Montreal airport, she had been nicknamed The Puppy, and she was in love with not only the track-and-field community as a whole, but with about 75 percent of the individual Olympic Team members. Eve could still recall the cologne of the javelin thrower with the crooked nose and slitty eyes, and the single, off-center dimple of the lanky pentathlete whose reserve struck her as elegance, and the swimmer with the broad, broad shoulders and no discernible personality at all, and the sprinter with the hard calves, and the long jumper who murmured some kind of performance mantra not only while competing but even on the airplane and at meals. The basketball players scared her a bit, but she obsessed about the point guard through two whole days and nights. That was before the reserved pentathlete finally spoke to her and Eve refocused her ardor. She was Cinderella, but rather than a trick of fate or magic delivering her to the ball, she had gotten there as a result of hard work. Eve supposed she could think of Nick as a kind of fairy godfather, dropping into her life at the right moment, but his guidance couldn't replace the thousands of hours (she'd estimated somewhere in the 5,000 range) she'd put in to achieve what she had achieved. And to receive attention which you feel you deserve is one of the most rewarding feelings in human existence.

Eve rarely talked about hard work at her lectures and workshops, and would never dream of quoting that number of hours, because that was when people's eyes glazed over. That was the part no one wanted to hear. But Eve hadn't exactly calculated the omission. She didn't talk about the hard-work part because it was the part she no longer wanted to look at, either. But that, too, was another home movie, the post-Moscow era, and now she was on her way to Montreal.

At the airport, the American team was met by a fleet of white vans that roared off like a presidential motorcade to take them to the Olympic Village. The Canadians shut down the freeways for them while Mounties on motorcycles rode out in front of their fleet of white vans, closing off-ramps as they approached, creating a vacuum of pure air for the athletes to travel through. Eve laughed and laughed and laughed.

Peaking too soon. That had always been her problem. That first night, wandering through the Olympic Village, greeting the elite of the elite, everyone loose with respect. It wasn't the kind of respect you have for your boss's opinion. Or for your neighbor's privacy. This was a knowledge that each and every person walking around that evening had spent years to become the most precisely excellent human body they could become for their sport. It was fantastic. It was like seeing a new continent. Like suddenly discovering you could fly. For Eve, it was enough. Walking that evening through the Olympic Village was simply enough.

Later that night, just a few moments before midnight, walking back to her room, escorted by both the javelin thrower and the pentathlete, a Finnish runner with white-white hair and long, lithe muscles stopped in front her. She put a hand on the side of Eve's face and said in perfect English, "So beautiful. May you have much luck."

Eve longed all her life to live in the feeling she had at that moment. To be anointed by another. To be the recipient of innocent goodwill. To believe that approaching physical perfection was the same as approaching spiritual perfection.

Because the City of Montreal had not finished its preparations for the Olympic Games, great cranes dominated the skyline during Opening Ceremonies. A lot of the athletes complained about the ugly setting, but as far as Eve was concerned, the cranes might have been the lovely birds rather than massive machinery. She stood in the sun for hours that day, awash in her love for the athletes and the sky, and listened to the endless speeches, seesawing back and forth between the familiar English and melodic French. She was far too happy to realize that she had become satisfied too soon. So that when she tried to use visualization, as the sports psychologist that Nick hired for her had instructed, her imagination took over. Still, she tried. As the hot sun baked her head and shoulders, she placed herself on the podium, higher than the imaginary women at her right and left, lowering her head to facilitate the medal being slung around her neck. But when she pulled her head back up again, it worked a bit like the control wheel of a small airplane, and her body began lifting into the air. She kept tilting her head back so that she could rise still higher, until she was a good fifty yards over the track, and then she spread her arms and sailed. Below her on the field, someone put the shot, coaches paced, one lone sprinter warmed up on the track. The last she remembered, she had soared off the coast of Nova Scotia and over the Atlantic Ocean.

Six days after Opening Ceremonies, Eve stood in her lane on the track toeing the start line for her heat. The sky was gray, but infused with a pearly light, and the track was red. Each blade of grass in the field, each molecule of that sky, meant something specific to her. She would use those molecules to run the fastest 1,500 meters she had ever run. She felt good, rested. She knew she was going to run fast. And she did. Her pace was perfect. At the finish line she had absolutely nothing left. She came in sixth and did not qualify for the next heat, let alone the finals.

Still, she was thrilled. She was there. She had run her best race. She was only nineteen years old. She had at least two more Olympics ahead of her. That moment wrote a whole book.

Eve thought she knew exactly who she was then. She was an athlete. Excellence meant something very specific to her. Something attainable. DIG—discipline, integrity, guts—it was easy. She didn't even think to look for herself back then because she thought she had herself in crisp focus. No discussion, no confusion, all the answers. Nick had found and plucked her at exactly the right moment. The first sixteen years of her life were left cleanly behind, like the roots of a picked flower.

Nick's flower, though.

Now, sitting in the holding vestibule at the Multnomah County Jailhouse, Eve didn't even have Nick anymore. How did that happen? It had been a slow slide—from hub of her life, her mentor, to her husband, to husband-in-name-only, to ex-husband-but-still-best-friend, to husband-once-removed-now-that-he's-engaged. Not that Eve couldn't handle the changes. Nick deserved a nice practical woman like Judith.

But Alissa. That was more complicated. He'd hired her to replace himself in Eve's life. Then he took her, too. At what point does a slow retreat become a betrayal?

Eve's toes and fingertips started tingling unpleasantly, and spaces opened up in her head, not breathing spaces, but blank spaces like the walls of this holding vestibule, hard cold vacuums. She lay down so she wouldn't pass out.

She wondered if Judith knew anything about Nick's newest diversion, the woman she made him hire because she was jealous of Eve. Then she wondered what Judith would do in her current predicament. Eve wasn't even close to the possibility of laughter, not even the nervous sputter she'd been capable of a few minutes ago with the officer, but if she had been, she would have laughed at the picture of Judith in jail. It would never happen.

But if it did happen, Judith would call her lawyer.

Eve didn't have a lawyer.

She could call Nick. But she was afraid he really wouldn't come, not this time.

How about Alissa? After the two pairs of earrings, she'd given Eve an ultimatum. But the ultimatum had been about their linked career. Alissa wouldn't rescue Eve Glass the product, but might she rescue Eve Glass the person?

But—and maybe this was the crux—she didn't *want* Nick or Alissa.

Eve wanted someone who would see her, the real her. Finally. But that person was too far away. Would she even consider coming? And if by chance she did make that long journey, requiring a ride to the airport, a flight across the country, a taxi to the county jail, would she find enough irony in the situation to make it worth her while?

For the lady who hawks grace like a fishmonger sells cod has now stolen a purse. A *purse.* Like a common thief. Jewelry, scarves, trinkets, well, that was childlike, getting her head turned by bright, pretty things. She could excuse the thieving in that, if not the lack of self-control. But a purse. Not only had she taken it, she had watched and schemed for the opportunity. Worse: she knew that if she had the moment back, even if she knew about this cell, she would do it again. She had no choice. That purse represented her last hope, a kind of possibility.

Someone was opening the door to the holding vestibule. Eve remained horizontal with her eyes squeezed shut until she heard a woman's voice say, "Eve Glass."

She sat up and faced the starched voluminous bosom of a deputy uniform.

"Gotta get you outta these clothes," she said. "Sorry, but you can't be wearing suggestive clothing in the jail. If you were wearing some trousers, and something covering you up top, I could let you keep your clothes."

She didn't speak unkindly, though when Eve looked up into her eyes, they were expressionless. Eve reached for something, and all her hand could find was the officer's wrist.

The officer shook her off, hard.

"Please," Eve said.

"You don't want to be in here in no miniskirt," she said. "Come on."

"Please," Eve repeated, but she didn't even know for what she begged. Whatever it was, it was a lot bigger than being allowed to keep her own clothes.

The officer motioned with her head toward the door, and Eve walked out of it. The hallway was empty, and she kept walking, waiting for the command to turn left, or to open a certain door, or to stop. Before, when she had been here, she'd found a way to deal with the situation. There had been Nick or her own finesse. Not that, once she was here at the jail, she could talk her way *out* of anything, but she had managed to talk her way *through* it all. It was like surfing, riding the wave, staying on her feet, staying on the surface of the water, actually, secretly, enjoying handling each lurch and surprise, keeping her balance, making the exact right, sometimes minute, moves. Today was different. The waves were already washing over her. Eve felt as if she were about to get pinned to the ocean floor.

Another deputy was coming down the hall toward them with a prisoner in tow.

"I thought it was clear," Eve's deputy said to the other prisoner's deputy.

"You check?"

"No, I didn't check, but I called down."

"We just finished. You can go on."

"Oh, mama, I want some of *that*," the prisoner said to Eve.

"Don't talk," said his deputy.

"See what I'm talking about?" Eve's deputy said. "You don't want to be in here in those clothes. We're trying to spare you." She stepped in front of Eve and opened the door to a room, then gently prodded her into the room. "Strip completely," she said, unlocking the handcuffs.

"Can't I just—?"

"Strip completely." The deputy kept her eyes dead, but Eve found a corner of kindness in her voice, a part of her that really did want to spare her. Yet Eve didn't think she could go through with this. She turned to the side and vomited. The deputy acted as if she hadn't. She asked, "What size you wear?"

"Ten," Eve whispered.

"You got to take everything off. Once you get assigned

redressing, it's the whole shebang." She dropped some pink briefs along with baggy blue cotton pants and a blue cotton top on the floor beside Eve. She remained standing while Eve finished undressing.

If black holes are the birthplaces of stars, then maybe white holes are the graveyards of stars. This place stripped Eve of her light. She stood naked, like a larva, grayish pink, quickly drying up in the harsh environment. Would the officer shine artificial light into her cavities? Eve dry-heaved, bent at the waist, became woozy-headed, and began to sink to the floor.

"Cut the theatrics. Put on the clothes."

"I've been sick."

"Put on the clothes."

Eve put on the pink and blue jail clothes as the deputy dropped a pair of plastic sandals at Eve's feet. She slipped into them and, after the deputy recuffed her hands, shuffled after her to complete the booking process. The starched bosom disappeared during her medical exam, fingerprinting, and picture-taking. Eve convinced the nurse that she wasn't suicidal and arranged her face to look as unlike herself as she could for the photo, which was laminated into a wide plastic bracelet that they fastened around her wrist. Then came the moment when she was supposed to be given a court day and be released. She had been before. But the plastic bracelet, these pale blue clothes and plastic sandals suggested a longer stay.

Never, Eve's thieving logician noted, shoplift in revealing clothing again. She wasn't surprised when the starched bosom returned and led her to another cell.

"What about my court date?"

The deputy ignored her.

"Why am I being jailed?"

"Two priors. And this time it's theft, not shoplifting."

The deputy fumbled with her keys at the door to the cell, quietly cursing her own clumsiness. Eve kept her eyes trained on the cell door, afraid of the confinement and wanting the enclosure, both. Men's voices drifted from around the corner, an escalating argument. *Motherfucker. Cracker-ass dirtball. Pussy-fag.* A smack. Probably fist on skin, and then a crack. Skull on cement? Eve could close her eyes, but she couldn't close her ears. The loud growling of an officer interfering. Eve's own officer still fumbled with the key, now wondering out loud why it wasn't working. Another inmate with her own private deputy stumbled by. Eve looked at her and saw a woman approaching middle age with a black eye and a cut on her chin. She wore a T-shirt and sweatpants. Around her neck hung a gold chain with an open heart looped through it.

As they passed, the inmate stopped briefly and swung her cuffed hands toward Eve, extending a finger to touch her hip, the only place she could reach. "You look so scared," she said. "Just remember, you can't push the river."

The woman's deputy urged her on and Eve's finally opened the cell door. She stepped into the center of it and stood there in her blue suit, hands forcibly clasped behind her back, and thought of one more person whom she could call. If she had her number.

At first Eve had been frightened of Joan. She knew Nick was. She'd even asked Audrey to quit writing her at home, to send the letters to her P.O. box, because of the time Joan had left a note in her mailbox. But then she got used to Joan showing up. Joan became a boundary that Eve needed. A line she wouldn't cross, but one she needed to see. Sometimes Eve pretended that Joan was a secret service agent, hired to haunt the perimeters of her life, keeping watch, protecting her. Eve knew this was a fiction, of course. She made sure she never acknowledged Joan, never smiled at her. But lately, when she saw her—like this morning, as Eve left for the mall, Joan was sitting in a car near her house—Eve felt something she could only describe as a sense of comfort. She was sure that Joan would come if she called her.

The deputy unlocked her handcuffs and Eve fell onto the single green plastic mattress which rested on another cement shelf, as if onto a rubber raft. *You can't push the river,* her fellow inmate had told her. She closed her eyes and felt the surge of the rapids below her, the rough touch of fast water against her back as she raced along on top of it, her destination entirely unknown. Perhaps she would never even get there, perhaps she would capsize and drown, but in the meantime, there was this feeling of speed, and trees spinning by, and water splashing her face. The sun, too, infused her world with bright yellow light. Let it spin, spin, *spin*.

"Any calls you want to make are collect."

Eve opened her eyes and looked at the wall-mounted phone. "How long am I going to be in here?"

"Maximum in a holding cell is seventy-two hours."

"I mean *me*. How long am *I* going to be in here?"

"Consider yourself lucky you got an individual cell. You don't want to be in the tank."

Maybe she did. Maybe she wanted someone to talk to. Maybe the woman with the gold heart looped through her chain would be in the tank. She could ask her what she should do. Eve liked people who gave advice.

The door shut and the deputy locked it. The stench of urine and clothes worn far too long was not erased by the smell of strong disinfectant. The smells hovered in layers, one above the other, a high-rise of stink. Besides her green plastic mattress and the telephone, she had a stainless steel toilet and matching sink. The floor was cement and the walls were, once again, white cinder blocks.

Eve needed to use the toilet, but anyone could look in her door window. She stripped off the loose-fitting top and held it up over the window, but there was nothing she could use to make it stay there. She quickly put it back on and looked at the toilet.

This was very frightening.

Maybe Nick was right. Maybe there was a way to see where one has taken the wrong path. If she could only find that intersection, maybe she could walk back there and take the correct path. Oh, but Nick *wasn't* right. They've already proved that a mere butterfly flapping its wings can change the course of world history. Each blink of an eye triggers who knew how many paths, probably an infinite number. There was no going back, ever.

But they've also proved that energy never goes away. It just changes form. If that was true, then Eve's joy still existed, somewhere, just in another form. Maybe an orca was dancing her joy in Antarctica? Maybe a stone in Central Park was bursting with it. But how did that joy leave *her*? What path did it take to get to that orca or that stone?

When you've lost something, try to think of the last place

you saw it. Glimpses don't count, at least not in the case of joy, only full embodiment. That would be Galisteo, New Mexico, in June. That night Audrey let herself be vulnerable. She shed her nationally honored poet veneer, that great pride she wears to shield herself from the harsh light of critics, and to protect her delicate, newborn poems from abuse. She let Eve see the lonely woman who lives by herself on the coast of Maine. Her bones were heavy with fatigue in Eve's arms, and her skin felt well used, as if she absorbed the world through her pores. When they made love, she repeated the words *oh my,* and at least for that one night she didn't question wanting Eve.

Audrey rose very early in the morning, perhaps needing her habits to know that she was still there. Maybe in all those celibate years of hers she had forgotten that everyone loses herself in extraordinary lovemaking. That can be frightening. Eve knew Audrey was frightened when, in the morning, she awoke alone. It was still very early, maybe half past six. Eve found her sitting outside with her notebook and pen in the fragile first sunlight, her chair sunk into the dew-wet grass, writing. She didn't see Eve, or at least didn't look up, so Eve padded like a cat quietly back to the room. She changed into running clothes and left by the front door of the inn, and then ran, ran as she had run years ago, ran so long Audrey would miss her and wonder where she'd gone. She took a road that bends past the small adobe church, past an old cemetery, and climbs to a rise where one can look out over the entire Sangre de Cristo Mountains. They were purple like in the song.

Audrey had told her the night before that she'd had a lover for over twenty years who had died. She told Eve that she carried the woman's soul in her left shoulder, that's where she felt her, like a perched bird, only *inside* the shoulder, between the heart and the catch in her throat. She said her grief had not prevented her from loving again, quite the contrary, had taught her that love was not a pursuit but instead an ether, a medium in which to live.

Pretty words, but Eve didn't buy them. She asked her why, if love was an all-encompassing ether, she hadn't had lovers since.

Audrey said she *had* had lovers since, just not for a while, and that the question was entirely beside any point worth talking about.

Poets, Eve thought, spend their lives thinking about truth, but maybe that was because they were so prone to lying.

Early that morning in Galisteo, Eve ran, and that running was joy. Even though she ran too fast for too long, so that her muscles were drowning in lactic acid. As if she didn't know better, she somehow exulted in the excess, even when she had to stop, bend at the waist, heave and pay for the oxygen debt. When she finally made it back to the inn, Audrey was less scared than she had been in the earliest morning hours. Eve found her in the room, where she had had a fresh pot of coffee delivered.

"Someone told me they saw you leave for a run," she said, smiling.

Eve was disappointed that her plan to make her worry had been so easily foiled.

Audrey also said, "I missed you."

Then Eve flew home to Portland, Oregon, and Audrey flew to Portland, Maine, where a neighbor picked her up and drove her home to her bloodhounds in the cottage on the coast. After that weekend, Audrey was as eager a correspondent as Eve was, but there was often tension.

Eve only wanted her to enjoy herself a bit more, so she'd once written, "Eat a piece of chocolate for me today, sweetheart."

Audrey, bless her acerbic soul, wrote back, "For god's sake, Eve, you can do better than *chocolate.* That's such a cliché. You could title one of your books that: *Eat Some Chocolate for Me Today,* by Eve Glass."

It didn't feel mean to Eve. She'd spent the better part of two decades drowning in sappiness. Audrey's bite was delicious. Eve wrote back, "I like that. Would you write a cover blurb? Then I could get the intellectual set reading my book, too. All twenty of them."

"Oh, that hurts," Audrey wrote back. She'd meant to be sarcastic, but Eve suspected that it actually had hurt, and she was sorry she'd said it.

"Audrey," Eve wrote next. "I know it's hard for you to care so much for a trashy motivational writer. But I want you to know something: I'm not stupid. I scored very highly on intelligence tests as a girl. I wrote stunning papers, according to my teachers."

"I'm sorry," she answered. "I know you're not stupid. Oh, Eve, you're brilliant. Truly. I felt it when I touched you. As for your being a motivational writer, well, I'll be honest. I do wish you asked more of yourself."

That had angered Eve. She wrote, "I love having an audience. I love having a *big* audience."

Audrey didn't answer that letter at all and Eve regretted the whole absurd exchange. She picked some roadside lilacs and pressed them into a card. On the inside she wrote simply, "I love you."

She didn't hear back for three and a half weeks. And when Audrey did write, her letter was newsy and light, never mentioning Eve's card. Even so, the handwriting felt like love-making to Eve, with her lined yellow legal pad paper as the bed and the trail of ink her fingertips.

Eve looked at the green plastic mattress. She didn't want to sit on it. Who knew what had occurred there. So she paced like a real prisoner. Maybe she should do calisthenics or recite Bible verses to keep her mind active. Would they give her a Bible if she asked for one? She could read about the fall of the original Eve and see if there were any hints she should have taken from that lady who, thousands of years ago, also followed her pleasure. But an *apple.* You'd think a woman could bite into an apple. Why, exactly, was a life of joy such a fucking mortal sin?

Eve wanted to howl. She wanted to shake bars. She wanted to start scraping at the cement with a stainless steel spoon. She had been in the cell somewhere in the neighborhood of thirty seconds to four hours, who knew, they also took her watch, but it wasn't a long time. It wasn't a day or even an evening. Yet she was losing something vital. She needed to get out of there. What exactly had she done wrong?

"I would have given the purse back," she whispered, just to hear how it sounded. What would happen if she shouted that? Nothing. No one would even hear her. There were no bars here, just a tiny multiple-paned window through which the guards could watch her urinate, if they so chose. She said, "I had only wanted to read the woman's letters."

Eve looked at the shiny white wall of cinder blocks.

"I'm talking out loud," she said. "Already talking out loud."

Where do they get off locking up people? This wasn't right. It was dead wrong. Audrey had it all wrong, too. She wasn't Molly Malone who died of a fever. She was *Eve.* She would pick every apple on that tree, stack them into a perfect pyramid, and then chomp into them, starting with the one at the very apex. She'd eat apples until she had a stomachache.

Four minutes or five hours in that place, however long or short, she was thinking like a crazy person already. Those women at Powell's had been the worm. They had been the divergence Nick would have looked for. If he had been looking. But that was just it. He had stopped looking out for her. Even with Joan hovering.

Maybe being locked up wasn't the worst possible thing. Instead of Nick or Alissa, now Eve had her deputy. She pressed her face to the small window in the door of her cell. She could see practically nothing, but at least there was no other face looking in. She quickly pulled down the cotton pants, as well as the pink briefs, hung her behind over the stainless steel toilet, then went ahead and sat on the ice-cold seat. She was far too tired to hold herself above it. Peeing was a relief. There was even toilet paper. She guessed there wasn't much damage an inmate could do with toilet paper.

Emptying her bladder made Eve feel a little less crazy, a little more capable of constructive thought. She eyed the wall-mounted phone.

Suddenly, it was easy. She dialed zero and her number, and then waited for Audrey's voice. What did Maine look like in September?

After a lot of rings—Audrey would never have an answering service, nor a computer, and not even a television—she answered! Was she wearing her black glasses? Was there a book in her hand or garden soil ground into the knees of her jeans? Perhaps she had an armful of blueberry branches, laden with fruit, just in from the cold autumn air. Was it dusk? Eve strained her ears, the moment after she said she would accept the charges, and thought she could hear the clicking nails of her three hounds who had surely gathered around her legs to find out who had called.

"I'm sorry to call collect," she said, knowing Audrey wouldn't think to wonder why she wasn't using her cell. "I got a wild hair and drove up the Oregon coast. I'm at a pay phone right on the beach and just had to call you. Listen, you can hear the surf from the phone booth. Wait. I'll hold out the receiver."

Then she did. She held the phone out toward the door of her cell for a moment. Then, "Did you hear that? Could you hear the waves?"

"It's nice to hear your voice," Audrey said. She sounded sad. "Are you staying overnight on the coast?"

"I might. I haven't decided. I just had to get away."

Audrey was silent, waiting.

"Is it all right that I called?"

"It's lovely that you called. It's just that Whit, my youngest hound, was hit by a car today." Her voice cracked and she said, "Aaah."

"Oh. Oh, Audrey, I'm so sorry."

"I needn't be so tearful really. He's okay. Just bashed up a bit. Not even any broken parts, the vet doesn't think. It really will be okay. It just . . . it just scared me."

"Yes. Is he home with you?"

"The vet wanted to keep him overnight. Just to be sure. The other two miss him so. They keep sniffing around the house looking for him. Tell me what you see from your phone booth, Eve. How can a phone booth be on the beach?"

"This one just is. In one direction I see miles and miles of waves. It's a calm day, so the waves are small, just tight little lines of rolling white. In the other direction, maybe a mile off, there's a big headland. I can't see much detail, but it's brown and rocky."

Again Audrey was silent.

"I'm glad Whit is going to be okay," Eve said. "I'm having rather a hard time myself."

"What's wrong?"

"Some women laughed at me at my event last night. They thought I was a complete joke. They reminded me of you, actually."

More silence.

"Are you there?"

"Of course I am. I have never laughed at you."

Ha. She could have quoted Audrey her own poem, listened to her stammer out an explanation, defend her Art, maybe even try to tell her that she wasn't the subject of that poem. Lie. Take away the only part Eve had liked: that she had moved Audrey enough to become a poem.

But that wasn't a conversation Eve was ready to have, so she only said, "I'm not sure about that. But it's given me a good idea. Listen to this: I'm thinking of going in a completely different direction. For my next book. Remember DIG? This time it'll be LAF, for *longing, affect,* and *fear.* What do you think?"

Eve sat down on the edge of the green plastic mattress, breathing in the stink-saturated air, and listened to the lovely silence of Audrey.

"I don't know whether you're joking," she finally said.

"I'm a fraud, Audrey. You know that."

"No, you're not."

"I depend on you to not lie to me. You know, after I first met you at that conference, I wanted so badly to call you and ask you what you thought grace was. What do you think it is? Tell me now."

A big guffaw. "But you wrote the book."

"I don't define grace in the book. I only say how to get there."

"Then you know how to get there?"

"No."

To package and sell grace. That was like pimping one's own child. Or stealing from Buddha. The ultimate greed. Eve had told herself that she was sharing the wealth. As if she held out hands dripping with jewels and gold nuggets. "Let me show you where I found this loot." Maybe, though, light itself was the one thing that couldn't be illuminated by light. Eve's hands were completely empty now. And those women who'd laughed at her had known that. They'd seen her empty hands.

"I want to see you," she told Audrey. "Soon."

She waited for Audrey to say something. Something honest. She who chided Eve for hawking grace claimed to deliver truth in her poems. Let's have some now. Eve hated her hesitation. She would give her a count of five. *Five . . . four . . . three . . . two . . . one.* Eve hung up.

She grabbed a length of toilet paper for her tears and lay

on her back on the green plastic mattress. She didn't know if her full seventy-two hours had passed, or only a couple, when she was awakened by the sound of the key turning in her cell door. Her own deputy stood in the doorway and said, "Okay, you're cleared. We'll get you your court date and clothes, and you can go. There's someone here for you."

There is? "Who?"

"Don't know. Just said she's here to pick you up. You call someone?"

For a moment, Eve thought she had come, had seen through the Oregon coast lie and known exactly where she was, had gotten the neighbor to take her to the airport, flown across the country, taken a taxi to the county jailhouse. Had heard her when she said, *I want to see you. Soon.* For a moment, she had the two of them in a rental car, racing down the highway, truly going to the Oregon coast, where they would buy a dinner of fresh salmon at a table with a view of the surf and laugh at her silly poem. Where she would see Eve and Eve would see her.

Eve took the piece of paper telling her when to appear in court. She stripped off the jail suit, no longer self-conscious in front of the deputy, and put back on her purple miniskirt and white tank top. At the last moment, the deputy gave her back her shoulder bag, though not the purse of the woman in the chocolate brown pants who wanted the cream blouse, and also her jewelry and watch. It was almost six o'clock. She had been in jail less than four hours.

Having recovered from the fantasy of Audrey, the only other possible "she" was Alissa. Eve stepped into the visitor's waiting area and looked around for her.

Instead she found Joan.

Eve thought of her fellow inmate's advice. If she were to stop trying to push the river, she would have to ride out the rapids of Joan.

She put out her hand and said cheerily, "Joan, thank you for coming."

Joan stepped back. "You know my name."

"Oh course I know your name. You're the *New York Times* reporter who wants to interview me."

"Right," Joan said.

Eve cocked her head, made herself look pleasantly puzzled.

"You really don't remember me, do you?"

"What can I do for you?" Eve knew she looked ridiculous standing there in the county jail's waiting room, pretending she wasn't disheveled, acting as if Joan were just a reporter.

"The *Times* hired me to do a story on you."

"Yes, I know. Surely you have plenty of material."

"I still need an interview."

Eve looked for help. Maybe her deputy. Or her fellow inmate with the gold heart around her neck. But there were only the families of other inmates waiting for the release of their loved ones. If life was a river, and this stretch of it a rapids, then Joan was the only raft offered at the moment. "Okay. How about now?"

"I can give you a ride home."

"How'd you know I was here?"

Joan hesitated. "Actually, I came by your house this morning to get the interview. I was tired of trying to get past the roadblocks of Capelli and your manager, so I thought I'd just show up. You were just leaving, and I followed you to the mall."

"Lovely. My own paparazzi."

Joan shrugged. "You're right. My conduct has been a little over the top. To be quite honest, I'm sick of the whole thing. But I've put in a lot of time on the story, and I can't write it without an interview."

"So at the mall, you saw . . . everything?"

"No. I never went into the mall. I waited for you in the parking lot. I saw the detective arrest you."

"This ought to please your editor."

Joan shrugged again. "I figured Capelli or Alissa Smith would rescue you. But when I checked, I found out they hadn't."

Eve could say no. She could walk out onto the street. She could call a taxi to take her home. Once there, she could call Audrey again. She would apologize for hanging up on her. She would not ask to see her again. She would wait for her next letter. She would go to the Wild Spirit conference next week in Los Angeles, where she was scheduled to deliver the keynote. She would resume being a national expert on attaining grace. She would make her court date in a couple of weeks and accept whatever sentence the judge gave her. It would be easy.

But that fever came back. The hot dry flush. For a moment she thought she might die of it. *She died of a fever, and no one could save her, and that was the end of sweet Molly Malone.* The bare lightbulb and the stalker. It would be so much better if someone finished off the job.

Eve wanted to tell Joan: Do me a favor. Destroy me. Set me free.

Joan held the door open for her, and together they stepped out onto a street of downtown Portland. Sunlight and air. Eve wanted a shower, a long, hot shower with lots of lemony soap, and a good hard sleep between clean, high-quality sheets. But she didn't think she could bear, just yet, being alone.

As Joan's eyes scanned her dirty tank top and short skirt, Eve wished it were dark outside. She saw her own desperation register on Joan's face.

"Um," Joan said, hesitating, looking quickly in both directions as if she wanted to bolt, as if the fact of Eve was a little more than she'd bargained for.

"Where's your car?" Eve asked.

"Right around the corner."

"Lovely!" Too eagerly.

"All right," Joan said, looking her over again, and then shrugging, as if to say, what the hell. She touched Eve's elbow. "Let's go."

"The last time you touched me was on the track twenty-five years ago. You tapped my back as you passed me."

Joan looked like she had been poked with a cattle prod.

"I'm not a moron. Of course I remember you." Eve laughed at the sight of her stalker looking almost frightened. "Maybe you'd prefer if I *didn't* remember you?"

"Look, Marianne. I don't know what games you're playing with yourself, but all I want is an interview." Joan checked her watch. "Let's go. I'll do the interview on the way."

It felt strange to walk at Joan's side, after all this time of avoiding her. She wore a black leather jacket with silver zippers that looked like thin menacing smiles, a white boy's T-shirt, and Levi's. Her face was like an apple with its soft, rounded features. That freckle still floated above the right side of her mouth, as if to remind anyone who gazed at her that she once had been a girl, despite everything else that had changed. Eve easily saw her as she had seen her years ago, with her head full of self-cut curls and her lightning eyes. She had been a big thundercloud passing through Eve's life, luminescently beautiful, threatening, potentially consuming. But she had passed, and passed quickly.

Where had she gone? Eve remembered perfectly that tap just above her right kidney. It was as if Joan were saying, "You're it." Instead of rising to the challenge, Eve had handed herself over to Nick. And Nick had taken care of everything, including Joan. Eve had never asked him where Joan had gone.

But now she was back. After opening the passenger door of an old, beat-up Toyota, Joan put on a pair of wire-framed sunglasses with green lenses. She waited until Eve had buckled her seat belt before pulling into the traffic and heading down Third Street too fast, the park blocks a blur of green. Shortly before they reached the YMCA track, where Eve had run thousands of miles, she turned onto the freeway. Eve closed her eyes. My stalker, she said to herself. I'm being abducted by my stalker. What if they just stayed on the freeway? The ocean was only ninety miles away. If she went there now, she wouldn't have been lying to Audrey, not really.

Joan looked angry, and she drove too fast.

Well, Eve wanted to say, I didn't ask you to come get me. Instead, she said, "Aren't we going to talk?"

"I need to take notes. We can do it at your house. I don't need to come in. Outside, in the car will be fine." The car slowed as they approached the freeway exit for Eve's house. Eve smiled at the idea of Joan knowing exactly where she lived.

"Don't turn off here," she said.

"What do you mean?" Joan asked, but swerved back onto the freeway. "Is there a better exit?"

"I want to go to the beach."

"What are you talking about?"

"Take me to the beach, please."

"I'm not your chauffeur."

"You're my abductor. You might as well do it properly."

"Abductor," Joan snorted. "In your dreams." But she didn't take the next exit, nor the next. She turned on the radio and then snapped it off. Whatever was *she* so angry about? Eve adjusted her seat to make it more comfortable, and then relaxed into the silence of the ride. When Joan turned onto the highway to the coast, Eve closed her eyes again. Was there such a thing as consensual kidnapping?

"So you remember," Joan said eventually, "the time I beat you in the 1,500." She laughed. "I've entertained a lot of friends telling them I outran Eve Glass once."

"Nick should have given you a chance. That was wrong."

Joan looked at Eve for a long time. "You know it wasn't about running."

"What do you mean?"

Joan huffed and shook her head.

Eve said, "My whole life from that moment on has been about running."

"Everything? Your *whole* life? About running?" Joan glanced back and forth, between the road and Eve's face, as if she were waiting for a real answer.

When she didn't give one, Joan said, "What about Audrey Boucher? A running buddy? I don't think so."

"Off-limits."

"Ah!" Joan said, as if she'd struck pay dirt. "That poem she wrote about you was intense, wasn't it?"

"Look, Joan. I said I'm sorry about what happened twenty-five years ago. Maybe we should go back to Portland."

"You did? I missed it. Anyway, you forget. I'm *abducting* you."

"I said I'd give you an interview. But there have to be rules. I won't talk about Audrey."

"If the poem had been about me, I would have been hurt, too. But really, being objectified in the *New Yorker* isn't altogether a bad thing. Seriously, Marianne. I doubt more than, oh, let's say 3 percent of the people who read that poem even had an inkling it was about you. How many *New Yorker* readers would also have read *IGIG*?"

"Igig?"

"Your book. *If Grace Is the Goal.* I bet Audrey Boucher—kick-ass poet, by the way—counted on your never seeing the poem. Wait. *Did* you see it?"

"Take me back to Portland."

"Ah, then you *did* see it. I'm sorry. I know what betrayal feels like."

Eve tried for silence but she couldn't keep herself from asking, "How do you know about Audrey?"

"I was in Santa Fe, remember? Even though you pretended you had no idea who I was. I saw the two of you together. It was obvious. But the postcard was proof."

"What postcard?" Eve knew she was being reeled in, but couldn't unhook herself.

"Remember my first request for an interview? The postcard was in your mailbox when I left off the note."

"And you read it." As Eve had suspected.

Audrey's postcards were lovely poems, as if the open-air format made her feel less hemmed in, better able to express love. There had been only two postcards, and both had been more expressive than any of her letters.

"It was a *postcard.*"

"It's still illegal."

"I doubt it."

"You really have been stalking me."

"Don't flatter yourself."

Eve wanted to say "Take me back to Portland" again. But Joan might do it. Riding in this car with her felt like that tap twenty-five years ago. Eve felt the ghost of Joan's hand on the small of her back. "You're it." She wanted to tell Audrey about that moment. She wrapped her arms tightly around herself and felt sorrow gather in the base of her belly.

Joan chuckled. "Her poem made it pretty clear that she feels sort of, well, *humiliated* to have a thing for you. *No* one likes to think of herself as so shallow as to love someone purely for their physical beauty, but someone like Audrey Boucher, whose work after all as a poet is to name the highest forms of beauty, she must *really* feel like a schmuck being thrown off her feet by a babe." Joan grinned at Eve. "You *are* a babe, Marianne. You always were."

"Shut up," Eve said, and the sobs geysered up.

"Jesus. I'm sorry." Joan grabbed a handful of her own hair. "I *am* sorry. I have a fatal tendency to fall for babes myself, that's all." Joan glanced at Eve, who was still hugging herself and trying to control the tears. "Um, my life is sort of falling apart. I guess we have that in common. But you don't want to hear about my life. I'm supposed to be interviewing you.

We'll do that as soon as we get to the coast. You still want to go?"

Force me, Eve wanted to say, but she remained silent.

"Do you?" Joan pulled the car off the road and watched Eve for a moment. "This is scary," she said and made a U-turn, screeching back onto the highway headed for Portland.

Eve felt as if a giant vacuum had sucked out her entire self. Nick had handed her off to Alissa. Alissa would drop her permanently now that she'd been booked for theft. To Audrey, she was no more than an emotional embarrassment. Even Joan, even her stalker, didn't want her enough to carry out an easy kidnapping.

One desire persisted. To be where she had told Audrey she would be. To have told the truth, this once, at least retrospectively.

"Wait," she told Joan.

Joan accelerated a bit.

"I do still want to go to the coast."

Joan acted as if she hadn't heard.

"I need to go to the coast."

Joan took a deep breath, once again pulled the car off the road, and said, "So you want to kidnap *me*?"

"No," Eve said without a trace of irony. "How could I? You're in the driver's seat. I want you to kidnap me."

"You don't know the first thing about me. This could be very dangerous."

Eve managed to smile. "Actually, I do know the first thing. But only the first thing."

"What's that you think you know?"

"I don't have words. It was an authenticity about you."

"What do you know about authenticity?"

"You'd be surprised what lacking something teaches you about it."

"I'm sorry," Joan said again. "I don't know that I'm in any condition for a trip to the coast with anyone, let alone you."

"You don't know the first thing about *me*." Eve smiled as she stole Joan's line.

"You know, at first I thought you were letting me stalk you, for lack of a better phrase, because your ego was so big even a stalker was a welcome fan. But you know what I think now? I think the reason you've let me is because you're curious about who you were when you knew me, when you were sixteen years old."

"Lovely. Now you're a therapist."

"So am I right?"

"Maybe you've been stalking me because *you're* stuck on who *you* were when you were sixteen years old."

Joan stared out the driver-side window for a long time and then turned back to Eve. "That's possible. Yeah, it's possible I'm stuck on who I was when I was sixteen. Here's another possibility: there are some things going on in my life that have nothing at all to do with you."

"I hope so."

"You've been a diversion. An intriguing little story to follow."

"What do you want from me?"

"How many times do I have to tell you? An interview."

"So what do you want to know?"

"I want to know if there's a real person inside you."

"Me, too. I'd also like to know."

Joan made a sarcastic face and fiddled with the gear shift. Finally she said, "You seem kind of vulnerable. That scares me. I'm not very trustworthy today."

"I don't care."

"I could be a serial killer. You really *don't* know the first thing about me, even if you think you do."

"I don't care."

"My girlfriend is leaving me for her boss."

So that was the anger. "I'm sorry."

"I just found out last night."

Eve looked at Joan's face in the late-afternoon light. The anger sizzled right under her skin, twitched in her fingers. She swung abruptly around in the car seat to face Eve. "You know what I really want from you?"

Eve shook her head.

"I want you to tell me what grace is."

Eve laughed.

"It's not funny."

"It is to me."

"Why?"

"Think about it. I'm the expert on grace. Ever since the book came out people have been sniffing around me, thinking I have a chunk of grace in my pocket. Now *you're* outright asking me for it."

"What makes *my* asking so hilarious?"

"You're not a fan. You're my kidnapper."

"So maybe the ransom is grace."

"Ah. And if I don't give it to you, then you'll have to carry out the kidnapping plan. Until I do."

"That's right," Joan said, giving the engine far too much

gas. She made another U-turn, and they were headed west once again.

Soon they were entering the national forest of the coast range, barreling between the Wilson and Trask rivers. It was late dusk and the dark green trees reached up to the nearly black sky. Eve could see a few stars between the treetops. Alder seedlings lined the highway, sprouting in the road cut, the predecessors to evergreens. She knew their leaves had been golden, just a couple of hours ago, before sunset.

Out of the silence, Joan said, "I was totally broadsided. Didn't see it coming."

"The girlfriend and her boss?"

Joan nodded.

"That really sucks."

Joan coughed out a laugh.

"What?"

"Your using the word *sucks*."

Eve shrugged.

"That's why I'm agreeing to kidnap you to the beach. If I stayed in Portland, I think I'd kill them both."

Eve remembered now: she'd loved Joan's passion. The focus of it. The tornado of it.

Joan said, "I would have killed Capelli, too. Back then. If they hadn't sent me away."

"Killed Nick?"

"You feign innocence so well."

"Because he never acknowledged your beating me in that first race? Because you never got a chance to prove yourself running?"

"I don't think I can take this. Let's go back."

"No. You'll kill the boss. I wouldn't be able to return the favor of springing you from jail. Not for murder."

That got a small smile. Then, "Tell me the truth, Marianne. What do you remember?"

"My whole life I've been jumping on any life raft that drifted by."

"Evasive, but okay, let's stick with the water metaphor. Why did you and Capelli have to hold my head under?"

"I don't know what you're talking about."

"Come *on,* Marianne."

"I never knew where you went."

"No? What if I had killed myself?"

"You wouldn't have done that. You were way too tough."

"Ha."

"Where'd you go?"

"You know, I'm getting a little feeling that you're for real. That you really *don't* know what happened."

"I remember you wanted a lot from me I couldn't give."

"So you held my head under."

"Nick did."

"Did what?"

"Took care of the problem."

"You sound like the mafia. What if Nick decides Audrey Boucher is a problem he needs to 'take care of'?"

Eve decided Joan was joking and smiled. "He probably would if he could." She enjoyed the glance Joan threw her, baffled and maybe curious. "He thinks I'm vulnerable, that only he can protect me. I'm his creation."

"Made from Nick's rib. Why didn't he change his name to Adam when you changed yours to Eve?"

Eve laughed. "So what *did* happen to you?"

"Busted for being a dyke. Threatened with being burnt at the stake. Sent to another high school."

Eve was quiet.

"Silence," Joan said. "The killing silence."

Eve guiltily enjoyed Joan's anger, like the solidity of an actual wall in a house of mirrors. She leaned against it.

"We need gas." Joan pulled off the road in front of a small country store with a single gas pump. As the attendant disengaged the gas nozzle from the pump and jammed it into the car, Eve got out and walked to the edge of the highway. She took out her cell phone and then turned to face Joan, who was watching her.

There was no one to call. She punched in the number for the time lady, pretending to be calling someone who cared. A Pontiac slowed on the highway and a guy with a mane of blond curls, a red bandanna tied around his forehead, leaned out the passenger window.

"How's it going?"

She didn't answer, but neither did she move away from the highway.

"Need a ride somewhere, sweetheart?" The driver now leaned over his friend to look at her. Wraparound shades, big grin. Blondie hefted a six-pack from off the car floor and held it up for her to see. She had to laugh. Was a six of Bud enough to lure some girls into a car? She wondered, What if I opened the backseat door and got in?

"Got you some coffee," Joan called out, emerging from the store.

Eve stepped back from the highway. The Pontiac slunk

away. It was cold now that the sun had gone down, and she wished she had a sweater to cover her white tank top. She took the Styrofoam cup from Joan.

"You call Capelli?" She peeled the lid off her own cup and took a loud slurp. "Didn't it ever feel queer to you, the way he was your father and coach and lover all in one? Didn't you ever feel uncomfortable with that?"

"Shut up."

"Whoa. Another hot topic." She tossed her cup in the big green trash barrel, and the coffee sloshed out. "Shitty coffee."

Eve turned again toward the highway.

"Fine. Hitchhike wherever you want to go." Joan got in the car, slammed her door, and started the engine. Eve pulled open the passenger door and got in. A jangled collection of light—hazy red from the neon beer sign in the store window, sallow yellow from the halogen above the gas pump, and a stabbing white from oncoming headlights—invaded the cramped interior of the car.

"I wasn't hitchhiking. I'm not struggling. I'm coming along with you."

"I noticed that."

"You're so angry."

"That's why I've kidnapped you, remember? You're going to show me how to find serenity in a world full of cheaters."

Joan turned on the radio, and a scratchy Marvin Gaye troubled the airwaves. She sang along, "We're all sensitive people, with so much to give . . . Let's get it ooooon."

"I've never liked that song."

"It's so *explicit*, isn't it?" Joan turned the song up, pressed down on the accelerator, and slid onto the highway, entering the darkness of the forest once again. No stores, no houses, no oncoming headlights. Even the Toyota's headlights were turned off, so that they drove in darkness, like a mole tunneling underground, Marvin Gaye's voice writhing in the car.

Eve stared ahead at the broken white line, shining in the starlight, and sometimes out at the forest that seemed to have bits of sparkle even in its blackness. She took comfort in the speed, in the way they hurtled down the corridor of evergreens, on their way to the edge of the continent. She needed to feel the cool sand on her feet, see the waves glowing in the autumn night, hear the ocean's music obliterating all other sounds.

She wondered what Audrey would be doing right now. If it was 8 P.M. in Oregon, then it was 11 P.M. in Maine. Audrey wasn't much of a sleeper. She read late and rose early. Maybe she had walked down the path she had described to Eve, the one made of broken bits of pearly shells that brooded with light at night, the path that led to a small headland from which she could hear but not see the surf. On very still days, and these occurred only rarely, she could also hear a colony of seals on the rocks far below. Perhaps tonight she listened to the surf and thought of how the oceans were all one, how the same body of water that crashed onto the cliffs below her feet was sloshing toward Eve's feet as well, because of course she thought Eve was on the Oregon coast, standing on the beach, as she would be soon.

But when they finally had driven as far west as they could drive, Joan did not go to the beach. She turned right on Highway 101 and kept driving. After a few miles, the highway swung to the edge of the land and Eve saw the ocean in moonlight, the waves crashing in big autumn tumbles, but Joan didn't stop. She reached across Eve and dug her cell phone out of the glove compartment, used her thumb to enter a number.

"Don't call her." Eve took the phone away from Joan's ear.

"How do you know who I'm calling?"

"The look on your face."

Eve put the phone back in the glove compartment, and a moment later, it rang.

"Get it," Joan said.

Eve retrieved the phone and read out the number of the caller.

"It's her."

Eve handed her the phone.

"Yep," Joan said, and then listened for a long time. Eve could hear a woman's voice calmly explaining something, too calmly. After a while, Joan turned the phone off and handed it back to Eve.

"What'd she say?"

"It's almost funny," Joan said. "She said that telling me sooner would have been the decent thing to do."

"Decent. That's such a cold word."

"Yeah."

"What else did she say?"

"She didn't say she was sorry."

Joan's tone was flat and accusatory.

Eve said, "Aren't we going to the beach? It would be soothing, don't you think?"

"Ha. Soothing. Another good word."

Joan drove faster and faster, and she still hadn't turned on the headlights. What if they were pulled over by highway patrol? Afraid to disturb her, Eve watched Joan's face in the light of passing beach towns. Still as a statue, she gripped the steering wheel at ten o'clock and two o'clock. From a distance, she would appear utterly composed. But sitting next to her in the car, Eve could practically hear the ticking of the bomb.

She leaned back in her seat, giving in to the ride. It was getting late and she'd had a long day. She'd already shopped for several hours, heisted a purse, been arrested and done time, gotten kidnapped, and now journeyed to the shore. She hadn't eaten since breakfast. She realized she was exhausted.

When they reached the town of Rockaway, Joan slowed, checking out the salty, run-down buildings. Twice she pulled over, as if she had arrived somewhere, but then veered back onto the highway. Finally she turned into the parking lot of a brightly lit, dilapidated establishment. A huge sign made of white light bulbs, many of which had burned out, read "Penny Arcade."

"We can eat here," Joan said.

"It doesn't look like the food would be very good. That Surfside place back down the road looked nicer."

"Nice has never interested me much."

"I don't want to eat fried frozen food."

"You know, Marianne. I don't know how to break it to you, but this isn't a date. What you want isn't the foremost concern of mine."

"I'll pay at the Surfside."

"You can pay here at the penny arcade."

"Look, Joan. I'm not your girlfriend. Don't take out your breakup on me."

Joan was quiet for a long time before she said, "True. But there are some nice parallels, aren't there?"

She got out of the car and walked in the front door of the

penny arcade. Eve considered yet again the possibility of deserting her kidnapper. She could walk back to the Surfside. Then what? One look down at her dirty purple miniskirt and dirtier white, low-cut tank top reduced her options to zero. What had been fun and a tad risky at a Portland mall on a Saturday morning would play as small-town whore on a Saturday night on the coast. She probably even smelled like the jail cell by now.

Eve followed Joan into the penny arcade. The junior high school crowd, with their too-big pants and bad skin, were doing primal dances with the pinball machines and video games. Joan walked right through the kids and they parted for her as if she were the town librarian. But as Eve passed through them, she looked into their faces and smiled. They didn't move out of her way. The tallest boy laughed.

One girl, who wore so much makeup that her face shined and tight jeans with bells so big and long they were ragged from dragging on the street, asked the boy, "What are you laughing at?" and grabbed at his crotch. He slapped her hand away.

They were children, not more than fourteen years old, but Eve wished she could be with them. She longed for the anonymity of childhood, for living in a broken-down town on the Oregon coast, for spending dead-end nights at a penny arcade. Eve directed her smile at the made-up girl and felt that she knew her. The girl smiled back.

"Got any money?" one of the boys said to her back.

She found Joan in the far, unlit reaches of the arcade, the area used by the owner for storage. There were stacks of cardboard boxes, a couple of old couches, some car parts. Joan stood in a dark hallway that led to two bathrooms, men's and women's.

"I found her," Joan said.

"Found who?"

"Laughing Gertie."

Stashed in that dark hallway was a big glass case containing the upper body of a mechanical woman. She had breasts as big as Eve's deputy's and wore a red dress with huge white polka dots. Her hair was a brown plastic hat of hard curls. In front of the glass case was a dashboard with a slot for pennies.

"I need a good laugh," Joan said. "But she probably doesn't even work anymore." She dug in her pockets. "Shit. No pennies."

"I have some." Eve pulled her coin purse out of her bag and gave Joan a handful of pennies. Joan dropped one in the slot. Nothing happened. Maybe thirty seconds went by, and Eve thought Gertie's failure to laugh might be the last straw for Joan, who sank down on a pile of hubcaps.

But then Gertie's hinged mouth opened. A hysterical canned laughter filled the dark hallway. The mouth shut and reopened. The woman's arms rose and fell, her hands like weapons, like ready-made karate chops. Laughing Gertie was laughing, wildly. All the light bulbs ringing the inside of Gertie's glass cage were burned out. Only a bit of moonlight came in the window on the other side of the arcade, striking the floor and reflecting mildly off Gertie's hard plastic cheek. Joan plugged five more pennies into the slot. Gertie laughed and laughed and laughed.

Eve didn't like the mechanical lady. She was predatory, her mirthless braying like some kind of net. Eve backed up until something hard dug into the small of her back and a bell rang. She'd been stopped by a dead pinball machine. Just then, midlaugh, the arms stopped pumping and the hinged mouth snapped shut, and Gertie stopped laughing.

"I want to go," Eve said.

"Do you have more pennies?"

"No."

"Let's get something to eat at the snack bar."

"Can we go back to the Surfside to get something to eat?"

"They have food here."

"I can't eat here."

"Again, Marianne, this is not a date. You don't have a choice."

The burgers and fries smelled rancid at the penny arcade snack bar, but Joan wolfed hers down along with a chocolate milkshake. Eve made the mistake of ordering clam strips which she couldn't eat.

Back in the car, the fatigue and hunger and loneliness swirled a vortex in Eve, and she thought she was beginning to hallucinate. Gertie's mechanical laughter replayed, over and over, in her head. She kept seeing dark shapes beside the road and felt sure they were going to lunge in front of the car. Once she saw the shapes clearly, a little girl and a man in a black suit, black tie, white shirt, black plastic glasses, greasy black hair. The man stepped onto the highway, pulling the little girl with him. She had blond pigtails and she resisted, pulling back on his hand. The man was stronger, though, and Eve's whole body clenched in anticipation of the dull thump as Joan's car hit them. But it never came. The man and little girl weren't there at all.

"Turn on your headlights," she said.

"I'm driving without headlights? Whoa." Joan grinned at her.

"What's wrong with you? Turn them on."

"I like a little danger with my Saturday nights."

"If the police pull you over, I'll tell them you're kidnapping me."

Joan swerved onto a gravel turnout on the side of Highway 101. She reached across Eve and opened her door. "I'm tired of you. Get out. Go on. You're free. You and your stupid fantasy of being kidnapped."

Eve stepped out of the car and shut the door gently, realizing too late that she shouldn't have. The Toyota's tires spat gravel as Joan shot back onto the highway. Eve stood completely alone in the black night. Above her were an infinite number of stars. Beneath her feet jagged stones. Somewhere, not far to the west, was the ocean, but she couldn't see it. She couldn't even hear it.

Eve sat down on a log and pulled out her cell phone. Somehow she'd have to do the impossible: convince Nick one last time to come get her. She listened to the phone's musical opening and watched the screen. No service.

"Shit!" She snapped the phone shut, stood up, and tossed it as hard as she could in the direction of the ocean.

Not a single car passed as she waited on the side of Highway 101. She lay on her back on the log and looked up at the stars, draped a hand over the side to caress the grasses. She had nothing. Was nothing. Just a woman on a log in the darkness of a coastal night.

Her eyes were closed and maybe she was even dozing when she finally heard a car barreling north on the highway, toward her. She remained on the log, as invisible as possible, but still the car slowed and pulled off onto the gravel turnout. A car door opened and shut. Footsteps crunched on the rocks. Eve hoped he had a knife and would slit her throat immediately. That, or a badge and handcuffs, the power to arrest her and give her a bed for the night.

"Sit up. Make room."

Eve sat up and Joan sat next to her on the log.

"Were you scared?"

"Is that what you wanted? For me to be scared?"

"No. I just feel a little foolish, Marianne. I mean, I'm forty-three years old, just been dumped by my girlfriend, and am driving around on a Saturday night with someone who I was obsessed about a few decades ago. It's just really weird."

"That was cruel, taking me to that laughing woman."

"Cruel?"

"You were at Powell's."

"What's that have to do with anything?" But her voice was small; she knew.

"Laughter can be a knife."

Joan nodded. "Yeah. I used to go to Laughing Gertie as a kid. It was sort of like cutting myself."

"I'll give you your ransom. Then you can take me home."

"You're going to give me grace? In some kind of ceremony like that little one by the creek when we were kids?"

The woman really was a tornado. If she insisted on blowing violently across everything in her life, anything that had meaning, how did she expect people to not leave her behind?

"No ceremony. Just words."

"I'm listening."

"About Nick. He was my coach and I was his athlete. That was the purest form of our relationship. Our baby was a kind of grace. We did find that together. But I dropped her from a fifty-story building. I beat her. I gave her lie detector tests, and she flunked them. I abandoned her. Maybe I killed her. Maybe Nick and I killed her together. But we pretended she lived.

"It was okay for a while after Moscow. I went on the European tour with the Olympic team, and also to the Pan American Games. After that, I trained seriously for maybe six more months. Then sporadically for another two and a half years. I quit pretty much altogether a year before Los Angeles. I didn't even go to the trials. I hadn't competed in months."

Eve stopped and looked at Joan sitting beside her, the starlight faintly touching her eyes. She was listening carefully.

"Nick never gave up on me, though. I fucked up the Olympics. I fucked up everything, and he just kept believing.

"He'd beg me to train. And I would, for a while. I'd start all over again, start lifting weights, run my miles, really believe that I was going to do it that time. Then I'd get into some kind of trouble, and he'd have to come rescue me." Eve laughed. "He wouldn't admit this, but for a long time, Nick enjoyed rescuing me. I was his mission in life.

"But he won't come again. He's finally figured out that the girl he idealized hasn't existed for years.

"So, Joan, I have nothing at all to give you. It's like where Audrey's poem quotes the folk song: *Her ghost wheels her barrow through streets broad and narrow.*"

Joan shrugged. "Ah. So you don't have the ransom."

"No."

"We agreed, Marianne. We agreed on grace."

"If the ransom was a million dollars, and you discovered your victim didn't have it, what would you do?"

"Kill her?"

Eve was shivering from cold. She walked slowly to the car and got in the passenger seat. Joan followed, getting in the other side. Headlights shining south flooded the insides of the car. In the glare Joan and Eve looked at one another, and both of their faces were stripped raw.

"I don't think either of us can face Portland yet," Joan said. "What do you think?"

Eve was quiet.

"I know, I know. You prefer the kidnapping scenario. Going with me of your own free will implies that I might have something to offer *you.*"

Eve wished she had a comeback.

"Aren't you afraid I might publish this stuff you've shared with me?"

"That's blackmail."

Joan laughed. "Kidnapping *and* blackmail. It's getting good now, isn't it? But no, actually, it would only be blackmail if I were demanding something from you in exchange for my silence. What I'm doing is a simple, straightforward threat."

"But you do want something from me. I just don't know what it is."

"You don't believe that all I want is an interview."

"Not really."

"Or like I said before, to find out who you really are."

"Why would you care?"

"Sixteen is a very impressionable age. I thought you were very important then."

"What if you just admitted to yourself that you were wrong?"

Joan reached over, got her phone out of the glove compartment, and looked at it for a long time. She tossed it in the backseat and said, "Capelli called me crazy. Actually, he called me a 'crazy bitch.'"

"I don't believe that. Why would he?"

"He wanted you. You were a closet case. So he made me the crazy one."

"You do seem a little nuts to me."

Joan almost laughed.

"When did he call you a 'crazy bitch'?"

"In the school hallway. The day before all the shit came down."

Eve spoke very quietly. "Okay, tell me. What exactly happened?"

"Oh, come on."

"Joan. Honestly. I don't know what happened. Tell me."

"Nick—and I thought you—went to the principal. Remember Mr. Ubik? Reported my 'behavior,' which, admittedly, was pretty extreme. Except that if you or I'd been a boy, no one would have thought twice. I was offered counseling with the hideous Mr. Frisch or another high school. I took the other high school."

"I didn't know. I'm sorry."

"How could you not have known?"

"Nick protected me. He just handled things. I was only sixteen."

"But you said you loved me. Why weren't you curious, or even worried, about where I'd gone?"

"Wait a minute."

"You did."

"I thought we were talking about Nick and the principal."

"Now I'm talking about us. You did say that."

"We were *children.*"

"Call me crazy. But it felt like a much bigger betrayal than Meredith fucking her boss."

Joan pulled onto the highway, gently this time, as if the car were an animal they were riding. She headed south, not toward Portland. Fine, Eve thought, let's go all the way to Mexico. She wouldn't have to worry about her court date. She could take a new name. Again. Start a new life. Alissa was right: she was good at constructing herself. She could do a whole new person.

"Okay, I *was* sixteen," Joan said. "Which admittedly makes everything a little neon. But I'm *not* crazy. I have a successful career. I've published in a lot of well-respected newspapers and magazines."

Eve laughed.

"What?"

"Equating a successful career with sanity."

"You have a point there. No relationship between the two. Nevertheless, I'm not crazy. Just very pissed off. Driving feels good."

"It does," Eve admitted, and closed her eyes. She slept then, awakening occasionally to see Joan still at the wheel, the car swallowing pavement, the black night passing. Once the cell phone in the backseat rang, but Joan didn't reach to get it. Some time later, when she woke briefly, she found that Joan had put her seat back and laid a sweatshirt across the top half of her body. Eve twisted around in the seat, her back to Joan, curled herself in a ball, and slept some more.

Finally the car stopped and Joan tapped her on the back, just above her right kidney, and then got out, slamming the car door shut. Eve slowly emerged from her own side, stretched and shivered in the cold starlight. She could hear surf, but directly in front of the car was a body of placid water, not the sea.

"Where are we?"

"Salmon River estuary. Are you hungry? I stopped at an all-night Safeway in Tillamook while you were sleeping. Bought you some apples and milk and bread and peanut butter. Oh, and another cup of coffee."

"What's this?" Eve held up the lavender sweatshirt. On the front it said "Tillamook" in gold, glittery letters above a rubbery picture of surf and rhododendron blossoms.

"A sweatshirt I bought for you. You looked cold."

Eve pulled it on.

"The lavender goes with your skirt. A little souvenir of the evening."

"Thanks. It's lovely."

"Are you being sarcastic?"

"No, but you are. What are we doing?"

"Go ahead and have something to eat."

Eve crawled into the backseat with the brown bag of groceries. Using her finger as a knife, she made a peanut butter sandwich. She drank milk from the carton. She also drank the lukewarm cup of coffee she found in the cup holder. She felt much better after eating.

Joan was gone when she got out of the car. The road ended here at the river, so Eve began walking back in the other direction. But the tall Douglas firs grew thicker, shutting out the starlight, and so she returned to the car. The river looked black and harmless, and the gentle slope to the water's edge was covered with big round stones. She saw a dark shape hiking downstream, toward the mouth of the river.

Eve called out, "Where are you going?"

"I think I see a boat up here."

"A boat," she said quietly to herself, and then a sudden peace overtook Eve. There was no moon at all yet, just deep sky with stars. The air moved over her skin like silk. In the distance she could hear the Pacific Ocean caressing the west coast of America. The only raw edge in the seduction of the night was the sound of the river stones clunking and chiming under Joan's feet. The feet were moving away from her, though, leaving her alone with the luscious elixir of seaweed and salt, the surge of the river, the den of her own body, rested and fed.

Eve sat down on the biggest, flattest rock she could find and let herself travel into fantasy. She imagined that she held in her hands a translucent green bottle, with a slender neck, pleasingly round body, and tight cork. She would write a note to Audrey.

"I saw the poem." That's all she would say. Fold the piece of paper into tight squares, stuff it into the bottle, secure the cork, and then toss the bottle far out to sea. A freak storm would blast the message down the west coast, around Cape Horn, and up the east coast to Maine. Audrey would find the bottle rolled up against a sleeping seal.

Audrey's return note would ask, "Who is this?" As if she didn't know.

"The gracemonger," Eve whispered. "The waif on the street with cheap spiritual fixes."

A long silence followed. She'd rendered a poet speechless.

Eve imagined her sitting on the top of her cliff, the colony of seals below, hearing Eve's words, which traveled in the wind this time, no bottle necessary, and being stunned into silence.

"I'm sorry," Audrey finally whispered in response.

"You didn't think I'd see the poem."

"I wrote it a long time ago. Right after we first met at that silly conference. Before I really knew you."

"But you didn't withdraw it from the *New Yorker.*"

"I'm sorry." Eve actually heard the whisper, as if the words had been spoken next to her.

"But why? You enjoy publicly dissecting the souls of your lovers?"

"I don't have lovers."

"Oh?"

"I mean, lovers plural. I don't have lovers plural. What happened between us in New Mexico is very unusual for me. These days."

"And it was just too much for you. So you sliced it off into a poem."

"Something like that. A lot like that."

"Tell me something. Is your life just one big mine pit? You just keep digging away, looking for nuggets you can sell? We're not all that different, are we?"

"I'm sorry, Eve. I truly am. If I could take it back, I would."

"What happens when you've mined yourself dry? When you hit bedrock?"

"Listen. Once I've finished a poem, it no longer has a relationship with the thing it was about. That poem isn't my version of you. It's a poem. And you're you. And I think of you every day."

"Hey!" Joan's voice punched through Eve's auditory vision. "It *is* a boat! A canoe!"

Eve tried to ignore the voice. She tried to recall Audrey on the cliff, listening to the wind messages, but the spell was broken. Audrey would not be on the cliff at this hour, she'd be asleep in her bed. Trying to picture that, Eve saw her under a big down comforter, the three hounds on the bed with her, a rustic rocker in the room, the air so cold her breaths came out in puffs. Alone.

It was so easy to forgive her.

"Marianne!" Joan shouted again. "Come here. Hurry."

"I'm wearing sandals," Eve yelled back. "I can't walk on these stones."

"Hurry up!"

Eve began picking her way across the rocks, falling twice as the slick soles of her sandals slid on pieces of kelp. She could hear Joan dragging the canoe across the rocks, the dull thumping of wood on stone. When she finally got close enough to see the canoe, Eve said, "You can't just steal that boat."

"Watch me." Joan climbed back up the riverbank and began scavenging along the high-tide line. "Perfect," she said, dislodging a rotted board from some sedges. "Have you ever noticed how many answers there are right at your fingertips? You only have to look. That sounds like something you should put in your next book. This board will make a perfect paddle."

"I'm not getting in that canoe in the middle of the night."

"I thought you wanted to see the ocean."

"Where is it?"

"Across the river. On the other side of that sand spit. You can hear it, right?"

"Yes."

Joan pushed the canoe into the river, all but the pointy stern, which she straddled, pressing her hands down on the boat to steady it. "Climb in."

The tide must have been very low because the stones closest to the river's edge were slimy with seaweed. Eve gripped the edge of the boat and threw one leg in. Her back foot slipped on the seaweed and she fell forward, onto the bow seat.

"You okay?"

"This is beginning to feel like an Outward Bound experience."

"Ah. Character-building."

Eve's character, at the moment, felt like a damp piece of kelp, rubbery and slick. She knew she should fight this course of events, but giving in felt sweet, in spite of her bruised shins and scary guide.

"Okay," Joan said. "Now hold on tight while I get in." She pushed the boat away from shore and leaped in, nearly tipping the canoe over as she landed inside. "Ouch."

"You're reckless."

"This is a place I came to a few times many years ago. When we were in high school. After you." Joan got herself onto the stern seat, but their combined weight held the canoe firmly against the river bottom. She used the scavenged board to push off.

"Whoops." The rotted plank slivered into several pieces, but the canoe dislodged from the rocks and slid into the current. Joan leaned out over the water, tipping the canoe again, and rescued a piece of the board. With this, she dug into the water, paddling hard, but the current was swift. The canoe raced toward the mouth of the estuary.

"Whoa," Joan said. "I'm feeling a little out of control."

Eve didn't want to drown. Yet there was something soothing about the river taking charge.

Joan held the driftwood paddle over her head with both hands and grinned.

They'd traveled at least a hundred yards downstream. Eve could see the mouth of the river now and the white surf just beyond. "Hadn't you better paddle?"

"I could try, but I don't have much to work with."

"The water's getting rougher."

As the river turned the bend to the ocean, a series of standing waves snapped against the canoe. Joan wasn't grinning anymore and she tried hard to paddle, but they hit a stretch of white water which yanked the piece of driftwood right out of her hands. The canoe jostled along on the crazy water toward the sea.

"There was a time in my life I thought I would die for you. Looks like that might happen."

"That's not funny."

The canoe shot out of the rapids at the mouth of the river and hit an eddy, which spun them around and spit them out to the side. The canoe gently rode up onto a shallow sandbar. Joan yanked off her sneakers and jumped into the water. She grabbed the bow and hauled the canoe to the beach.

"Okay," she said. "I'll hold the boat. Take off your sandals and get out."

The cold ache of the Pacific Ocean seized Eve's legs, like a too-hard hug.

"Thank you," she said when they were both on shore.

"Low tide. We'll have to pull the boat high or we'll get stuck over here."

"Aren't we stuck over here anyway? Without a paddle?"

"Nah. I'll find something. The water will smooth out, too, once the tide comes in a little."

"Your jeans are all wet."

Joan glanced down at the bottom half of her jeans and shrugged. Then she took hold of the boat and pulled it far up the beach, toward the crest of the spit that was covered with grasses. Eve tried to help by pushing, but Joan moved too fast for her.

"That's good," Joan said, patting the canoe. "And it's not even that cold out."

A three-quarter moon was rising and Eve could now see the two headlands, black bulky shoulders, on both sides of the estuary and sand spit. They walked across the wet sand toward the ocean, and Eve didn't stop when they reached it, but walked right into the water, enduring the icy ache again. She stayed in the shallow surf, walking south, letting the wavelets splash her legs, relieved that at last she was in the truth of what she had told Audrey. She was not only at the coast, but in the ocean.

Joan walked parallel to her, higher up the beach on dry sand. They walked like this for twenty minutes, until they came to the end of the spit, when Eve turned to join Joan. "It's beautiful here."

Joan held up another found board. "Our paddle for going back. It'd be best, though, if we let the tide turn around. It'll carry us up the river."

Eve imagined herself yanking the "paddle" out of Joan's hands, running to the canoe, hauling it into the water. She had already survived the rapids at the mouth of the river. Why not paddle the canoe down the west coast of the Americas and through the Panama Canal. Up past Jamaica and the east coast of Cuba. Ride the Gulf Stream to Maine. Why not?

She loved the way thoughts of Audrey delivered her so fully outside the circumstances of any moment.

"Let's walk up there and get out of this breeze," Joan suggested.

"You must be cold in those wet jeans."

Joan glanced at her, as if checking for sarcasm, as if a kind remark from Eve was impossible.

The spine of the spit was covered with alders and pines, surrounded by a border of beach grass. Joan found a big dimple in the land, a pocket of sand surrounded by the spiky grasses, and she lay down in the soft bowl. Eve sat at a distance, clasping her thighs to her chest and resting her forehead on her knees. Not only were they out of the wind, but the sand had absorbed the sun all day long, and even now, hours after sunset, still held its warmth. Eve stretched out to feel the warm sand against the length of her body.

"You know," Joan's voice jumped too hard on the softness of the moment. "Your refusal to be accountable for your behavior back then really riles me."

"We were sixteen years old. Like you said: everything is neon then. I don't have to be accountable for anything I said or did when I was sixteen."

Joan rolled forcefully onto her side, facing Eve. "Technically, you're right."

"It's kind of crazy for you to be still so, as you say, riled about it."

"Not really. You're still all dewy about Capelli. That was when *you* were sixteen years old, right?"

"I'm not dewy about him. He's been a lifetime friend."

"Who's deserting you now."

"Unlike you? Loyal to the bitter end?"

"No, loyalty has nothing to do with anything right now. But since we're stuck here, indulge me. Tell me what happened between us. Then. In 1973. Before you started fucking the coach."

"Nick and I didn't sleep together until I was nineteen years old."

"Who cares. I want our story."

"You were faster. Nick was wrong to have chosen me. I'm sorry I didn't make him see that."

Joan sat up, a look of incredulity on her face. "Why do you keep insisting that *running* was what it was about?"

"Because that's what it *was* about for me."

"You said you loved me."

"That again."

"I didn't take it lightly."

"Apparently."

"God, you're a bitch."

Eve laughed. Being called a bitch was refreshing. She got up and climbed to the ridge of the sand bowl where she could see the ocean. She knew she'd traveled here, to the sea, not because Joan had forced her but because she had wanted to be on the edge of the continent, like Audrey was, and because she wanted to have told the truth. More, though. She wanted the truth from Audrey in return. More than anything, she wanted for Audrey to acknowledge what had passed, and perhaps what was still passing, between them. She wanted from Audrey exactly what Joan was asking of her.

She turned and looked down at Joan lying in the sand bowl.

"You look like a goddess in the moonlight," Joan said.

"A goddess bitch?"

"Exactly."

"It was spring," Eve said.

Joan sat up and Eve walked back down into the depression. She sat next to Joan.

"We were the two smartest students in Mrs. Fisher's Advanced Placement English class. You were in the artsy crowd and I was a loner, but we started doing our homework together."

"In the social studies lab."

"I liked you. You were very, very serious, and yet at the same time, always pushing the envelope. You liked to wear weird clothes, usually all black. With a purple bandanna tied somewhere funny, like around your calf. In class you always argued with the teacher and sometimes won. I thought you were cool. I admired your authenticity."

Joan flopped onto her back, her hands beneath her head and her elbows out, looking at the sky. Eve saw again the entire girl she had known twenty-five years ago all there in the woman beside her, and something about that incorruptibility broke her heart. Eve had made so many compromises in her own life she didn't know who she was.

Joan was patient, waiting for Eve to continue.

"We started doing that thing that happens when you have a crush, laughing at everything. We got kicked out of the social studies lab a couple of times for being too rowdy, and then we would go out on the grass behind the school, because it was spring, late March, and if you stood directly in the sunlight it could be warm. We didn't sit on the grass, though, because it was still spongy from months of rain."

"What about under the bleachers?"

"On rainy days, yeah."

"What'd we talk about?"

"You would smoke cigarettes and tell me about your family. I told you that I only had a future, that my past was nothing more than a jet stream."

"I thought that was cool. Back then. Now I think it's bogus."

"My mother died when I was a baby. By the time I met you, my father was slowly losing all touch with reality. He would have taken me down with him if I didn't cut all ties. You know a little about the absolutes of sixteen-year-olds."

"Yeah."

"I saw him a couple of hours ago."

"What do you mean?"

"By the highway. Trying to pull me in front of our car."

Joan was silent.

"Do you want my truth or not?"

"Yes."

"I have visions sometimes."

"Okay."

"So once when we had gotten kicked out of the social studies lab and were, that day, under the bleachers, I told you I thought I might try out for the track team. You asked why. I said because I liked to run. You said, 'I guess you'll start hanging out with jocks, then.' I said, 'I doubt it.' Then you told me being a jock was stupid because I could be anything I wanted to be, a homecoming queen, a Rhodes Scholar."

Eve laughed. "I remember being surprised that you thought a homecoming queen was something to be."

"I know. I remember being embarrassed I'd said that. I wondered where it'd come from. Except that it was true. It seemed to me that you had so many choices. Such a range."

"Then you told me I was beautiful."

"And you got all teary. I didn't understand why."

"I would have given anything to have your guts and resolve. You were so smart and artsy and eccentric. So sure of all your opinions. I wanted you to see more in me."

"Well, I did say Rhodes Scholar, too."

Eve shrugged. "Then you kissed me." She remembered the kiss being very different from the ones she'd had from boys. It was as if a bowl at the base of her belly filled with honey. "I liked it. A lot."

Joan cleared her throat, and Eve smiled at her discomfort. "Isn't this what you wanted? For me to tell you what happened?"

"Yes."

"After my last class that day, you were waiting at my locker. We went over to your house and you locked the door to your bedroom. We made love." Joan had been very tender, and Eve had been very willing. "That afternoon I did say that I loved you. You were right about that."

"Did you mean it?"

"Probably not." Eve flipped over on her side so that she faced Joan. "I take that back. I probably did."

"Truth is more important to me than placation."

"I'd already slept with several boys—and a couple of men—by then. Love wasn't something I could afford. Nick was the exception. He was the only one who didn't try to sleep with me. You have to understand that. He gave me running. And I've been running hard ever since."

"I'm sorry."

"Sorry?"

"I guess there was a lot I didn't know."

"There always is."

"Can I ask you a question?"

"Yep."

"Afterwards. When I walked you home? Remember that sort of ritual by the creek? With the handfuls of water?"

"Yeah."

"Did I disappoint you? By running away?"

"Yes."

"Oh."

"I wanted you to see all of me. I hoped that with all your eccentric brains you might be able to understand things I didn't. About me."

"And if I had let you know that I saw all of you—if I had emphasized the Rhodes Scholar and been able to bear your glow, or whatever it is—would things have been different?"

"Probably not. You weren't exactly a safe choice, Joan. And I needed a safe choice. I had no family, nothing. Nick offered me everything. I can't imagine anything that would have caused me to turn that down. I'm not brave."

"Who is?"

"You are."

"Ha."

"Those letters you wrote were very brave."

"The crazy letters I pushed through the vent slats of your locker?"

"Yes."

"Brave?"

"You were completely unafraid of your own wild passion."

"Ugh. Even now I cringe at the thought of those notes."

Eve smiled. "They were a little frightening. Even so, I was awed that anyone could give herself that much freedom of expression."

"Even back then you were awed?"

Eve nodded.

"What about the time I broke your bedroom window throwing rocks at it?"

Eve laughed. "I told Joanna, the woman whose home I lived in, that I'd done that with the vacuum cleaner handle."

"No way. You did?"

"Yes."

"But when I painted 'I love you' with nail polish on your locker . . ."

"That got a little scary."

"That's when Capelli turned me in."

"He found the notes in my locker."

"He *read* them."

"Yes."

"The little prick."

"He and the principal opened my locker that night. I would have hidden the letters, if I'd known they were going to do that."

After a long pause, Joan said, "You really would have?"

"Yes, of course."

"So what'd you say? When they confronted you about the letters?"

"No one ever confronted me. I just found both the paint and the letters gone the next morning. Nick told me that he and Mr. Ubik had 'cleaned out'—as he put it—my locker. I was afraid to ask anything else and we never talked about it again."

"How'd that make you feel? Them snooping in your locker."

"Relieved, in a way."

"Relieved . . ."

"I know it's hard for you to understand how badly I wanted to be taken care of."

"At any price."

"At any price."

"And what do you think about that price now?"

"It was very high."

"It's nice to know that *you* didn't turn me in. It's very nice to know, actually. I always wondered why they didn't come after me later, after I transferred high schools, when I'd sometimes wait for you by the creek in the woods, on that path you used to walk to school."

"You never tried to talk. You'd just follow a few yards behind."

"You must have been creeped out."

Eve shrugged. "Actually, not. It felt a little like it's felt these past months."

"What do you mean?"

Eve touched Joan's temple and trailed her finger down her cheek. Joan didn't move, didn't breathe. "I'm glad you stalked me. Then and now."

"I wouldn't call it stalking," Joan said very quietly.

"It's like you stopped me. I quit competing as a runner years ago, but I've never stopped hurtling forward by any means possible. It's like I needed to be physically restrained."

"I haven't forced you to do anything."

"Yes, you have. You've insisted on seeing me."

Joan cleared her throat and got to her feet. "The tide's probably coming in good now. We should go."

"I liked it better when you were kidnapping me."

"We'd better go."

Eve reached for Joan's hand and pulled her back down to the sand. She held her head in both hands and kissed her tenderly on the mouth.

Joan reared back. "Jesus! What are you doing? Is that what you think I want?"

"No."

"I can't. Not now."

"My stalker," Eve said quietly and smiled.

"Don't play games with me. My girlfriend just . . ."

"I know. Dumped you. Just hold me, okay?"

Joan stared, didn't move. The whole story passed across her face. Eve saw sorrow, regret, a fleeting moment of joy, the possibility of pity. If she'd settled on the pity, Eve would have pushed her away. But then Joan smiled the smile of a forty-three-year-old woman, a smile of complexity and compassion and anger. She put her arms around Eve's shoulders and pulled her close.

"Don't worry," Eve said. "I'm not going to cry or anything."

"Couldn't we just wrestle?"

Eve laughed and they fell back, lying side by side. "You've always had so much fight in you."

"Okay," Joan said. "Just once coming from me." They kissed for so long that Eve thought they were going to make love, after all, but Joan finally pulled away. "We're not sixteen anymore," she said. "Let's go back to Portland."

When Joan dropped her off early in the morning, Eve found her house exactly as she had left it less than twenty-four hours earlier. But finding it so was oddly shocking. Everything else had changed, and she felt as if her house, too, should have changed. It would have been more fitting to find it empty, cleared of all its furniture and clutter, or maybe entirely refurbished with new stuff. But it was just her house, plain and serviceable, and looking at it now, she thought it wasn't the house of a motivational speaker, an expert on grace, a wise woman. It was the house of an extraordinarily ordinary woman, a woman who caught each moment like a juggler caught torches, trying, trying, trying to not drop any, failing all the time. Out of habit, she called Nick to tell him about her arrest and court date. Judith answered the phone.

"It's me, Eve."

"Hello, Eve." That strained voice she always used with her, particularly when she called at times Judith deemed inappropriate, like Sunday morning.

"Is Nick home?"

"Of course. I'll get him." A finality in Judith's voice, as if she were confident she wouldn't have to hear much more from Eve.

"Eve! How're you feeling?"

She'd nearly forgotten about her fever and the aborted Powell's Books event. "I'm fine. I'm sorry to call Sunday morning. I'm sure you and Judith are busy."

"We're about to go for a run."

"Are you okay? You and Judith?"

"Sure. Of course."

"You're still getting married?"

"Of course. *Yes.* What's up, Eve? Do you still have the flu, or whatever?"

Eve wondered what it would it mean for Nick to suppress Alissa. "I'm fine. Except that I've gotten into trouble again."

He didn't say a word, which was how he expressed impatience, but Eve told him the story anyway, of taking the woman's purse and getting caught, her time in jail, but leaving out what happened after she was released.

"It's theft this time," she told him. "A little more serious. Plus, the priors."

"You're bragging about this?"

"No, no, no. I just want you to know everything, that's all." Full disclosure. The terms of her life were no longer negotiable.

"Eve. I'm going to call you back in a minute, okay? Don't move. I'm going to call you right back."

"It's okay, Nick. I'm fine. Go for your run." She wished she had never called him. So much fluster.

"Stay right there." Nick hung up.

She knew he was clearing the time with Judith, asking if it was all right if they went for their run in a half an hour, maybe swearing that this was, finally and really, the last time Eve Glass would interfere with their lives.

A moment later, the phone rang. She imagined him on another extension where he could talk privately. She had never in all these months been inside Judith's house, where Nick now lived.

"Hey. Look. I'm worried about you. I think it's that poet in Maine. I don't like how she's been affecting you. Now I know we've always stayed out of each other's, you know, personal lives, but—"

"How can you say that? We were *married*. How does that constitute staying out of each other's personal lives?"

"I mean since then. I mean recently. I don't meddle with who you're seeing. But this woman, she's under your skin. Alissa said you write her constantly, and that she writes you back."

"Since when is letter writing dangerous?"

"You know what I mean."

"I don't think I do."

"I saw the poem in the *New Yorker.* Alissa showed it to me. That was cheap. The woman is mocking you."

"She's mocking Eve Glass."

"Yeah. So? That's what I'm saying."

"She's not mocking Marianne Wade."

After a long, dull silence in which she knew Nick puzzled over what she'd said, he continued, "I don't think she has your best interests at heart."

"Go for your run. And Nick? From what I've observed, you might not be the best person to be doing relationship counseling right at the moment."

"What's that supposed to mean?"

"Go for your run with Judith." She put a lot of emphasis on the name.

Uncomfortable with this turn in the conversation, Nick said good-bye.

"Good-bye, Nick." She held her hand on the receiver long after she had hung up.

Eve took a hot and sudsy shower and put on her yellow flannel pajamas. She left the shades up in her bedroom so that the sunlight could stream in while she slept. And then she dreamed long and hard, about people she had known before her life started, before she began recording the making of herself. There was her father, and the stepmothers, even her real mother in a flash of wild hot light, and then deep pools of sunlight, like the one gathering on her bed as she slept. It was a waking kind of death.

She got up in the afternoon and packed a small bag. In the past, she had always traveled with several bags and most of her clothes, but today she took only a toothbrush, her favorite lemon soap, jeans, and a thick, woolly sweater. Then, because she could no longer imagine how she might dress for Audrey, she dressed against her. She pulled on red cowboy boots over bare legs, a purple dress with faux Western sequins, a denim jacket. She stuffed three copies of *IGIG*, as Joan referred to the book, in her bag. Then she called a cab.

The small castle in which Alissa and Seth lived throbbed with music. It was eerie, hearing classical music pumped up like rock. The place was like some kind of church run amok, civilization gone heathen. Eve sighed, thinking of Alissa. The poor thing didn't understand her own voraciousness. Her red Jaguar was pulled up to the top of the driveway, the trunk open and loaded with boxes of CDs. Eve slipped two of them, by exotic-looking musicians she'd never heard of, into her bag.

"What are you doing?"

Busted.

Alissa's hair was pulled back in a messy ponytail, and she wore sweats, a T-shirt with damp armpits, and no bra. She was carrying another box, which she dropped by the Jag and sat on. "Take all of them, if you want."

"I'm sorry." Eve pulled the two CDs back out of her bag and held them out.

Alissa waved them away. She nodded her head toward the street and asked, "What's the cab for?"

"I'm going to the airport. I came to say good-bye."

"The Wild Spirit conference isn't until next week."

"I know. Are you okay? You look awful. What are you doing with all these boxes?"

"I'm moving out." She stood, and though she carried nothing now, Alissa looked burdened as she climbed the stairs to her front porch. Eve followed her into her office, which contained only a rolled Oriental rug, the blaring stereo, and some papers on the floor next to a packet addressed to Eve. Alissa turned down the volume of the music and said, "I was going to drop this by your house. It has the name and number of the organizer for the Wild Spirit conference. Your hotel reservations and plane tickets. Eve, look. I'm quitting. It doesn't have anything to do with the *Times* story. It's for personal reasons."

"What *Times* story?"

"What *Times* story?" she deadpanned. "You know perfectly well 'what *Times* story.'"

Eve shook her head.

"Next week. Something like, 'Eve Glass Revealed,' by Joan Ehrhart.

"Eve, you're smiling. I can't believe you're smiling. You do know what'll be in this piece, don't you?" Alissa snatched the handful of papers off the floor and waved them above her head. "That woman left excerpts from the transcript of the interview on my porch a couple of hours ago. Same thing on Nick's porch. He's shitting bricks. You know, Eve, like I said, I'm quitting for personal reasons. I was packing before these arrived. But there was a real breach of trust here. You promised to not give any interviews that weren't okayed by me."

"I didn't do an interview."

"So she made this up? Because if that's the case, then you can sue the living bejesus out of her."

Eve shrugged. "It's that bad?"

"It's definitely not pretty."

While Eve had slept, Joan had typed up her notes. There was something perfect about that. Complete. Eve slept. Joan wrote.

"It's only her notes," Eve said to comfort Alissa. "You don't know what she'll write."

She might spike the piece with the worst—Eve's betrayal of a childhood friend, her admission of hypocrisy, her shoplifting and theft convictions. But it was equally likely that she would get her kicks by doing just the opposite, overplaying Eve's beauty, her aura, her potential. Joan might ballyhoo her utter honesty in the "interview," a willingness to talk about her own foibles. She probably knew that perpetuating the myth, boosting Eve's career, was better revenge. Either way, people had been fabricating her story her whole life, and none of it mattered.

Eve smiled again. She couldn't help it. The picture of Joan typing furiously in the brilliant morning light! Then she laughed out loud at the thought of Joan yanking the notes out of her printer, barreling through Portland in her pea green Toyota, slipping the sheaf of papers onto Nick's porch, ringing the doorbell, and running away.

Alissa sighed and shook her head, interpreting Eve's smile

and laughter as grit. "Well, it's not why I'm quitting," she repeated.

"I know. You're quitting because of Nick."

Alissa looked at Eve, appraising, then gave in. "Nick is bedrock. I was just a small seismic slip in his life. *Small.* You know that as well as I do."

Eve wasn't so sure, but what she thought didn't matter. "Then why are you leaving Seth?"

"He left me."

"You told him about Nick?"

She shook her head. "There's nothing to tell. Anyway, it's probably more about you than about Nick."

"Me?"

"Seth wants money, kids, an au pair."

"What's that got to do with me?"

"He thinks I'm going soft on him. New Agey. That I can't toe the appropriate lines. My taking you on as a client represents my drift toward the fringe."

"You? You're totally hard-edged."

"Yeah. I know. But he doesn't."

"Alissa, honey," Eve laid a hand on her arm. "What do you want?"

Alissa moved her arm away and nodded toward one end of the rolled red Oriental rug. As Eve helped her carry it down the stairs, she answered, "A kiss that lasts long enough. Music that's loud enough. No, what I want is simply *enough*. Why doesn't that word ever have meaning for me?"

She jammed the rug into the space between the two seats, one end resting on the dashboard, and then went back and locked the front door of the miniature castle.

As she got behind the steering wheel and started the engine, Eve, standing on the driveway, asked, "What about the stereo?"

"I have a good CD player in the car. Get in. I'll take you to the airport."

Eve paid the cab driver and got in the Jag.

"Where're you going?"

"Where do you think?"

"Maine."

"Bingo. You?"

"Missouri."

What would it be like to have a "Missouri" to return to? "Do you think Missouri is going to be 'enough'?"

"I just want to see my family. I'll see after that."

"Nick wouldn't have been enough, either."

Eve thought Alissa was the type who couldn't cry, but her eyes filled. "He might have been."

Above them, a big steely airplane descended toward the airport. Another plane skidded to a landing on their right as a white one soared into flight on their left. Alissa loved airports, and once they arrived she perked up. Getting in her last five minutes of managerial licks, she said, "Promise me one thing. Promise you'll make it to the Wild Spirit conference next week. You're the keynote, Eve. It's a huge gig for you. There are over three thousand registered for the conference. The publisher has mailed as many copies of your book. It was a real coup getting this speaking engagement."

"Maybe I should cancel."

"Did you hear what I just said?"

"But what with the *Times* piece coming out and all."

Alissa finally smiled. "Any press is good press. It'll be a humiliating story to *you,* maybe. But to everyone else it's good juice. You're human. You have to make sure your audience knows you know that. This Joan Ehrhart is an aberration. You'll outlast her."

Eve thought of telling Alissa that she had spent all of last night on the beach with that aberration, kissed her even. Instead she said, "And what if I don't go to the Wild Spirit conference?"

"That's not an option. You'll be considered defeated. It'll confirm everything Ehrhart says in the article."

"And what if it's all true?"

Alissa pulled up to the Departing Flights curb and yanked the parking brake. It was late Sunday, and people were anxious about the conclusions of their weekends, the impending Monday, the idea of travel itself. They honked their horns. They screeched to the curb and away from it.

"'True' is a relative concept. Don't worry about it. Look, Eve. I liked you from the moment I met you. You built a person named Eve Glass. The difference between successful people and unsuccessful people is the knowledge that that's possible. There is no 'true' person. Most people leave themselves to chance, which is why *de*struction is what most people get, life being like waves beating down a cliff. But you can control the elements, *con*struct yourself. We've both done that. We both understand point A and point B."

Eve thought about the "con" in the word *construct* and wished she could stay a few more moments in the cool enclosure of the Jaguar with its soothing leather upholstery. But a traffic cop in his fluorescent orange vest and white gloves appeared at her window, beckoning them to move on. More cars honked. So Eve turned to say good-bye. Alissa's disheveled hair and dirty T-shirt made her look even younger than her thirty years. Her face was composed, entirely confident in what she thought she knew, but behind that Eve saw anguish, as if there were an entire orchestra in her heart that she was ignoring. Soon, though, the music would break through, she wouldn't be able to control it. Alissa would be okay.

"My parting advice," Alissa said, oblivious to her own vulnerability. "This Audrey Boucher. I don't trust her. Nick would kill me if he knew I was taking you to the airport to see her."

"But you took me anyway."

Alissa's eyes filled with tears again. Eve pet her tangled hair, then leaned in and kissed her cheek. "Drive safely to Missouri."

Alissa reached for some Bach concertos and plugged the CD into the narrow slot. She looked straight ahead as Eve climbed out of the car and dragged her one small bag from the backseat. Eve stood on the curb and waved at Alissa in her red Jaguar, already pulsing with music, as she drove away.

Once she landed in the other Portland, on the Atlantic coast, she rented a car and bought a map. She drove north, filled with a fear as orange and bright as the dawn. Was it only yesterday's dawn that she lay in dunes next to the Pacific Ocean? It was. How very different this dawn was, coming to life over the sea, a brilliant orange light shocking the interior of her car. She had slept deeply on the plane, and now felt clear-headed, painfully aware of what she was doing.

And now she was here.

Eve recognized Audrey's property right away, even before seeing the number on the mailbox by the road. She left her car at the beginning of the long drive. Still wearing her purple sequined dress and red cowboy boots, needing the inappropriateness like a child's drawing needs thick, darkened outlines, she walked toward the ramshackle house in the distance. To either side of her were the dew-wet, wild fields of her poems, dusky blueberries thick amid the weeds. She saw also the two white pines of which Audrey had written, off to the side of the house, and the stand of beech, their yellow leaves now iridescent with the morning light. She heard the barking hounds of her poems and smelled the salty wetness.

Soon she would see Audrey, too, and it seemed that she had to figure out who she was in the measure of time and geography before then. She was no longer the pure Greek form, the essence of body, the perfect runner that Nick had loved. Nor was she the product that Alissa professed, just a few hours ago, to still believe in. Audrey came closest with her street merchant girl and a cart of wares. Maybe that identity left her the most room, for at least the wares were in the cart, the girl separate and mysterious. To herself, though, Eve was simply the woman who bites the apple.

The dogs, just two of them—Whit must still be at the vet's—bounded from the house, their barking a prelude to their walk. Audrey herself followed in knee-high rubber boots, a corduroy jacket, a wool hat. She stopped when she saw Eve, but her dogs didn't. They hurtled themselves down the drive toward her, no longer barking, eager to meet the guest. Audrey stood on the porch, waiting. Eve couldn't see from the road if she was smiling, but she strode forward anyway, as eager as the hounds, though scared, more scared than she'd ever been in her life.